THE
FOREST LAKE
MYSTERY

T0159840

Palle Rosenkrantz

TRANSLATED FROM THE DANISH
BY
DAVID YOUNG

Lightning Books

Published by
Lightning Books Ltd
Imprint of EyeStorm Media
312 Uxbridge Road
Rickmansworth
Hertfordshire
WD3 8YL

www.lightning-books.com

First published as *Hvad Skovsøen gemte* in Denmark in 1903 by Gyldendalske
Boghandels Forlag (F. Hegel & Søn)
Translation copyright © 2018 by David Young
This translation first published by Abandoned Bookshop in 2018.

Cover design by Ifan Bates

No part of this publication may be replaced, stored in a retrieval system, or
transmitted, in any form or by any means, without the prior permission in
writing of the publisher, nor be otherwise circulated in any form of binding or
cover other than that in which it is published and without a similar condition
including this condition being imposed on the subsequent purchaser.
This book is a work of fiction. Names, characters, places and incidents are
either a product of the author's imagination or are used fictitiously.

British Library Cataloguing in Publication Data
A catalogue record for this book is available from the British Library

Printed by CPI Group (UK) Ltd, Croydon CR0 4YY

ISBN 9781785631641

Introduction

THE FOREST LAKE MYSTERY was first published in Denmark in 1903 as the second of Palle Rosenkrantz's crime novels, this one containing a number of parallels with his own life. He had felt inspired by the success of his first, *The Murder at Vestermarie*, which was based on an actual murder case from 1836.

Palle Rosenkrantz was born in Helsingør (Elsinore) in 1867, the son of Baron Iver Holger Rosenkrantz and Julia Louise Mackenzie of Tarbat. His parents had met in Italy during his father's brief period as a Danish diplomat and they married in Turin in 1864. The connection with Italy is one of the themes which is echoed in *The Forest Lake Mystery*. The family was not a member of the wealthy landed aristocracy and tended to maintain their standard of living by incurring debts and getting help from relatives. Back in Denmark, the family moved house frequently, which Palle later referred to as 'my childhood's nomadic lifestyle'. He was to be equally nomadic in his adult life.

When his father died in 1873, Palle was only six years old and the four sons of the marriage went to live with their maternal aunt in Rome for an extended period, while their mother was visiting her Scottish family, a practice she continued intermittently. Palle was thus brought up by a succession of servants and was sent to various Danish private schools for his education. He studied law at Copenhagen University, from which he graduated in 1891 with a rather mediocre grade. He later admitted in his memoirs that he spent most of his student years on 'a far too lively student life, (involving) irresponsibility and a taste for some not always innocent pastimes.'

Despite his poor exam results, Palle succeeded in gaining legal positions out in the provinces, including one as a lower court magistrate where he took part in the investigation of a child murder, the details of which have also found their way into *The Forest Lake Mystery*. He continued the family practice of living beyond his means, relying on help from family and friends. In 1892, he married Edle Christiane Nielsen, the daughter of a merchant and two years younger than him; they had their first child in 1893 and three more were to follow. While working in the small town of Nakskov in 1898, where as a sideline to gain more income he began his writing career with theatre and concert reviews for the local paper, he lost his magistrate's job because his new boss considered that he had misused public funds. With help from friends, he managed to repay the missing amount and the charges were dropped. However, this also resulted in him having to declare bankruptcy with debts of 70,000 kroner (around £3,800 at historic exchange rates), a considerable sum in the late 1800s. In addition, the scandal made it difficult for him to find a position in the legal sphere. At this time, along with a few minor legal positions in commercial enterprises, he became a writer out of necessity in order to provide for his family. In 1899, he became involved in another legal case where he agreed to be a witness for a friend who had been accused in relation to a vanished cheque. When he appeared in court, he was treated very condescendingly by the investigating magistrate, Axel Petersen, who subsequently accused him of stealing the cheque, even though he had not been anywhere near the crime scene at the time. After this fact had been verified, the charge was dropped, but Rosenkrantz felt he had been humiliated by an arrogant and haphazard justice system. Along with earlier cases of corrupt police and legal practice he had witnessed while working as a magistrate, this experience set Rosenkrantz off on a theme which pervaded much of his crime writing, including his first novel which was an actual case involving a miscarriage of justice. *The Forest Lake Mystery* is something of an anomaly among his crime novels, in that it contains no polemic about the injustices of the Danish legal system.

In the early 1900s in Copenhagen, Rosenkrantz was part of a literary group which included Georg Brandes, the prominent literary critic of his time, and his brother Edvard Brandes, at one point editor of Politiken, one of the major newspapers for which Rosenkrantz wrote articles, especially about the justice system. This group was critical of the national-romantic literature of the time and believed that literature should create debate about pressing social issues, a demand which Rosenkrantz lived up to through his crime novels.

Although it is the detective stories he is best known for today, Rosenkrantz was also prolific in writing romantic and historical dramas based around the aristocracy and country estates, tales for which there was an avid readership. Having inherited the title of Baron from his father, the Danish nobility and their country estates were subjects dear to Rosenkrantz's heart, in that his extended family owned some of them, making him a frequent visitor, and he wrote articles about them for tourist magazines. In addition, he wrote plays for the stage and later for radio, and manuscripts for films. He has also translated a number of works to Danish from Italian and English, including Dashiell Hammett's 1932 novel, *The Thin Man*.

His success as a writer changed his financial fortunes and he was able to buy an impressive house in the upper-class suburb of Hellerup, and later bought a large plot of land in the same district where he had another, even grander, house built. It also gave him time to engage in the debate about the Danish justice system. He wrote articles and gave lectures on its iniquities, particularly on the necessity of separating the judiciary from the public prosecutors to prevent them colluding and trying to press confessions out of accused people using inquisitorial methods. Whilst he was an enthusiastic supporter of reform, he wasn't in favour of the jury system advocated by some other reformers, believing that legal decisions should be taken by people with a legal background and that juries could be too easily swayed by a charismatic lawyer. The reform campaign was eventually successful with the passing of a new law in 1919. After this law was passed, it is interesting that both the quality and the frequency of Rosenkrantz's crime writing dropped and he concentrated on the romantic, country house dramas and his translation work.

During the First World War and immediately after, the Danish economy suffered, including that of the publishing industry, and Rosenkrantz was forced to sell the property in Hellerup and the family resumed its nomadic existence in rented accommodation. They often spent the summers in the resort town of Løkken on the west coast of Jutland, moving back to Copenhagen for the rest of the year. Løkken held a Palle

Rosenkrantz festival in 2018 in commemoration of the author's links with the town.

Although it could be argued that Danish authors wrote novels about crimes before 1902, it is generally accepted that Palle Rosenkrantz was the first Danish author to use a police detective as the principal character. As can be gleaned from reading the novel, and some of the short stories also featuring Eigil Holst, the profession of 'detective' was viewed with much suspicion in early 20th-century Denmark and was not considered a reputable job. Rosenkrantz was also the first to earn much of his living from crime writing. It is this that principally swayed the Danish Crime Writers Association in 1987 to name their annual prize for the best novel published in Danish after Palle Rosenkrantz. The prize includes translations into Danish from other languages, and the winners have included such luminaries of crime writing as PD James, Ruth Rendell, John Le Carré, Colin Dexter, Ian Rankin, James Elroy and Michael Connelly. It is no doubt because of the interest generated by the prize that many of Palle Rosenkrantz's novels and short stories are now being reprinted or released digitally.

In a number of instances in the novel, Rosenkrantz has used German. This German has been retained in the current translation of the text, with English translations supplied in the endnotes.

DAVID YOUNG, TRANSLATOR

PART ONE
Forest Lake

I

ONE DAY IN MAY 1902, shortly after the woodlands had unfurled their spring finery, Eigil Holst decided to reward himself with a trip out into the Zealand countryside north of Copenhagen. In addition to being in dire need of fresh air in his lungs and an escape from the daily grind and the dust and smoke of the capital, he was feeling tired, on edge and run down by all the hard work.

Holst was twenty-six years old and the only son of a military officer whose family hailed from Jutland. Both his parents were dead and he hadn't moved to the capital until he was twenty-two, exchanging the silver-plated uncertainty of a Second Lieutenant with the less resplendent but somewhat more reassuring prospects of a Copenhagen policeman. Eigil Holst was destined for this path from childhood. As long as he could remember, police novels had been his favourite reading, the history of crime his greatest joy. He had read every volume of François Guyot de Pitaval's famous causes célèbres in the German editions. As he grew up, he carried on this reading systematically, studying German and English works on criminology; indeed, his passion for the subject went so far that, with the support of a cousin who was a grammar school teacher, he acquired enough knowledge of French to study the famous Jean Macé in the original language, and of Italian to follow the interesting criminal theories of the Italian school.

His greatest sorrow was that his father hadn't allowed him further study. He had ardently wanted to become a lawyer and, eventually, a judge, and had intended to work gradually without outside help towards acquiring a high-school diploma. But his parents had died just as he had turned eighteen, and he had had to remain in his position as an assistant in a bookshop, which he had taken up on his father's insistence after passing the preliminary diploma. He had stayed there until he had been called up to national service and, as he was a tidy, bright, disciplined young man, he was detailed as a Second Lieutenant and did service as such for a year. During this time in service, he had become a much sought-after and popular guest in the garrison town's best homes, but was wise enough to realise that life as a soldier could only be an intermediate stage for him.

His company commander, an ageing, kind soldier who was related to one of the capital's senior police officers, procured employment for him in the police force and Eigil Holst once again began slowly but surely to work himself up from the bottom to a position that could both satisfy his ambition and earn him a living.

The first years were a disappointment, but tough and persevering as he was, he pursued his goal and eventually worked his way to recognition as an exceptionally efficient person, far ahead of his colleagues in education, proficiency and innate knack. He kept himself to himself, lived a quiet life in a boarding house in the middle of the city and, because he didn't seek out the company of his colleagues, wasn't particularly well-liked but was considered irreproachable in his conduct. The others said he was a dry stick who had no interest in anything except work and his mouldy books, and that was probably fair enough, for he just focused on his goals and didn't mix with anyone.

Eigil Holst was an unusually handsome young man, with brown, curly hair and dark, slightly dreamy eyes, lithe and strong, healthy of body and well-trained in various sports. Women admired him, but he passed them by without a second look. He was self-sufficient and his work was everything to him. He loved long walks in the countryside and had ridden almost the entire length and breadth of Zealand on his bicycle. He liked North Zealand best – the region around Gurre and Esrum and the forests north of Elsinore, where the Kattegat and the Sound meet and Kullen raises its jagged ridge in Sweden across the blue water.

He had found himself a favourite spot by a small marl pit on the edge of a forest, closely fringed with trees, but with a partial view over the smiling countryside to the blue sea in the distance. This spot was adorable, especially in May, and he would sit for hours alone with his thoughts, staring down into the small, dark lake and over the flowering bushes and thorns.

He almost regarded this spot as his own, somewhere unknown to everyone else, and he felt himself master of the place. He had made a bench for himself under a tall beech where the water had carved out an inlet under the embankment, which was supported by the latticed network of tree roots.

He was thus immediately discomfited when, on that day in May, he was awakened from his reveries by the sound of voices.

He rose involuntarily to leave, but at that moment the speakers stepped forward from the bushes and blocked his way. He remained seated to let them pass.

It was a man in his fifties and a young woman dressed in light colours, by the look of her, not yet twenty. The man was tall and most meticulously dressed, with wonderfully sharp eyes in a rare classically shaped face bearing a short military moustache. He stood in front of the bench and leant slightly towards Holst to apologise briefly for any inconvenience their arrival might have caused.

He spoke Swedish, though with the intonation of a man who had been living in Denmark for a number of years. Holst lowered his head with a muffled God preserve us and got up to go, but the stranger clearly wasn't disposed to allow it; he was very eloquent and apologised profusely for his and his daughter's intrusion, while adding with a smile that the bench provided enough space for them all. Holst bowed politely, the two strangers sat beside him, and the Swedish gentleman said that this spot at Forest Lake was their favourite and that they were staying for a short while in a farmhouse nearby.

The young lady joined in with a little chuckle, remarking that it was especially her 'Pappa' – she pronounced the word with two distinct p's – who would head for this small, shiny lake several times a day; it was admittedly adorable, but she preferred the wide-open countryside, the view of the sea and Kullaberg in the distance. She laughed once again, revealing some charming white teeth, while a little twinkle in her eye was on the lookout for whether or not her smile and laughter had disarmed the young man's restrained hostility.

She looked a little disappointed.

Holst responded mostly with monosyllables and was really only waiting for an opportunity to retreat with honour. The

Swedish gentleman seemed to enjoy his shyness, while his daughter cast an occasional glance at their taciturn neighbour.

They talked about this part of the country, its nature and the green trees, and the Swedish gentleman was generous in his praise of the beautiful, lonely spot on the edge of the forest where they were sitting.

'I love this little lake,' he said. 'It lies here, fenced in by green trees, like an idyllic protest against all the harshness and ugliness in the world out there, shining and clean like a virgin's desire, while the sun's rays play on its surface during the day and the stars of heaven are reflected in its depths at night.'

The young lady laughed once more.

'Pappa is being poetic.'

Holst shrugged.

'I dare say this lake is very deep and there is hardly a fish living in its cold, clear waters,' continued the elderly gentleman. 'It is peace itself, untrodden, untouched and very, very quiet.'

The young lady took a large stone and threw it high in the air so that it fell with a splash into the lake, causing rings to rise from the water, spreading, subsiding and vanishing once again. She threw another stone and stepped close to the edge. A blush rose in her cheeks, which had earlier been rather pale.

Holst looked at her and found her beautiful; quite slender but harmoniously built with uniform facial features, fresh lips and large laughing eyes. It was a shame though that, like all women, she was conscious of her appeal and used her physical virtues to flirt.

The old gentleman looked at her with a mixture of tenderness and pride. She picked up a huge stone in order to hurl it into the lake, but it was obviously beyond her powers. Involuntarily Holst got to his feet and stepped over to her in order to prevent the weight of the stone taking her over the edge.

15

She smiled at him and asked if he could throw the stone out into the middle of the lake.

He lifted it with a shy smile. It was very heavy, but he tensed his muscles and took a firm stance on the ground. Her eyes were resting warmly upon him; she found pleasure in this game of strength and didn't attempt to hide it.

He hurled the stone, which fell with a hollow gulp, and the large rings rippled the surface of the water with a light foam which subsided.

All three of them stared instinctively out over the surface of the water and watched the ripples as ring after ring formed. Suddenly a squeal escaped from the young woman.

'What's that?'

She pointed down at the edge where something white had appeared and took an instinctive step back. Holst bent over the edge and looked sharply down into the water. He straightened up slowly.

'I think the young lady should go back from the edge,' he said seriously. 'This isn't the sort of thing that young ladies are comfortable with seeing.'

The Swedish gentleman stood up, twitching nervously and came swiftly over to the edge of the quarry.

'What is it?' he asked breathlessly.

Holst turned towards him. 'It seems to be a child's corpse that has been lying at the bottom of the lake,' he said in a hushed voice. 'The stone has brought it to the surface. I have to get it brought on land, but since I can probably manage it alone, I would advise you to go. Your daughter will hardly find the sight particularly appealing.'

The Swedish gentleman smiled.

'A child's corpse – well I never – so this idyllic lake is hiding dark secrets in its depths. Perhaps there are more than this one.

Do you really want to get involved in this? Let it be – it's not our business to meddle in such things. We pay the authorities to handle this kind of work.'

Holst smiled.

'Precisely – and I'm one of those you pay.'

'You!'

The Swedish gentleman took a step back and inspected Holst.

'Yes – I'm employed by the investigative police in the capital – and I'm not the type of person who just says, like the bailiff in *Brand*, "This isn't in my district." But you probably have little interest in a bailiff's work and I'd like to spare you any further trouble. Nevertheless, the body has to be fished up and brought into the custody of the local authorities – and I'll take care of that right away.'

The Swedish gentleman shook his head with a smile.

'This means that you, sir, have made a catch, set your foot on a trail which you intend to pursue in order to lead a poor man to the bar of justice – or perhaps the bar of injustice, who knows? Ulla,' he said turning to the young lady, 'go home, please. I will help Mr Detective here to get the catch ashore.'

The young lady had drawn back to the bench. At the word 'detective' she looked up in surprise. Something resembling disappointment drifted across her face and she nodded a kind of farewell before walking away slowly along the path behind the forest fence.

The Swedish gentleman turned back to Holst and, taking a small visiting card wallet from his breast pocket, he handed Holst his card with a smile.

'It's probably best we become familiar with each other before we start our task together.'

Holst glanced at the card. Under a five-pointed crown were the words: Arvid von Ankerkrone, former Captain of Horse with the Scania Dragoons.

Holst bowed.

'I'm sorry I'm unable to reciprocate. I have no card with me. My name is Eigil Holst, a sergeant with Copenhagen police – and,' he added with a smile, 'previously a Second Lieutenant in the 9th regiment.'

The old gentleman held out his hand.

'A soldier like me then – it's my pleasure to make the acquaintance of the Lieutenant. Let's get to work.'

They did. First they took off their coats – the Captain hung his with great care over the bench and rolled up his dazzlingly white shirt sleeves. They armed themselves with some broken branches and after a few minutes of work they had managed to bring the little corpse into the bank.

Holst bent over the corpse – it was an infant that hardly looked full-term and had evidently been lying on the bottom of the pit for some time. It was completely naked, like a little mummy with a flattened face, but still not decomposed apparently. It looked as if its neck bore a strangulation mark. The sad story was not difficult to tell; it was the old one – moral laxity, betrayed promises, shame and financial difficulties.

'What will you do next?' asked the Captain.

'Make sure that this little human corpse is placed in a crate and sent to the judicial officer for the district. Any further action can be left to the area authorities.'

'Won't you have anything to do with it yourself?'

'Hardly,' said Holst. 'It's usually a very easy matter to track down the perpetrator of this kind of crime and it won't take long for the poor mother to be found. Poor thing – they'll be tough days for her, but there's nothing else to be done.'

The Captain looked keenly at Holst.

'What if we did nothing about it? Let the corpse lie here?

18

The foxes would certainly devour it before daybreak and then…
then no one else will get to know anything about it.'

Holst shook his head.

'The Captain knows a soldier's duty. My duty here is the same
as the soldier's. It's a different matter for you. You of course don't
have to do any more.'

The Captain smiled a little despondently.

'You're quite right. We humans have a way of becoming a
nuisance to each other in pursuit of a greater good. So let's be a
nuisance – for the Good Lord's sake.'

He turned towards the lake and said as if to himself, 'Who
knows whether this smiling, silent lake is hiding other riddles
within her? You should empty it, Mr Detective, and arrest it
immediately if it proves to be complicit in more crimes.'

'That would be a lot of hard work in vain,' said Holst. 'No,
what we already have here will have to be enough for now.'

He covered the little corpse and the two men went to
the nearest farmhouse. Accompanied by a groom with a
wheelbarrow and a crate, they returned to the spot where they
placed the body in the crate and transported it to the farm. Once
here, it was placed in a coach house while Holst promptly set off
for the district magistrate's house to report their discovery.

Captain Ankerkrone went back to the lake and sat for a while
in deep thought, his eyes trying to penetrate the water and get
the lake to reveal any more secrets it may be hiding.

He looked very dejected when he came home and his daughter
tried in vain to dispel his heavy mood. She was herself actually
more affected by meeting Holst than she was by the incident. It
pleased her to hear that the young man was a Lieutenant; that
is, a gentleman who could probably become chief of police or
suchlike. He was exceptionally handsome and well-mannered;
she had never really imagined a 'detective' to be like that.

II

THE CASE PROGRESSED very smoothly and quickly. Immediately after the notification, the magistrate began the investigation in a professional manner. As Holst had predicted, they quickly succeeded in identifying the murderer, a peasant girl from a farm lying close to the lake and forest. She seemed almost relieved and confessed immediately. The child had been born in December of the previous year and she had stifled it immediately at birth. She had then wrapped it in some clothes, taken it to the lake and sunk it near the bank where it had been found.

Holst and the Captain gave their testimony, which in the circumstances was not of major importance to the case, but it led to the magistrate and the Captain becoming acquainted. The magistrate, an old bachelor who lived alone most of the time, took great pleasure in the grand, aristocratic Swede, who seemed to be very interested in everything to do with the administration of justice. The magistrate was most chivalrous in excusing Miss Ulla from appearing in court, and while the case was progressing, the Ankerkrones and the magistrate met each other frequently. Miss Ulla often enquired about the handsome young 'detective', as she and her father referred to Holst, and the magistrate smiled a little haughtily, though he admitted that the young police officer was a highly cultivated and courteous young man.

However, something happened that complicated the matter and caused the magistrate huge inconvenience. The Captain had been invited over for the evening – they were both passionate bezique players – and during a break in the game, the magistrate expressed his irritation about the nuisance the seemingly well-publicised case was causing him.

The Captain was slouched in a wicker chair enjoying one of his host's very best cigars, while sipping a glass of 'punch' which the magistrate had had brought out for his guest. The magistrate walked nervously up and down the floor, speaking rapidly.

'You see, my dear Captain, these blasted doctors create nothing but trouble. The district medical officer, who just between you and me is a clown, has found out by opening up the little corpse that the child had taken nourishment. Another equally sagacious lackey of the species medicus has backed him up. I have the girl's statement that the child was killed immediately, but as our wise penal code distinguishes very distinctly between greater or lesser speed in the expedition of such a small creature to the hereafter, the facts must be established clearly. If the girl is correct in her statement, says medical science, the child we've found isn't Marie Andersen's – that's the girl's name – but a completely different one. Since Marie, however, has confessed that she has given birth to a child and killed it, there is a possibility that there may be another child at the bottom of this damned marl pit and that must be

21

investigated. The girl insists on her story and the wise doctors on theirs, so the lake must be emptied.'

The Captain laughed.

'Do you really think, my dear sir, that it's necessary to empty the quarry to ascertain that? Suppose that you found a whole regiment of children's corpses on the bottom, what would you do about it?'

The magistrate scratched his head.

'Try to find a corresponding regiment of child murderers, I suppose. With the morals our society has, there's plenty of that sort of thing around, you know.'

'Oh – is Denmark really such an immoral place?' asked the Captain.

The magistrate shook his head.

'Oh no – I actually think there's an excess of so-called morality rather than the opposite. The way society and the law treat a poor girl who gets into trouble, it's really not a surprise that she becomes anxious and strangles her baby. Ah well, it's not me who has to make the laws – let's leave that to those who do. I just have to reach judgement according to them. I've got to get to the bottom of the case even though it would annoy me if I was forced to empty the quarry. The district medical officer, that ossified... – enough said – maintains that if the girl's child was killed immediately, it isn't this child, and just to convince – and be rid of – him as soon as possible, I'll have to set an Archimedes' screw in motion, probably tomorrow. By the way, I've written to the young policeman, Holst, who's a protégé of one of my friends in the capital, and who's supposed to be smart at finding out about similar cases on the quiet. Those people in there have such a wealth of material and the doctors seem to have finished annoying the life out of me. They do nothing but bloody pester both the living and the dead.'

22

The Captain leant back in his chair and blew large rings with the cigar smoke.

'Empty the lake? Well, that's one solution, I suppose, but if I were in your position, I wouldn't do it. That business about nourishment is a matter of little importance and since the girl has confessed, the case seems clear-cut to me. No, I definitely wouldn't do it. Suppose, as I say, that the bottom is covered with bodies – what then?'

The magistrate laughed.

'Oh, there's not much danger of that. It's all rather simple really. Draining it is easy, as the lake is high up and there's a deep ditch which runs past the forest. We can go up there together tomorrow and watch.'

The Captain called his daughter, who was sitting at the piano in the living room playing for the magistrate's housekeeper, an older relative.

'Ulla,' he said, 'now they're going to empty the water out of our lake up there in the forest, so we might as well go home to Malmö immediately.'

Ulla laughed.

'You'd think Pappa was in love with that lake. In the three weeks we've been here, he's visited it every single day. I thank you very much, sir, that we will now be free of it – it was beginning to bore me. That young detective was just as captivated by the lake as Pappa. He'd probably be just as annoyed if he came back and found it empty.'

Ulla blushed slightly at the thought of the young 'detective' and turned her head away.

'The young lady can ask him herself,' said the magistrate with a little smile. 'He's coming up here tomorrow, in a work capacity. If you want to renew your acquaintance, you could do me the honour of lunching here, along with the Lieutenant.'

Ulla blushed even more.

'Is he going to help with emptying the lake up there?' growled the Captain.

'Not exactly,' said the magistrate, 'but I have some matters I wish to discuss with him. Afterwards we can go up and look at how the work is going.'

The Captain got to his feet.

'Shall we play another round, sir?'

They did. Later that evening, as the Captain and his daughter were taking the fifteen-minute walk home from the magistrate's house, the Captain was in a bad mood. Ulla asked with a smile if Pappa had lost many games.

'No,' he said, 'but now I must leave. That idea of emptying the lake is just too absurd for words.'

'But that doesn't have to have consequences for us, Pappa,' objected Ulla.

'No, it doesn't,' he replied sharply and walked on in silence.

Ulla thought Pappa's mood had become worse since the day they found the child's corpse up there and met the 'detective'. Ulla blushed; she was spending rather a lot of time thinking about the young man, but he was handsome and very courteous. Tomorrow she would get to meet him once again.

III

EIGIL HOLST RECEIVED the magistrate's invitation to come to the lake with some surprise; he had thought the matter closed. It was not very complicated and he had seen in the newspapers how everything had gradually come to light. But since it was possible that there was something or other with the evidence that they wanted his opinion on – it was he, after all, who had first reported the case – he easily got official permission to attend and he was happy for the opportunity for a trip to his favourite spot. The gentlemen criminals in the capital were already beginning to go on their summer holidays and there wasn't terribly much to do in town.

The magistrate received him warmly and invited him to lunch, which Holst gladly accepted. He had a very sensitive nature and the bureaucratic rigidity with which some of the judges treated him when he came into contact with them in their official capacity made him feel uncomfortable. He found the divide that qualifications and rank raised between superior and subordinate police officers unreasonable. When working, he was courteous and carried out the orders he was given precisely, but it pained him that the majority of his superiors seemed to completely forget that he, with his training and his service position in the Army, might feel offended by this lack of respect.

The magistrate perceived their relationship quite differently. He treated Holst with the utmost courtesy and kindness and, while lunch was being prepared, he seated him in a comfortable chair in his large private office with a good morning cigar and brought him up to date with the ridiculous dispute between the legal authorities and their medical counterparts. Holst smiled; it wasn't the first time he'd come across this sort of thing. Doctors always found it difficult to appreciate that their divine knowledge had limits and nowhere had their authority been more exuberantly embraced than in forensic medicine. In all probability, the district medical officer's 'discovery' of the remnants of food in the child corpse was of very little importance. Now that it had been determined that the corpse had been in the water for five months, it could very well be that different decompositions or water which had seeped in had resulted in the so-called remnants of food, and as the girl was telling the truth about everything else, there was little reason to believe that she would be lying about this.

What the magistrate actually wanted with Holst was to persuade him to discreetly present their case to the medical authorities in the healthcare council, which he had learnt that Holst happened to have good access to through the different occasions when he had had the opportunity to convince the council or the chairman of the committee. They had already discussed this together when Holst had reported the find. Holst was happy to promise to do what little he could, and by degrees tried to dissuade the magistrate from having the lake emptied.

Admittedly it was infatuation, sentimentality even, but he wanted so much to retain his little spot in the forest. He didn't reveal this but it lay behind his efforts. However, the magistrate wouldn't budge on that point. He was rather pedantic, and since the district medical officer had stated publicly that it had to be another child, it had to be documented that he – as the magistrate – was right, even if he had to have the much larger Esrum Lake emptied. Holst had half a mind to say that it was most fortunate that Esrum Lake was not in the magistrate's jurisdiction because he seemed to be a man who stuck firmly to his guns.

Shortly before lunch Captain Ankerkrone and his daughter arrived. The Captain greeted Holst kindly and Ulla sent him a little coy nod of recognition which he received with the honour due. Holst, as previously touched on, was not someone who paid much attention to the fair sex. He had few opportunities to meet women in their homes and the many women he was able to meet 'outside', as he called it, he approached with armed neutrality. In this case, it was another matter; he was the magistrate's guest in a friendly, pleasant home and strove to be as gracious as possible.

Ulla was slightly surprised at the apparent change in his manner, but, as she said to herself, he was so full of vitality that one forgot about the other thing. The other thing was him being a 'detective'. Holst and Ulla became really good friends; they sat next to each other at lunch and Holst took the opportunity on the sly to look into her bright eyes and enjoy her fresh, enchanting smile. Ulla took good notice and sparkled with even greater freshness, if that were possible.

The Captain was in low spirits. There was no way he could be persuaded to allow Ulla to come with them to the marl pit; one had no idea of what grisly horrors the pond could be housing in its depths, and although Holst laughed and assured him that the danger was very little and that, on the contrary, it would be most stimulating if the young lady would accompany them on such a beautiful stroll, the Captain was adamant and Ulla had to remain with the magistrate's housekeeper, not at all an amusing prospect for her.

By the time they arrived at the marl pit, the work was well underway. It was being presided over by the district constable, an old soldier who had served in both wars against Prussia as a warrant officer in the cavalry; a reliable man, but strictly limited as far as the intellect was concerned. He was an excellent organiser, both at bird shoots and work of a more representative nature, and knew how to put a sheen on local festivities. It was a pleasure to watch him marching at the head of the procession at the local bird shoots, and his speech in praise of the king on these festive occasions – the king of the country, that is, not of the birds – was something of an event in itself that was only impaired by the fact that he made more or less the same speech three times a year and had done it for almost the same period of time that the country's ruler had reigned. But each time he delivered it, he said that he found a new aspect to dwell on.

The emptying of the marl pit was something of an event for him and his organising talent had not let him down. The stone wall had been broken through at three places and three screws were working simultaneously, driven by the locomobile from the parish's cooperative threshing plant that was located at a farm near the forest. The town's blacksmith and 'mechanical coachman', as he was called, had constructed an axle which spun in a way which was a joy to watch, and while the townsfolk stood by the wicket fence, the constable, accompanied by the wheezing of the locomobile, was in charge of the 'systematic emptying', his way of referring to the work that was underway.

When the magistrate and his guests turned up, the constable's predominant attitude swung over into modest subservience. He observed Holst with some suspicion; it annoyed him that a police officer from the city had been invited to be a guest of the magistrate. He considered himself to be at least the equal of Holst who, when it came to it, was only a sergeant, while he could call himself an inspector if he wanted to – and he did want to, by the way, but did so mostly out in the country districts. The magistrate laughed at the technical arrangements and Holst hid a quiet smile, but immediately went over to the constable and expressed such an open and unmistakably favourable appreciation of the work that the constable's stiffness towards him disappeared and he felt a certain pleasure in being able to show the gentleman from in there what the local police was able to stage.

In the meantime, the quarry was slowly being emptied; in places it was fourteen to fifteen feet to the bottom and the slope of the bank was steep. There were no fish at all; it seemed quite uninhabited, nor was there any trace of the clothes that the girl had said she had wrapped around the little corpse.

Holst was standing by the fence next to the Captain and the magistrate, looking a little wistfully over the yellow banks that were being revealed as the water gradually ran out. Suddenly, he felt a pressure on his arm; it was the Captain, who had taken a cramp-like grip on his wrist, just for a second before letting go.

Holst looked at his neighbour in surprise; the Captain's face

29

was strikingly pale and his eyes were focused on the bottom of the quarry. Holst looked in the same direction and pulled himself up straight. That looked strange – what could it be?

At the same moment, there came a shout from the men along the fence – all eyes were turned towards the edge where the water had been pumped out of a hollow near the bench, approximately in the area where the child's corpse had appeared. Holst stared at the spot and in the surface of the receding water there was something dazzlingly white beginning to emerge, pliant and round against the yellow bank. The water continued to sink and, with his blood freezing in his veins, he saw the body of a completely naked woman, stretched on her back and held down by two heavy stones, one tied with a rope round her feet, the other round her neck. Everyone flocked forward as the magistrate made his way with difficulty down the steep bank. A deep hush descended, except for the hiss of the locomobile and the creak of the screws, while the assembled men stood speechless, uncomprehending and almost paralysed by their profound, silent horror.

Little by little, a whisper spread from man to man; the work stopped and slowly, without being commanded, the men approached the body, untied the ropes and took hold. They carried it up the slope and laid it down in the grass near the bench. Holst and the magistrate followed them up, while the Captain came over to the bench and leant against the back support; he had gone very pale. None of them spoke.

The magistrate was dumbfounded; think that such a thing could happen in his peaceful jurisdiction – a murder, and one committed in the very recent past. He already felt how the whole country's attention would be directed at what he was up to, anticipating the magnitude of a task with little prospect of a result. He turned to Holst.

'May the devil take that doctor,' he hissed softly between his teeth.

At that moment, by a strange coincidence, the district medical officer came over the fence by the quarry. He pushed through the assembled throng of men and stood in front of the corpse, face to face with his adversary. The magistrate soon recovered his poise; he bowed to the doctor with an ironic smile and gathered his intellectual superciliousness into a joke.

'It's certainly not Marie Andersen's child.'

It sounded jarring and sharp through the eeriness that was oppressing everyone.

The district medical officer gave him a serious look in return.

'No,' he said, 'but it could be the mother of the other child.'

The magistrate tensed his lips and turned towards the quarry.

'Kirkeskov,' he yelled to the constable, 'Get the water out of this damned pit, even if it turns out to be stuffed full of corpses. Let's get it all done while we're at it.'

The crowd retreated silently until only the magistrate, his guests and the doctor were standing by the body. Holst observed it thoroughly. It was a young woman of medium height, well-developed, with luxuriant, blond hair. Her features were harmonious and beautiful, strangely well-preserved, her facial expression peaceful, her eyes closed under the pale eyebrows; a strangely white, firm, marble body, more statue than corpse.

The doctor broke the silence.

'She hasn't drowned; she was already dead when put into the pit. There can therefore be no question of suicide.'

He bent over the corpse and examined it closely.

'No more than twenty-five – more likely younger – it's a murder, sir, a full-blown murder.'

'Thank you, Doctor,' snapped the magistrate. 'I can just about see that for myself – we can take the preliminary post-mortem immediately, if you wish! The full autopsy can take place in its own time.'

Holst stepped aside and rushed down the slope to take a closer look at the spot where the body had lain. It struck him that, in the clay where the corpse's head had been, there were some pieces of clothing and a cotton apron, apparently dragged down there by the stone that was tied round the neck. He motioned to the magistrate, who came down to him.

'Sir,' he said, 'aren't these the rags the child murderer talked about?'

'Yes, you're right...' The magistrate bent down and examined the clothes. 'Exactly that.'

'They were lying under the corpse's head – you can see the imprint here. That means,' continued Holst as if to himself, 'that the body of this woman has been lowered into the pit sometime after the child's corpse. Not all that long after.'

The magistrate looked questioningly at him.

'Why do you say that?'

'I think the child's body, gradually, as the clothes around it became saturated with water, disentangled itself from them and finally just hung loosely to them. The body of the woman was quite naturally lowered at the same spot, the only one where access to the water was fairly easy, and came to rest on the clothes around the child's body. So when I threw the large stone out the other day – that one,' said Holst, pointing to a large stone which had been exposed in the surface of the water, 'the movement in the water released the child's body and brought it to the surface.'

The magistrate nodded.

'That means that the murder – if it is a murder – must have been committed within the last five, or maybe only three, months.'

'Five – probably,' said Holst.

The magistrate looked acutely at the young man, as if inspecting him from head to foot.

'Lieutenant Holst,' he said, 'could you consult your superiors and get permission to be placed at my disposal in this case? You're a talented man, and we'll certainly be needing all the talent we can get hold of. This is a damnable story.'

Holst bowed.

'There's probably nothing to prevent it,' he said.

The magistrate turned around.

'Get going immediately, Lieutenant Holst. I shall issue the necessary orders.'

The magistrate went back over to the body. The Captain was in conversation with the district medical officer.

'Yes, gentlemen,' the magistrate joined in, 'we have some work to do here. You, Captain, were right in your judgement, though it wasn't a child's corpse we found in the quarry.'

'There's a possibility...' the doctor remarked drily.

'I'm sure there is,' snarled the magistrate. 'Nothing would surprise me any more.'

The work was started up once again. A tarpaulin was spread over the body while the locomobile hissed and the screw squealed. But there was an oppressive atmosphere hanging over the men, and little by little the crowd of spectators stole off while the magistrate and the district medical officer held the post-mortem and Holst and the constable carefully searched the area.

The quarry was emptied and nothing more was found. Only the poor, frayed rags that the child murderer had talked about, and the naked body of the young, unknown woman, bound with two short, strong ropes around the feet and neck, but without a single characteristic or a fragment that gave them a clue as to who the murdered woman might be, let alone where the murderer was.

The Captain walked homewards with the magistrate. He was, like everyone else, very unpleasantly affected by what had happened and emphasised strongly how sensible he had been to stop his daughter coming with them, on which point they were in agreement.

Holst stayed behind after the others had gone. His brain was working overtime; there was something to get stuck into here – and under conditions that suited him down to the ground. He promised himself he would leave no stone unturned and the trail would be found. He was at last facing a task that required a man's strength and engaged his commitment in working towards a real goal.

IV

THE NEWS OF THE MURDER spread across the country like wildfire. Correspondents and reporters from every newspaper came to the crime scene. The area around the empty quarry was so completely trampled down that all the vegetation was destroyed, and an excellent reporter from a major newspaper in the capital, whose speciality was the portrayal of forest idylls, had to go a couple of miles north to find some scenery that could lift his inspiration to the required heights of lyricism.

There was no peace, day or night, for the magistrate; he welcomed the journalists with exquisite goodwill, as well as cigars and refreshments, announcing that he was prepared to make information available to them and doing so conscientiously. They were allowed to see and photograph the body, him, the constable and the child murderer; in short, everything they wanted.

All the newspapers nominated the magistrate as the most

talented, humane and discerning official in the country – to the immense annoyance of his colleagues countrywide and especially to the district medical officer, who was secretive and unwilling to release any information, and therefore presented as being an ignorant fool, as the story of the food inside the child's body came out and was exhaustively discussed.

Holst was left in peace. A rumour asserted that the investigation was going to be entrusted to this talented policeman, who incidentally was not at all popular among the capital's crime reporters, but when the rumour was confirmed, Holst could hide behind his new superior with great confidence and his protected position was respected.

The woman's corpse preoccupied the entire country for eight days. Every newspaper contained hypotheses, dates and conjecture of every kind. The afternoon press brought new sensational revelations every day, the main content of which was the information they promised to reveal the following day, but the mystery remained unsolved. The autopsy showed that the young woman had been killed with a strong, fast-acting poison and was dead when she was lowered into the water, but nothing more than that.

Absolutely nothing was found in the quarry and its environs, which were searched and dug up. There seemed to be no information about whether the young woman had been seen in the surrounding countryside. Photographs were taken of the corpse, notices and descriptions issued, all sorts of people interrogated, but not one witness came forward or was found who ventured to say that the woman concerned had been seen in the area. When ten days had elapsed without anything new coming out, interest waned. Visits became fewer. The journalists began to assign the case to the ranks of the numerous undiscovered murders and the government opposition began complaining about confusion in the justice system and poor organisation within the police.

In short, everything carried on the same as usual, which was most reassuring for everyone.

But the magistrate and Holst got some peace; just what they had been waiting for. There was already a very large amount of material, admittedly mostly of a negative kind, but the preliminary autopsy and the investigations which had been set in train had provided them with quite a few areas to begin investigating, all of which were of such a kind that they were less interesting to the press and the public than to the few people actually working on the case.

These few were the magistrate, the district medical officer, Holst and Captain Ankerkrone. As far as the first three were concerned, their eagerness was perfectly natural; the Captain may not, strictly speaking, have been authorised, but he had been associated with the incident by circumstances, so he felt obliged to give his utmost attention to it. He was a sensible and serious man who never gave his opinion, but just listened, shaking his head approvingly or disapprovingly according to what was happening.

He was especially interested in Holst and what he was up to. He was well aware that Holst was a man who had great ambitions and was also very able. From the first day, he followed his work with the utmost attention.

Circumstances would have it that there was a room available at the farm where the Captain was renting accommodation. He drew Holst's attention to this.

Holst rented the room and although he insisted strictly on paying for himself, he gradually became the Captain's guest without him noticing it. Nor could he hide from himself that he was becoming increasingly appreciative of the time he was spending with these two people and especially, of course, with the young woman who, with her fresh, cheerful warmth, contributed strongly to keeping his spirits up when the task was beginning to dishearten him.

What particularly charmed him about Ulla Ankerkrone was the fact that she never said a word about the murder case, avoiding mention of it with genuine female tact, so that in her company he felt released from the daily grind and strengthened by the freedom and peace she provided.

The Captain on the other hand was, as mentioned, extremely interested in the matter; he never talked about it in his daughter's presence, but at night he frequently sat with Holst for hours and reviewed the material, without offering advice but always listening. Holst became used to regarding him as a silent colleague.

Twelve days had elapsed and it seemed that they had made no further progress. Holst had been given the transcripts of the interrogations for review in order to organise the material for new interrogations, from which nothing at all was expected.

The Captain came in to him as usual with a splendid strong cigar and a glass of punch. He asked Holst to repeat his account of the case and this he did – slowly and accurately.

'There's not terribly much we can be certain about. As for the victim, we know that she's a young woman, about twenty-five years old, probably not married, since, while her fingers do bear the imprints of rings, there isn't any sign of a broad, smooth, gold ring. Probably not from the so-called fine stratum of society; her limbs are indeed well-formed, her hands well-kept, but there are traces of previous employment and her feet are marked by footwear which wasn't always of the best manufacture. Her torso bears the marks of excessive use of corsets; her hair has undoubtedly been coloured, a chemical test confirms this – it was originally ash blond, but has been treated with strong cosmetic colouring. Her skin is fine and doesn't show any excessive use of make-up – on the contrary, her complexion was probably fresh and healthy. All the internal organs are normal, except for the effects of the poison. But the examination has also shown that the victim has undoubtedly given birth at some point, although it doesn't seem to have been immediately before she was killed, more likely rather a long time back. The deceased appears to have breastfed her baby. No external characteristics or specific marks have been found at all, except that it would seem that individual marks on the fingers of the right hand indicate that the deceased at some time in her life has kept herself busy with sewing. But her nails have been cared for in such a way that there seems to be no doubt that the deceased had not participated in any manual work for a long time before she was killed.'

Holst paused and took a breath.

'As you can see, not so very little when all is said and done,' he added with a smile.

The Captain sipped thoughtfully at his glass and exhaled a dense column of smoke.

'That is to say, a demi-monde lady or at least an 'easy' woman from the ordinary people.'

'Precisely,' replied Holst, 'a young woman who, while not belonging to the really loose spirits, has probably not excelled in virtue and chastity, though on the other hand she's been able to look after herself well physically and has not been encumbered with imperfections of any kind. Quite the opposite, she was as sound as a bell. That's the positive part.

'The negative aspect also provides one piece of information. She's probably not from this country. Very exhaustive examinations have been undertaken. Everything points to a child of the big city and yet not one of our capital's renowned street walkers has gone missing, not even one of those whom few people are familiar with. The time of death is established by the relationship to the child's corpse. The murder must have been committed after 15th December last year. I'm inclined to think well into spring, as the remains of the rags in which the child murderer wrapped the baby's corpse are very much decomposed and were compressed under the woman's corpse. No one has seen the woman in question here in the local area or in the capital – by which I mean, we haven't been able to find anyone who has the slightest knowledge of her; a number of the people we have had in mind have been confronted with the corpse, but not one of them recognised it, not even our officers in the health police, who have extensive contacts in that world. In addition, the corpse's face type was not really Danish. You will recall that you yourself immediately conceded that she was very likely to be a compatriot of yours.'

'I did not,' said the Captain. 'To tell the truth, I've hardly really looked at the body – it's a weakness of mine, but one that's easy to understand. You must be remembering wrongly there.'

'That's possible, although I'm in no doubt myself and the next step I took was to ask for information from Stockholm and Gothenburg, but it seems that not even there are they missing any lady from the sort of society I'm thinking about. Of course, it isn't impossible that I'm mistaken, but I don't personally think so at this point. That's what we know about the murdered woman – it isn't much, maybe, but you'll admit that it's something.'

'Yes, certainly. What about the murderer?' asked the Captain. 'What do you know about him?'

'Very little. I suspect there's jealousy involved – it's definitely a premeditated murder. The girl has been poisoned by a calm, restrained man who has thought about all the possibilities. He hasn't left a single thing on the corpse that could lead to it being identified. We've carried out excavations and used a dragnet in several water-filled pits in the forest. I hadn't expected much out of it, since I'm convinced the man has taken away everything that belonged to the corpse. This indicates that he must have prepared his plan rather well and I'm inclined to believe that he brought a suitcase or similar and committed the murder on the spot.'

'Why do you think that? Isn't it more natural to assume that he took the body out there?'

'No, that would be too difficult. He must have known the place and chosen it deliberately. I imagine that he arrived with the victim from Sweden to Elsinore and travelled here with her. I've authorised investigations to this effect but nothing has turned up yet. '

'Why should the murderer be Swedish too?' said Captain von Ankerkrone, addressing Holst in rather a sharp tone. 'Aren't you Danes equally capable of murder?'

Holst bowed slightly.

'I'm not saying the murderer is Swedish. Only that the victim was, and that they probably came here together from Sweden. However, I confess I know nothing at all about it. My following hypothesis is more interesting. I assume the man brought a suitcase out to the woods with him – that would look natural enough, wouldn't it? After the murder, he packed his victim's clothes in the suitcase and took it with him.'

'Well I never!' The Captain pondered a while, but had to admit that it was a possibility.

'But now it gets interesting.' Holst looked up with a glimmer of pride. 'So far the killer has conducted himself in a very intelligent way, but now he commits his first act of stupidity, which he no doubt considers to be a very clever act and which, by the way, is quite well thought out, provided that he's only dealing with total idiots.'

'So tell me, what does he do?' asked the Captain, who was finding the case increasingly interesting.

Holst collected himself.

'If the murderer does what I want him to do,' he added modestly, 'he calmly leaves the suitcase somewhere in a waiting room or train compartment and lets it be registered among the lost and found items, to later vanish without a trace by auction.'

'Well I never!' The Captain sipped his punch with a little smile. 'Yes, if these murderers are kind enough to do what the detectives want, it's not really all that complicated.' Holst smiled.

'Luck, Captain, luck – that's what it comes down to. And so far I've been lucky.'

The Captain rose and left the room. He muttered something into his beard about that detective being one hell of a chap, but there was something about Holst that he took to and the man was certainly very sure of himself.

V

HOLST DECIDED TO TAKE A TRIP to the capital to test his suitcase hypothesis, which was more a sudden idea he had had while in conversation with the Captain than an actual preconceived plan of campaign. It was raining, so he couldn't use his bicycle for the trip; it thus suited him rather well that Miss Ulla had an errand to go to the station to fetch her brother, who had suddenly telegraphed his arrival.

Their passage was slow up the sandy hill road as Ulla and Holst sat very comfortably reclined in the farmer's fiacre carriage, which had the hood up because of the weather. The two had gradually become really good friends and the conversation was fairly brisk between them on all sorts of inconsequential things.

Fourteen days spent at the same place ties many small bonds and weaves thoughts, out of which camaraderie and friendship easily grows, and Ulla's lively, cheerful bearing had quite got

43

the better of Holst's restraint. They talked about the brother who was arriving. Ulla adored him; he was actually a kind of bright, handsome Swedish hussar officer, now a landowner, as he had taken over his father's estate, which lay between Eslöv and Kristianstad where the Scanian manor houses are closely packed together between the forests and bogs.

The Captain had never run his estates himself, she told Holst.

'Pappa's an officer and loves to travel in southern Europe, and in that regard 'Gammalstorp', as the estate is called, is not exactly a beautiful or amusing place to be, and if it wasn't for my brother Claes being married to a very wealthy woman and having had everything appointed with such charm, he would hardly be able to stand the place.'

'So your brother's married?' asked Holst, who had now been offered the opportunity to make closer enquiries into the Captain's family for the first time.

'Yes,' said Ulla, 'to a conventional but very sweet young lady from England. She's extremely wealthy and very sweet – not exactly beautiful, far from it – but very sweet and very wealthy.'

'Has your brother been married long?' asked Holst.

'Four years, but Emily – my sister-in-law's name is Emily – has been ill and has been living in the south for two years. There was a baby – a small one – who incidentally was close to dying but has now fully recovered. Now then, you can't be interested in hearing about Claes's family situation and, besides, it's not all that pleasant.'

Holst smiled.

'Is that perhaps because your sister-in-law's wealth was the primary consideration? I thought you emphasised it so strongly.'

'Not exactly, but Claes is so bright, so handsome and so joyful, and Emily is so austere, such a philistine. Yes, well, you know us so well now, Lieutenant Holst, that I don't need to keep it from you that Claes and Emily have been on the verge of splitting up. Pappa intervened and Claes became more sensible – because he'd been somewhat imprudent and Emily is partly in the right, but she was sick too and…'

Miss Ulla had talked herself red in the face and completely down a blind alley from which she couldn't escape. It was all very charming, and Holst smiled, which only caused her to become even redder in the face and come to a complete halt. Holst came to her aid.

'You mean thereby that your brother may not have been the most devoted of nurses and that his frail wife has taken offence, but the clouds on the marital sky have now been removed and the credit for that should go to the Captain.'

Ulla nodded.

'Exactly.'

Holst interrupted.

'Excuse me, Miss Ulla, for touching upon a matter which I would not otherwise have referred to, but you know very well that, unlike your father, I am not in the countryside for the sake of my health.'

Ulla nodded once again.

'Good,' continued Holst. 'You'd be doing me a great service if you didn't mention this case to your brother. I don't want it discussed in the circles in which he probably moves at home – I have my reasons for this. I would ask you to tell your father on my behalf that it's important that the case isn't discussed. Perhaps, should I meet your brother, I can refer to it myself. Will you promise me that?'

Ulla looked extremely solemn and had a great desire to ask questions, but her father had strictly forbidden her to discuss the case with Holst, and besides, from what her housekeeper had said, there was something improper about it all. She thus held her questions back.

They sat in silence for a short while.

'Tell me, Miss Ulla,' said Holst to break the ice, 'how have you really dropped into this out-of-the-way spot? It isn't common for foreigners to find their way out here.'

Ulla greedily grabbed the new topic of conversation and told him in a very lively manner and with great verbosity how they had been at Gammalstorp and how, when matters with the young couple over there had been put in order, they had left haphazardly, having actually decided to go to Rügen or Norderney, but at the last minute, the Captain had suggested Northern Zealand, and they had found this excellent place where they would stay until the middle of July.

While Ulla sat there talking, Holst observed her occasionally and noticed how much she resembled her father. The fresh, cheerful face could suddenly become serious, almost sharp, and there was something robust and strong-willed about her movements that totally resembled the Captain's distinctively energetic bearing and conduct. But she was lovely, and Holst thought of Gammalstorp and the very sweet and very wealthy, but not exactly beautiful Emily. They had reached the station.

The train from the south came first and Lieutenant Claes introduced himself – a tall, fair Swede with an exceedingly amiable countenance and prone to bowing a lot. He was one of those Scanian cavalry types who are recognisable wherever one may meet them from the North Pole to the South; not in the least interesting, but very handsome and elegant.

Ulla introduced Lieutenant Holst as a friend of Pappa upon which Claes von Ankerkrone bowed favourably. He was no doubt longing for a refreshing drink and a private conversation with Ulla, so when the train arrived from the north, Holst hurriedly left the two siblings to it.

On the journey into town he continued thinking about Ulla. It wasn't until arriving at Gentofte that he remembered the suitcase, but he shrugged it off in favour of daydreaming.

VI

THE NEXT DAY AT THREE O'CLOCK Holst presented himself to
his superiors at police headquarters, his heart pounding with
nervous excitement. Something very strange had happened to
him. In the morning, he had approached the lost and found
office of the railway corporation, and through inspecting the
depot lists, he had found 'a suitcase with various items of
women's clothing', dated 28th March. When he had the suitcase
brought out, it turned out to be a lightly woven wicker suitcase,
with two handles but no lock; the size of a standard man's
suitcase. It contained a complete set of women's clothes, from
inner to outer – just a single set – underclothes, coordinated
outfit, boots, hat – in short, everything down to garters, but no
valuables, such as a watch, and in addition, a half-full cognac
bottle and a small glass.

Holst had almost been overwhelmed by his discovery. He
seemed to see in it a portent that he really would succeed in

reaching his goal, but to arm himself against any hasty action, he instructed the railway official to maintain a steadfast silence about the find, and immediately set off to police headquarters to make the necessary arrangements.

The chief of police was just as profoundly affected by the discovery as Holst. Of course, they had to investigate whether the clothes he had found fitted the dead body, but there was from the outset a high probability that they were on the right track, especially as the suitcase had been found abandoned in an incoming train from Elsinore and only contained one complete set of women's attire of very luxurious elegance and quality. They proceeded immediately to making a list of the discovered items, a list that was checked on the spot by Holst's superior officer before being handed over to the investigating magistrate along with the suitcase.

The suitcase itself was, as mentioned, made of woven reeds, rectangular in shape, two feet long by sixteen inches high and twelve inches broad across the bottom. It looked completely new, but was not equipped with any brand name that might betray where it was purchased or manufactured.

It contained a half bottle bearing a Hennessy & Co. label, half full of cognac, in addition to a very cheap glass, apparently acquired for use while travelling. The cognac bottle with its contents would be the subject of a special examination to ascertain whether poison had been added to the contents, which, if the discovery was linked with the murder, was likely. In addition, the suitcase contained:

> 1. A black straw hat with braiding in a fashion particularly used by English ladies, with two ostrich feathers crossed in front on the brim, and bearing a label with the name Jean Tissot, Rue de Rivoli, Paris.

2. A black, silk-lined jacket of strong English cloth labelled Redfern, London.

3. A grey silk blouse, trimmed with black lace and silk embroidery, lined with silk and labelled Jules Biester, Berlin.

4. A smooth, black cloth skirt with a silk lining without trim, labelled Redfern, London.

5. A thick petticoat with sewn pleats, of yellow silk without label.

6. An embroidered fish-bone corset, richly trimmed with lace and silk ribbons, and with a fairly long waist, labelled Bon Marché, Paris.

7. Linen and underwear etc. richly trimmed with lace and interleaved with silk braid and a pair of brown silk stockings.

8. A pair of thick, brown boots with low heels, labelled in the leather inside, John Clifford, Strand, London.

9. A pair of gloves labelled Ricotti, Milano.

10. A pocket handkerchief with lace, embroidered with 'A. C.' and a smaller handkerchief embroidered with 'Annie' with a crown,

11. And finally, a set of garters of ordinary, slightly worn elastic that contrasted somewhat with the other particularly exquisite linen. The clips were stamped with the easily legible lettering: 'A. Vikander. Västra Storgatan 17, Kristianstad' and underneath 'Silver Medal at Stockholm Exhibition 1897'.

Nothing else was found, but it was no small find anyway.

First, they had to examine whether the clothes fitted the corpse, which Holst immediately wanted to test as soon as he came back, since the body had been subjected to suitable treatment so that it wouldn't undergo any process that prevented its presence during the investigation. They would also have to investigate if any clues to identify it could be ascertained from the discovered articles.

Holst carefully reviewed the discovery with his superior and they were agreed that the information considerably reinforced Holst's hypothesis about the victim's standing and circumstances. Judging by the revealed luxury, the dead woman was probably a lady who had had easy access to money. The peculiar combination of the finest English and German dressmakers with little-known merchants in three European capitals, coupled with the strange fact that one handkerchief was embroidered 'A. C.' and the other 'Annie' under a crown, considerably reinforced the propounded theory.

The most interesting find, however, was the garters, because if they succeeded in following this trail, which led to such an obscure, out-of-the-way city as Kristianstad, it should be easy enough to work out the dead woman's identity, in which case it would only be a matter of time before the murderer was detected.

It would surely be highly unlikely that a woman whose clothes came from Redfern's famous salon in London, and whose blouse was designed by a certain Jules Biester, Unter den Linden, would travel to Kristianstad to acquire a pair of garters and later add these tacky elastic bands to her European splendour. It had to be a far more realistic course of events that a wanton young Scanian girl had gone out into the world by the side of one or perhaps changing cavaliers; as the journey went from one country to the next, she had gradually changed her feathers from the outside in, eventually retaining only her garters, which were probably a comfortable fit and a reminder of home and the old days.

This hypothesis was perhaps more than realistic and it had the advantage that it offered a solid starting point.

By the time Holst left his head of department to take the return trip, it had been decided that not a word of what had been discovered was to come out in public, in which regard the railway official in question was given very strict instructions. The magistrate was almost beside himself with nervousness and, in the greatest secrecy, he and Holst, accompanied by the county gaoler's wife, went to the cell in the gaol where the body had been placed under the necessary precautionary measures.

The county gaoler's wife, who was adept at every kind of task, clothed the corpse, albeit with some difficulty, with the most important of the discovered pieces of clothing, especially the linen, corset, stockings, shoes, gloves and dress, and it turned out, as Holst, incidentally, had not for a moment been in any doubt about, that everything fitted in the most precise way and that the corpse as it lay on the stretcher was what was left on Earth of Annie, a wanton young girl from Kristianstad, who had visited most of Europe, only to end her days in a forest north of Elsinore, buried in a marl pit on the edge of a forest and risen from the grave to demand revenge on her murderer. But they maintained their silence about all this and, believe it or not, the people in question could indeed hold their tongues – not a syllable came out.

VII

LIEUTENANT CLAES STAYED JUST A DAY with his father; he was passing through on his way south. Everything seemed to be well at home and the Captain was very happy over the news from his daughter-in-law, who was staying in a hotel in Copenhagen, waiting to continue the journey.

Holst only caught a glimpse of the Lieutenant; he was very much in doubt about whether or not he should take the opportunity to mention Kristianstad and Annie, but it quickly became apparent to him that it was out of the question. Although it had gone quite smoothly so far, one had to be prepared for the tree not falling at the first blow, and the case wasn't so simple that one could just start questioning the first available person.

On the other hand, he decided to ask the Captain to grant him a conversation, as he had something particularly important to impart.

The Captain met him as usual with his punch and his cigar.

He sat in the wicker chair and didn't even wait for Holst to begin.

'Now then,' he said with a charming smile, 'the Lieutenant has found the lady's suitcase with the lady's valuables and clothing, and now the Lieutenant knows both where she's from and what her name is.'

Holst laughed.

'If that were true, sir, what would you say?'

The Captain paused for thought.

'If that were true, I would say that you were the luckiest devil in the three fraternal kingdoms – but it's obviously not true.'

'Yes, it is,' said Holst triumphantly, 'but it's a deep secret.'

'God preserve us!' said the Captain, not turning a hair. 'May one ask the Lieutenant who the murdered lady is then?'

'Annie C – shall we say, Annie Carlson from Kristianstad,' replied Holst in the same tone.

'Was that on the suitcase?' asked the Captain.

Holst shook his head. 'The suitcase belongs to the murderer.'

'Really now – perhaps his name is on the suitcase?'

'It isn't,' said Holst seriously, 'but if I have anything to do with it, it will be put on it.'

'I'm sure it will,' said the Captain, looking earnestly at Holst. 'You're one hell of a man – I'm tempted to believe you're a wizard.'

Holst smiled.

'This is a perfectly natural turn of events – a lucky idea, which has given results. It could just as well have come to nothing, but it worked.'

'Where did you get the name from?'

Holst told him about the clothes and the different labels. The Captain nodded affirmatively and had to admit that it was all very plausible.

'What are you going to do next?' he asked.

'Head for Kristianstad and investigate the world of ladies of easy virtue there. Because I don't suppose I can get any information about it in the Captain's house, can I?'

The Captain shook his head and laughed.

'No, sir. I've long grown out of that.'

'It's a shame that Lieutenant Claes von Ankerkrone has left. Perhaps there'd have been a possibility of getting some information from him.'

The Captain suddenly became serious.

'Unfortunately, it is a possibility – but even if my son hadn't gone away for a long time, I would have asked you not to interview him. I'm afraid that even during the time when he had permission for that kind of thing, he has devoted a great deal of attention and far too much money to the world of easy women. I've managed to drag him out of it and I'd be reluctant – for his wife's sake, extremely reluctant – for this to be stirred up once again.'

Holst almost regretted that he hadn't spoken to the Lieutenant about Annie – maybe he could have got some first-hand information there – but he said nothing.

'Did the Lieutenant perhaps know any lady of this name?' he asked.

'I don't know anything about the ladies my son might have known. Fathers usually don't, do they, Lieutenant?'

Holst bowed.

'I beg the Captain's forgiveness. I have perhaps touched on a sensitive area – I didn't know and would ask the Captain to disregard my question.'

'By all means.' The Captain's face once again became kindly disposed and he raised his glass to Holst. 'Your health, Lieutenant, your continued good health. What next?'

'Kristianstad,' replied Holst. 'And now I must take this opportunity to thank the Captain for his great kindness towards me during the past few weeks. Now our ways part and God knows when we'll meet again. So thank you for the time we've spent together.'

Holst paused for a moment to think about Miss Ulla and the thought warmed his heart.

The Captain looked very seriously at him.

'It's not my custom to ignore someone I've met,' he said softly, raising his glass. 'We two will meet again – or rather, we must meet again. You're very probably thinking, Lieutenant, that you're close to your goal, but it could happen that the road to Kristianstad and back will turn out to be quite long. In which case, you must not go past my door without knocking on it. You have in me a friend – you should know that – and people always need friends. Especially when they least think it.'

Holst stood up and went over to the Captain. He held out his hand and spoke with a certain intensity of tone which suited his subdued, somewhat dark voice so well.

'My most heartfelt thanks for our good work together, Captain von Ankerkrone. You may be sure that I won't forget the friendship you've offered me; so sure that no one can be in greater need than I for friendship, for I stand as alone as any man can stand. I don't forget friendship, any more than I throw it away blindly, but if I didn't trust you, sir, as I do, we two wouldn't be sitting here together on a case which means as much to me as this one does.'

The Captain shook his hand.

'Lieutenant Holst,' he replied softly, almost in a whisper. 'We Swedes have a reputation for being bad at what we might call drinking a brotherly toast. I give you my word that on this point I'm not like my countrymen, and so I toast you – in brotherly friendship.'

Holst wasn't familiar with Swedish customs and as he drank the brotherly toast with the grand old gentleman, whom he had met under such special and strange circumstances, he fell into a solemn, yet warm, mood.

He felt it truly as a kind of consecration of a friendship, upon which he was building more than he was admitting to himself. Holst and the Captain spent that night talking and drinking together, until the day began to brighten in the east, and they parted as two men who had got to know each other and sealed a friendship that would last the best part of a lifetime.

The following day Holst began his journey by following the trail that led from the still, lonely Forest Lake out into the world where people circulate.

PART TWO

Annie

I

WHO IS NOT FAMILIAR WITH ESLÖV STATION, the centre of Scania, where rail tracks from all corners of the universe meet, where the barons, tenant farmers and businessmen of Scania cross paths and meet up with friendly nods to the extremely colourful mam'selles at the counters, where red crayfish and brown crispbread beckon, and where the station's bells toll to hurry travellers to the long, open platform and the 'snorting steam horse' – a popular Swedish figure of speech – which will carry the noble members of the Trolle, Bonde, Beck-Friis and Hamilton families in first class and the Perssons, Cettervalls and Lindkvists in second class and distribute them radially out across southern Sweden, even to its remotest parts?

This small railway station acts as the central square of the small town. Every time you stop there, you seem to see the same faces and it all becomes a bit humdrum, as if all the local men of note have agreed to meet at the same place at the same time, where a six foot 'guard' with a flaxen military moustache walks majestically up and down the platform, calling out, alerting people – and bowing to the upper classes and the especially generous travelling salesmen – and then suddenly, as if impelled by a higher power, starts bellowing:

'Train to Hässleholm, train to Lund, train to Billeberga, train to Klippan, train to Ystad, train to Kristianstad.'

And the Trolles, Bondes and Hamiltons nod to each other while the Perssons and the Lindkvists wipe the last drops of Wolke's punch off their bristling moustaches and take their seats – in first and second class respectively in the mainline trains or in first class 'private', because on the private line trains, Trolle and Persson are merged into a common travel unit and get along just fine.

The guard signalled the train to Kristianstad and Eigil Holst took his seat in a broad, comfortably equipped first-class compartment, while the bell tolled and the aforementioned 'snorting steam horse' began to move, foaming at the bit.

The train slipped out from the station, first along the broad, royally approved, glorious stretch of the mainline, before swinging to the north-east past fields where large granite stones seemed to be projecting out of the womb of the earth as if representing the only thing it could provide, past the red, medieval, towering walls of Skarhult Castle, before meandering through cultivated fields near Kristineberg to the banks of a glorious lake, Ringsjön, where the Beck-Friises' magnificent old Bosjö Abbey peered out between green trees across the sparkling lake.

Holst sat by the window and looked out over the smiling countryside where castles and cottages lay in the sunshine by fertile fields and meadows. Without bothering about names and places, he just took in impressions which were entirely fresh and new and didn't bring any old thoughts to mind – nor initiate any new.

They were purely reflective travel impressions, where one only sees but doesn't think.

Opposite him sat a small, elderly gentleman, clearly a former military man, slightly balding, but as stiff as a Prussian and swaying as if on a steel spring, ready to shoot out some information, but too ceremonial to tilt forward before a question triggered the spring.

He amused Holst – but Holst held his tongue. At Hørby Station, the spring failed to function and, as the train rolled on, the little man raised himself in his seat.

'The gentleman is Danish, I believe?' he asked respectfully.

Holst nodded.

'Been in Sweden before?'

Holst had not. The elderly gentleman, on the other hand, had been in Copenhagen countless times. He mentioned a dozen different cafés, unsullied memories that sparked a little twinkle in his slightly bloodshot eyes and galloped past a dozen well-known names until Holst took compassion on him and said he knew a Colonel someone-or-other who was his companion's most intimate friend.

Eventually Holst had to come out with his profession and his lieutenant title gave the steel spring the final crack. The Swede swung back and introduced himself with great congeniality as a former Lieutenant in the Vendes artillery regiment, Bror Sjöström by name.

Holst bowed with honour and had now acquired a friend in Scania. The landscape changed while Ringsjön disappeared in the distance, the track climbed over pine-clad hills and ridges, while the train rolled up at numerous small stations where blond Trolles and Hamiltons passed the compartment with a rudimentary nod.

'G'day, sir...'

Sjöström knew them all.

He took the time to say a little about each one, while pointing out over the district and mentioning the names of proud lineages and magnificent stately homes. Holst didn't recognise any of them and received the speech in the same way as the changing images: without reacting. They were now approaching Karpalund, a junction shortly before Kristianstad. Lieutenant Sjöström bent towards the window.

'Over there the Lieutenant can see Gammalstorp, a beautiful little property with some forest and several farms.'

Holst nodded.

'It belongs to a good friend of mine, Claes Ankerkrone,' continued Sjöström, 'that is, the old man is still living in Denmark somewhere – a charming old chap – former Captain of Horse, with a daughter – one of the most beautiful girls you could possibly imagine.'

Holst nodded mutely.

'Monsieur Claes is a lively lad, a handsome, charming friend, married to a sickly English wife, and hard to keep under control. There was gossip about him last winter – his father had to intervene.'

It was uncomfortable for Holst to hear this stranger talking about Ankerkrone.

'I know the family...' he interrupted a little sharply.

There was a pause.

But Sjöström couldn't hold back for long. He continued, as if cautiously feeling his way forward.

'The Lieutenant knows the Ankerkrones from Copenhagen?'

'Yes,' replied Holst abruptly.

'Very pleasant people – exceedingly pleasant people, and

especially since the Captain – but...'

Holst was a little unsure as to whether he should interrupt or listen. He decided to let himself be informed; all things considered, his acquaintanceship with Ankerkrone was completely one-sided and it could be quite interesting to hear about him from one of his own countrymen.

Holst turned to his companion.

'But...?' he asked hesitantly.

The Swede was equally hesitant.

'Is the Lieutenant very familiar with Captain Ankerkrone?'

Holst smiled.

'No more so than that you could put him in the frame for the assassination of McKinley, if you wanted to. It would be most interesting for me to hear what a dreadful person conceals himself behind his charming exterior.'

Sjöström looked up seriously.

'So you've heard?'

'Not a word,' continued Holst calmly.

His companion lowered his voice.

'Well you see, the matter's so generally well-known, everyone's talking about it here in Scania, otherwise I would need God's protection for talking about the matter, but as I said, it's public enough. Captain Ankerkrone was, as the Lieutenant knows, serving with the Scania dragoons; he's never been really wealthy but was quite prosperous and married an Italian lady quite early in life, a Countess Cassini, who was very beautiful, quite extraordinarily beautiful, in fact. I remember her so clearly from the Amaranthe balls in Malmö and from parties at the manor houses in these parts. At that time, I was a young lieutenant and spent quite a lot of time at Gammalstorp – it must be around twenty years ago now, I suppose. Let me see... Claes is twenty-six...and Ulla...is eight years younger. That's about right. Then Mrs Ankerkrone died suddenly – after a ball at Araslöv, the large manor house you can see down there by the woods.

'The Captain took it very hard apparently, since he travelled south – his wife was a native of Venice – and the children stayed with his sister, the old spinster, Miss Ulla Ankerkrone, who now lives in Trelleborg. Shortly afterwards, one of our regiment's most dashing lieutenants, Baron Cedersköld, died. He'd gone to Italy at about the same time as Ankerkrone. Rumour has drawn a connection between the two deaths. I'm telling you this only because the story is already so public. But many voices were raised to have Mrs Ankerkrone disinterred. The servants claimed emphatically that very moving scenes had taken place between the Captain and his wife. After the wife's death, it was established with tolerable certainty that an intimate relationship had existed between Cedersköld and the deceased but, as always when it comes to important people, the authorities turned a deaf ear. The case was never cleared up. Nor did we get to know the circumstances of Cedersköld's demise. Some people said he'd fallen in a duel with an Italian officer; others that he'd duelled with Ankerkrone somewhere in the Tyrol, but this surely can't be true. The majority believe that he was quite simply murdered, pushed off a cliff at Ferdinandshöhe near Bozen. It was never cleared up. Ankerkrone returned after a few years, but he never again took up residence at Gammalstorp; he mostly lived in Copenhagen and is said to be there still. He never comes here.'

Holst sat listening quietly. When the Swede had finished speaking, he smiled.

'And you believe this story?'

'Goodness only knows,' replied his companion. 'It's so long ago now, but people say Ankerkrone is in some ways quite different to how he was in the past. I haven't seen him for many years. The daughter is said to be very beautiful and resembles her mother.'

Holst remained silent.

The train was approaching Kristianstad.

'Where should one stay?' asked Holst.

'The Masonic Hotel,' said Sjöström immediately, 'the most beautiful and most comfortable house in the whole of Scania. I always stay there myself, and if the Lieutenant has some time available, I would be pleased to do the honours on behalf of my old garrison town.'

Having a man who was so familiar with the town struck Holst as being a rather practical solution and since his companion, with typical Swedish tact, hadn't posed a single question to him about his business, he decided to keep access open to anything the chance encounter could offer; if, for example, difficulties should arise in investigating the young girl from Kristianstad, whom he had christened Annie Carlson and whom he in his musings always referred to by that name.

II

THERE IS A CHARACTERISTIC LOOK about the façades of buildings in small Swedish towns that has an immediate effect. If one stays in such a town for a while, one soon realises that there is nothing that differs from our own small Danish towns, which is hardly surprising as it is a mere two hundred years or so since Denmark had to cede sovereignty of the area to the Swedish crown. For the visitor, they are just as hopelessly dull as Bogense or Ebeltoft, but the look is more elegant and the food is better. This applies to most small Swedish towns and it applies to a singular degree to Kristianstad. The town lies on the River Helge where, on its meandering from the highlands of Småland near Alvesta, it widens into the lake known as Hammarsjön; when approaching from the south-west, the highlands to the north-east give the impression of mountains behind a broad plain and the town is quite splendidly located with its canals and copses. Its old church was built by Christian IV of Denmark.

Legend informs us that this was because of a dream that the gracious monarch had on a hunt when he stopped for a rest on that spot; if Christian IV really dreamt or not must be left as an open question, but the church stands there, looking so much like Holmen's Church in Copenhagen that the people of that city instinctively look for the Stock Exchange and the statues of Tordenskjold and the mounted King Frederik VII in front of the castle ruins.

Instead of those famous buildings, we must make do with Kronhuset, situated magnificently on a square with cannons deployed and where the Scanian High Court resides. Alongside are the barracks of the Vendes artillery regiment and the residence of the provincial governor with its slender columns, in addition to a sizeable number of public buildings and the masonic lodge which rules its side of the square – broad, powerful and rich in good food and Swedish punch.

As previously mentioned, all together it gives the impression of a large city – particularly the Masonic Hotel which boldly dares to compete with major European city hotels, and where the Scanian nobility and officers of the Vendes artillery regiment contribute mightily to maintaining the illusion, which a glance at the rest of the rather quiet population in the county capital otherwise quickly destroys.

The impression doesn't last for someone who, after an excellent meal at the hotel, wanders out into the town, which, as suggested, quickly sinks back into modest rural restraint. Its proud buildings become simple details and all that remains in the memory is the glorious Christian IV who dreamt godly dreams, Hr. Gustafschiöld, born Abraham Hellichius, who together with King Gustav III of Sweden put his foot down with the Swedish estates, and the sad event a few years ago, when a specially hired train removed the Scanian Enskilda Bank with its cash in gold from Kristianstad, under the noses of its hungry citizens and indebted warriors, and took the reserves which the bank owned to Helsingborg.

The main street is called Västra Storgatan, but in no. 17 there was no A. Vikander, the supplier of the garter Annie had worn and the direct reason for Holst's trip to Kristianstad.

This was the next disappointment he experienced and it affected him more deeply than the town's, in his eyes, fading grandeur. Not only was A. Vikander not in Västra Storgatan, but there was no one of that name among the town's drapers.

This detail was of course quite unimportant, because even if Mr Vikander had been sitting in 17 Västra Storgatan in the best of health, selling his garters and enjoying his glass of Carlshamn punch, he would hardly have been able to remember the particular young lady who had bought garters off him that Holst was interested in.

Upon closer reflection, however, Holst realised that the fact that A. Vikander was no more might be just as interesting, and lead to indications about time that could further the investigation. It was a given that Mr Vikander had participated with honour in the Stockholm Exhibition in 1897 – so he must have been alive then. Now that he no longer existed, it was possible that termination of his existence could yield an important moment for the determination of who Annie had been.

Holst managed to learn that Mr A. Vikander had certainly lived and been an esteemed and distinguished citizen of the good town, but one year after the exhibition in Stockholm, he had died under such circumstances that the priest in Christian IV's magnificent church in Kristianstad could legitimately have repeated Anders Sørensen Vedel's memorable words at the funeral of that king's father: If the late-lamented gentleman's favour had been less devoted to the enjoyment of strong drinks, which was unfortunately beyond all common measure etc. etc. – and that one of the contributing reasons for the omission of this mild reproach was probably that Mr A. Vikander, as well as the late-lamented Frederick II incidentally, was hardly a unique case among the brave citizens of Kristianstad.

He had, however, died in 1898 and the business dissolved the same year.

Now part of Mr A. Vikander's stock of garters – not least in the light of the honour that had been bestowed on these useful articles in 1897 – could indeed have been transferred to his descendants, but these people would in all probability have taken the opportunity to link their own name as soon as possible to the distinguished article and it proved on closer examination that the excellent garter was in fact being sold as a patented article by a Mr Lindkvist in Arsenalsgatan, who had provided the original brand with the addition: Exclusive distribution by Oscar Lindkvist, 5 Arsenalsgatan, Kristianstad.

Holst was thus left with the hypothesis of 1898 or the autumn of '97 as the date and decided to try to ascertain whether, in the world that was enjoying life in Kristianstad in these years, there had been a young lady by the name of Annie, possibly Carlson.

To enquire further, he could have turned to the local authorities, but it seemed easier to him in this respect to use his travelling companion, and especially the latter's connection with the honourable Vendes artillery regiment, in that he reasoned that a lady like poor Annie, in the full spring of her youth, would probably have been known to the regiment's young men, and that their memories might be both brighter and richer in content than those of the local police.

Lieutenant Sjöström and Holst had agreed to dine together, and Sjöström had held out the prospect of a visit to the regimental

71

establishments, so Holst decided quite calmly to bide his time and take that opportunity to make enquiries. To pass the time he went for a walk in the area, and before long had taken in the whole town. His thoughts turned back automatically to North Zealand and the Ankerkrone family, and he had to admit that Sjöström's tale of family drama had made quite an impression on him.

He had become fond of the Captain, whose fine, sympathetic mentality had immediately fallen in with his, but he couldn't deny that, properly speaking, it couldn't be excluded that Captain Ankerkrone had good reason for spending the last years of his life in a foreign country, far from his ancestral estate. However, it seemed unlikely to Holst that he would have murdered his wife in jealousy, but it was evident from his own words and his bearing that he had lived through a grief that was more serious than usual. It struck Holst that Ulla had never talked about her mother, but little by little, individual traits appeared that made it more than likely that there was a so-called skeleton in the Ankerkrone cupboard and that this skeleton was the mysterious event that was associated with her mother's death.

As always, one thought led to another and, almost against his will, Holst was led to a series of reflections on the Captain's remarks on the occasion of the discovery of the corpse, and in particular on the examinations that had determined murder by poison, which admittedly could have been completely natural, but with reference to Sjöström's tale – that is, to the local gossip – took on a deeper, more troubling character.

These thoughts were gaining increasing ground in Holst, attaching themselves more strongly to the picture of the fine, handsome gentleman and leaving an involuntary stamp on this picture, so it wasn't such a big step from there to Holst making his final decision that, when time permitted, he would spend it investigating this other mysterious death and try to penetrate the events that had accompanied it.

For the time being, it was important to find Annie Carlson's murderer, but first and foremost to prise out everything that could cast greater clarity on who she had been.

Holst returned to the Masonic Hotel, where his travelling companion was waiting for him.

III

LIEUTENANT SJÖSTRÖM had arranged a party that turned out to be quite festive. Beside the obligatory 'smörgåsbord', he presented Holst to an older fellow officer who was still serving in the artillery regiment: Baron Holger Kurk, a tall, lean, very obliging and well-mannered captain whom Sjöström jokingly described as the entire region's uncle and the most sought-after cavalier throughout Kristianstad County.

Captain Kurk did nothing to harm his reputation, and the dinner, which included all the pleasures the most pampered garrison soldier could wish for, was both long and lively. The atmosphere was excellent; cheerful stories of garrison life and life in the capital crossed swords. It turned out that Sjöström had wound up as an equerry at a major feudal landowner in South Scania, on whose behalf he visited the regiment to acquire vulnerable older horses for breeding purposes. Holst was silent about his business, but allowed it to be understood that his visit was related to a legal matter, in that he stated that his occupation was connected to a department of state in the Danish capital, on behalf of which he was looking for some information in Kristianstad and other towns in Scania.

He had thereby primed them for his question, and when the men sat drinking coffee in front of the building where the young people of the town paraded across the square, past the beautiful, blooming borders, Holst casually asked whether any of the gentlemen remembered a young lady named Annie Carlson, who had probably played some sort of role in the small town a few years back.

No one knew her. Sjöström had a valid excuse, as he had already left the town at that time, but even Captain Kurk, who was a bachelor and, according to what Sjöström had testified, a pure encyclopaedia when it came to ladies, even outside family life, had to declare void. Holst easily sidestepped the matter; he didn't want to let on that he didn't know the name precisely and thereby expose himself to questions he didn't want to answer, but chance came to his aid, as the Captain didn't want to throw in the towel but kept coming back to the lady whom he wasn't supposed to be able to remember.

Holst eventually admitted that the name Carlson could be wrong, an assumed name, and this set the Captain's thoughts going in a lively retrospective. It was an impressive regiment of Amazons the old warrior conjured up, a not-insignificant addition to Vendes' famous artillery, and when Holst helped with a description of the person whose characteristics were very clear in his mind, the Captain's thoughts became gradually clearer.

He looked acutely and intently at Holst before casting a glance at Sjöström.

'Aha – so that's it,' he blurted out.

Holst could see that the Captain knew the correct name, but that there were circumstances that prevented him from mentioning it and, with great dexterity, he led the conversation totally away from the matter and avoided broaching it further. Sjöström was very clearly under the influence of the evening's festivities; he was determined to drink a brotherly toast with Holst, but the latter noticed that Captain Kurk, after the little incident that had quite escaped Sjöström's attention, had become very restrained and in between times cast sharp, furtive glances at him.

Furthermore, Kurk had made a considerable impression on Holst; he was a pleasant table companion who exercised strong moderation with regard to the festivities and didn't change his bearing despite the rather significant number of glasses that were emptied. Holst decided therefore to pursue his goal and, as the party gradually expanded with the arrival of more officers, while Sjöström's exuberant joy simultaneously began to assume overwhelming proportions, Holst managed to beat a retreat at an opportune moment.

The Captain stood up at the same time and followed him down the street. They walked instinctively towards the outskirts of the town and, as if the question had been burgeoning in both of them, they also stopped instinctively.

'I'll pre-empt the Captain because I wish to ask his forgiveness for being so restrained in front of the other gentlemen. Unfortunately, I found it necessary.'

Captain Kurk looked sharply at him.

'The gentleman is perhaps not Lieutenant Holst.'

Holst looked up.

'Yes, I am. Apart from the approach I made, as you will have noticed, as a pretext to gain your trust, I have no particular reason to hide my name.'

The Captain bowed. Earlier in the evening, Holst had made the discovery that Captain Kurk – quite naturally in a city like Kristianstad – was a freemason, like Holst himself.

'It's just a matter of the purpose of my presence here and of my question from before – the girl I asked about,' continued Holst.

Kurk nodded.

'The girl – Annie Cederlund.'

Holst looked up.

'So her name was Cederlund.'

'You didn't know?' asked Captain Kurk.

'No,' said Holst, 'I didn't know – but to come back to myself, I am, besides being a lieutenant, also employed by the Copenhagen police and it's in this capacity that I've come here.'

The Captain nodded once again – it struck Holst that his face took on the same expression as Ulla Ankerkrone's when he first mentioned his occupation.

'Aha,' continued the Captain, 'so the gentleman is a 'detective'.'

'Yes, I am,' replied Holst abruptly.

The Captain smiled.

'I suspected as much, by the way, when you asked about Annie. However, I had a reason not to mention her name while poor Bror Sjöström was present.'

'Oh – and that was?' asked Holst with interest.

'Well, Annie Cederlund has cost poor Bror most of his wealth and, into the bargain, his family's honour. So, what do you really want with Annie? Has she committed crimes in Copenhagen? The last I heard of her…' Captain Kurk suddenly stopped.

Holst looked intently at him.

'My dear Captain,' he began in a subdued voice, 'we two don't know each other and the Captain can of course reject my intrusion. I only have the operational way to approach this, you see, and I don't expect very much out of that. If, on the other hand, the Captain would show me the trust that, in accordance with what he already knows, I have a claim to, I might be able to take care of my business here as early as this evening and leave town as quietly as I came, without a word about the sad events that have brought me here needing to be known to anyone else than the Captain himself. It is an urgent prayer concerning a very important matter.'

Captain Kurk was silent for a moment; the moonlight fell on his upright figure, while his head was bowed and his thoughts were churning round.

'Lieutenant Holst, there are reasons, very serious reasons,' he said, throwing his head back and emphasising every word, 'that could compel me to reject your request. I know quite a bit about Annie Cederlund and her name is one I'd rather not mention. I can give you my word of honour that I don't know where Annie is now, but I can say just as certainly that I can only give you information about her that is several years old. That doesn't mean that I don't know anything about her since then, only that I'm unable to tell you anything. Will you from your side give me your word that you won't request any further information from me than that I can, and will, give you?'

Holst thought for a moment. There was something solemn about this conversation beneath the moon, while light was flickering sparsely from individual lamps and the water in the lake inlet lapped against the shore.

He raised his eyes and looked firmly into the Captain's.

'Will you for your part give me your word of honour that you don't know where Annie Cederlund is at present or what her final fate may have been?'

The Captain maintained eye contact with Holst – his face was fully illuminated, bearing a seriousness that made it clear that what he was about to say was the truth.

'You have my word of honour, Lieutenant Holst. Come home with me, and I'll tell you what I know and what I feel able to tell you about Annie Cederlund. That name contains more for me than you can imagine. Is she dead?'

'Yes,' said Holst softly. 'She was murdered in Denmark in March this year.'

Captain Kurk went as pale as a corpse but said nothing. The two men went to the barracks together.

IV

Captain Kurk lived in a flat in the artillery regiment's barracks, which in its consummate, Spartan simplicity was no small contrast to its resident's exquisite elegance. The complete contrast certainly made an impression on Holst, but it was as if the furniture and walls in the large, square study quietly but convincingly testified to the Captain's rule-bound and completely trustworthy comportment.

The household effects had been kept strictly in the Biedermeier style from the years 1820-50 – dark mahogany, mostly without inlay, a broad but hard sofa with storage, and black, leather-covered armchairs. The desk in particular, a delicate piece of mahogany furniture, was an outstanding specimen of this style. The windows were high and framed with austere, green damask curtains, the tops only covered by a pelmet. The floor was whitewashed and the living room, where an old moderator lamp, already lit when the gentlemen arrived, spread a gentle yellow glow, giving the space a sheen almost of purity and meticulous order.

On the wall above the sofa, a trophy display was assembled, consisting of numerous shiny weapons; an extensive collection, in part of very rare slashing and stabbing weapons, and above this stood a bust of Sweden's reigning king in bronzed plaster.

The walls were tightly bedecked with copper engravings and lithographs, mainly representations of Sweden's kings and distinguished statesmen; one end wall was adorned with photographs of friends, and in the middle of this group hung a painting of a wonderfully beautiful woman with a fine oval face framed by black, curly hair. A black mourning crape was hung over the frame of this picture and in black letters on the bottom edge was a name: Giulia.

Underneath the picture was a large photograph that showed three men in uniform in front of a camp tent; a wreath of rather withered everlasting flowers had been laid over the black frame, and as Holst ran his eyes over the picture, he saw that one of the men was his host, the second, who was bending over him with a hand on his shoulder, was Captain Ankerkrone, while the third was unknown to him.

Captain Kurk watched him closely while he stood in front of these pictures and, as Holst turned to him to ask about them, he sensed such tight-lipped melancholy in his host's face that the question died on his lips. The Captain asked him to take a seat and an old, composed servant brought in a tray of refreshments, which he quietly placed on a table between the two of them, after which he noiselessly retired.

The Captain opened a drawer in the large, beautifully inlaid mahogany writing desk standing between the tall windows and handed Holst a miniature portrait made of ivory mounted in a slim, gold frame.

'That was Annie Cederlund,' he said with a sad smile. 'That's how she looked in 1885.'

Holst looked up in surprise.

'1885? I thought she was only a little over twenty.'

'She was born on 7th June 1866 in Bäckaryd by the River Laga, close to Ljungby in Småland. Her father was a corporal and a gamekeeper in the big hunting districts that some English lords have rented in this part of the country. He's dead now, but her mother is still alive and lives in a small house by the Laga. Some old friends of her husband, me among them, give her an annual support payment; she's now childless, as Annie was her only child. As promised, I'll tell you as much of this unfortunate girl's story as I can, even though unfortunate is hardly the word to use for a creature whose conscience has had to bear such heavy burdens as Annie's.'

The Captain pushed the carafes of whisky and water over to Holst and, having made himself comfortable in his armchair, proceeded to tell Annie's story in a subdued, serious voice.

It struck Holst that the serious man sitting opposite him in his austere, soldierly quarters didn't much resemble the handsome, smiling officer his travelling acquaintance had presented to him, and he recalled the Captain's remarks about the beautiful people he knew with surprise. Now it was as if his mouth had never smiled and he didn't look anything like a brave conqueror, a happy soldier in peace time.

Holst listened while the Captain spoke and the hands on the large mahogany grandfather clock moved slowly towards the midnight hour.

'As I said, Annie was born in Bäckaryd in 1866, her father's name was Bengt Bengtson and she was known as Annie Bengtsdotter, according to the customary tradition of Småland. As the only child, she was the apple of her parents' eye, especially

82

of her father's. She didn't learn much in school, but this just made her all the more eager to go out with her father in the forests and heather-covered clearings. She learnt to know the shriek of the reindeer, the call of the bull and the cry of the roe deer in the summer; she learnt to recognise the tracks of the game, to hunt foxes and hares in the clearings in the autumn, and no forestry assistant could have been a better marksman and hunter than she. She was straight-backed and lithe, and furthermore as beautiful as a shepherdess in one of Watteau's paintings, and just about all the young lads of the parish courted her... Indeed, the magistrate's son in Bäck even took his own life because of her scornful response to his courtship. I first saw her in 1880 when I was a hunting guest with a couple of friends on grouse shoots in the clearings by the Laga. She was only fourteen years old, but fully developed and dazzlingly beautiful.

'We were guests there two years in a row. Besides me there were two gentlemen whose names I won't mention, since the circumstances make it my duty not to mention their names in connection with her. During the second year, Annie left her home with one of these men.

'Her father's anger was boundless; he implored me to get his daughter back and I tried as hard as I could, but in vain. Then he went to the town where his daughter had taken up residence, but Annie refused to come back home with him. Two years passed, Annie had a child, and her father attempted to kill the man he regarded as her seducer, but failed, and one night in the county gaol he hanged himself while his guard was asleep.

'He was a brave soldier and a loyal, skilled hunter.

'The case attracted a lot of attention and Annie and her lover went away. He, who was an officer of the regiment here, had his pay stopped, but a couple of years later, he was forgiven by his superior officers and returned to the town.'

The Captain paused for a moment before continuing.

'Strange things happen in this world, and he went back to his debauched lifestyle – to the sadness and distress of his best friends. Shortly after his return, an event took place here in the district, something which remains another person's secret, so I cannot and will not explain it to you more fully. A respected family of high standing was ravaged by a sad incident, in which Annie's lover played an enforced, if ugly and humiliating, role. A friendship that tied him to one of the best men in his station was broken – Annie was to blame, but the events that occurred removed him forever from Annie and the country and cost him his life abroad.'

The Captain's voice became even more subdued and serious and Holst noticed with surprise how intensely he was moved by the memory. It was almost as if tears were blurring his gaze.

He broke off abruptly before resuming at a brisker tempo.

'Annie left the country for around ten years. No one knew where she had gone and her name, which had been on everyone's lips in those days, was forgotten by everyone. Then, one fine day, she showed up once more in town. She called herself Annie Cederlund and she opened a dressmaker's workshop in this name in Voldgatan. The middle classes were distrustful in having her back, so her business could hardly have been particularly extensive. But she was dazzlingly beautiful, her figure was now stately and fully developed and her ability to coerce men and lead them where she wanted was so rare that I still don't quite understand why she hadn't tried to find her place in the demi-monde of a large city, which she could easily have achieved as a first among equals. Ah well – but she had that child, a girl who had been brought up here in the town – and that was no doubt one of the reasons she had returned.

'However, she may have had other reasons for choosing

Kristianstad for her home. I didn't look her up – the events I have only hinted at to you separated us like a deep, insurmountable chasm. On the other hand, she seemed to want to seek me out and, as I consistently rejected all her approaches, she took revenge by forming a close attachment to a young man for whom I harboured a fatherly friendship, the younger brother of our dear fellow tonight, by the name of Hugold Sjöström, who was my first officer at the Armoury, which I was commanding at that time.

'Hugold was a handsome, spirited lad with excellent abilities, but without any strength of character and weak as a kitten when it came to women. Annie pressured him to advance himself, step by step, without any love, I believe, just out of a desire to stir up trouble. Then her little girl died and, as if trying to drown her sorrow, she abandoned all restraint and indulged in orgies that caused a stir in the town, but as she was free and independent, there was no power that could stop her – and unfortunately not him either. Hugold Sjöström took money from the regimental cash box which he was in charge of, signed fake bills of exchange for a considerable amount, and the respectable Bror only managed to save his brother from dishonour through great sacrifice involving most of what he owned. Hugold was dismissed from the regiment and went abroad with Annie. This happened a few years ago in the autumn of 1898. Since that time I've only heard from the couple occasionally. Sjöström slid further and further down; he was still Annie's companion, but there is no doubt that the funds for his upkeep were solely raised by her, and her sources have hardly been the purest.

'I saw them once myself in Paris a year ago. Sjöström tried to avoid me, but Annie nodded to me in recognition and laughed. The couple were on that occasion accompanied by a young man whose fate was close to my heart. I warned him about Annie.

But… Well, I suppose that kind of warning doesn't usually bear fruit.'

The Captain finished with a sigh.

'I don't really know any more…there isn't any more either… no… There's no more.'

The Captain stood up and paced nervously back and forth.

Holst bowed to him.

'Thank you, Captain, for what you've told me. Unfortunately, it would seem that what is of most interest to me is what you have held back.'

The Captain nodded.

'I told you that, Lieutenant Holst. I told you there were things I had to withhold which no human power could force me to speak of. You may well argue that you could learn something about this by other means. I think it unlikely. Besides me, there is only one other person who knows all about this matter and he will know how to keep quiet, but if he wants to talk, he has the right. I do not.'

'You can't even tell me his name?'

The Captain shook his head.

'Nor the name of Annie's first lover?'

The captain hesitated for a moment.

'Well, yes, I suppose I can – his name was Cedersköld and he died 16 years ago.'

Holst was silent for a moment.

'Would it be of any use to ask Lieutenant Sjöström about the matter?' he asked gently.

'Which one? Hugold – yes, if you can find him – he would probably be able to provide further information. But God knows if he's still alive, or if he's at liberty, for his ways led him close to the walls of prisons. It was such a shame because he was a handsome soldier once upon a time.'

'I was thinking of the equerry,' interjected Holst.

'I doubt it,' replied the Captain. 'He probably doesn't know as much as I've already told you and it will only bring him embarrassment to talk about the matter.'

Holst sat for some minutes in silence, then got up and walked over in front of the Captain, who was leaning against the writing desk.

'Captain, what you have told me is something, albeit only a little,' he said firmly. 'I've given you my word that I won't impinge on you by demanding more information. I can tell you that my first trip will be to Bäckaryd to find out what Annie's mother may know about what you feel unable to tell me, and about the last information she had from her daughter. I certainly don't expect much from this journey, but I don't want to refrain from it either. The only thing I want to add to my thanks is that the day will probably come when we will meet again and talk more openly about Annie Cederlund and the men whose fates have been linked to her. My word binds me and I won't seek additional information from you. I just ask you if you will tell me the name of the officer whose picture is hanging under the painting – the third one – the young one sitting in front of the table in the photo bearing the wreath of everlasting flowers.'

The Captain cast a sharp look at Holst.

'Him?'

He fell silent, as if undecided. Holst put his hand on his shoulder.

'Cedersköld?'

The Captain didn't answer, but Holst turned to leave.

'Why are you asking about that?' snapped the Captain suddenly. 'It's a picture of me and a couple of friends.'

Holst interrupted him with a mild smile.

'Captain Kurk – we two still don't know each other properly

but with time we may remedy that. Thank you once again for everything you've told me. I will be leaving early tomorrow morning and will not inconvenience you any more. You are right. I will try to find out the information which your duty as a friend and brother officer prevents you from giving me from someone who is a much closer acquaintance, the person who is most familiar with it and to whom I will convey your brotherly greetings.'

Captain Kurk looked at Holst in astonishment. He stood with Holst's hand in his own without really being able to clear his thoughts.

'I don't understand...'

Holst smiled once more.

'It doesn't matter, Captain. He will understand.'

'He? Who?'

'Arvid Ankerkrone,' said Holst softly while freeing his hand.

Holst left with a mute nod. The Captain was left standing rooted to the spot; he made a movement as if to follow his guest, but stopped suddenly.

'God's will be done,' he muttered.

He heard the servant talking in the corridor, followed by steps on the stairs. Sinking into his armchair, he spent a few minutes looking at Annie's portrait which he had put down on the table. His eyes slid over to the picture on the wall and his lips moved gently.

'May God be with you too, Arvid.'

The morning light had risen before Captain Kurk went to bed. Around the same time, the train steamed off towards Hässleholm taking Holst onward to Vislanda and the clearings by the River Laga in the forested, hilly Småland.

V

THE JOURNEY BETWEEN Kristianstad and Hässleholm was uneventful for Holst. He was fast asleep. It was no wonder, as his body, after a night so rich in experiences, demanded its right and the landscape in the middle of Scania isn't attractive enough to hold a tired man awake.

Holst slept soundly; in Hässleholm he ate a reasonable railway lunch followed by an hour of good rest, and when the train came steaming in from the south to take him across the border to Småland, his thoughts were as clear as his eyes.

Scania ends at Hässleholm and Småland opens up for the observer. The Scanian countryside, especially the region around Kristianstad, is gently rolling and mostly reminds one of Denmark, now and then a little wilder, with large coniferous forests and fields with boulders like Bornholm, but not particularly alien.

In Småland a completely different countryside presents

itself. The railway line from Hässleholm runs through large tracts of coniferous forest, dense with low spruce and pine, and large birch forests; the ground is hard and stony, the boulders becoming larger, lying scattered on the hillsides as if giants had been playing ball with them; water meadows lie side by side and, down the slopes, streams trickle into lakes, which spread over the land and extend between Småland and Blekinge, forming a row that completely riddles the landscape with flickering surfaces.

In the beginning, the brown marshes appear and beyond them Lake Ballingslöv, followed by marshes and heaths alternating with large forests, where lakes are spread out near Älmhult and Liatorp; finally, after travelling over rocky, wooded hills, one reaches Vislanda, the junction town where railway lines run to the west and east coasts of the country. Holst was completely intoxicated by the strange, singular countryside. His gaze swept over hills and marshes, ponds and lakes, was captured here and there by red-painted wooden houses and farms, scattered beside streams or lakes, or up against a protective cliff. Here and there beside the clearings and the larger lakes, tall chimneys rose into the sky; it was as if civilisation was stretching its arms out towards the forest idyll, but gradually as the journey continued northwards, the forest idyll became the strongest impression and the wind bore the fresh forest scent towards the carriage windows. Holst was alone in the compartment, which suited him.

Little by little, he released his thoughts from the strong impression made by the strange countryside, returning coolly and matter-of-factly to the case and the purpose of his journey. He had learnt quite a bit, with the help of the lucky star that seemed to be watching over his quest.

He now knew that the murdered woman was an Annie

Cederlund, whose reputation was not exactly unblemished and whose fate seemed to him as full of adventure as any heroine from a novel. He also knew about the most important events of her life, and the visit to the little village by the River Laga ought to give him more information about what might still be hidden from him.

But more important than anything else, it seemed to him, was that strange meeting that had happened so suddenly and before he had any inkling of all that was about to be revealed, and had brought him together with a man who must be able to provide the most important contribution to lifting the veil that, despite everything he had learnt, still shrouded Annie's strange destiny.

Captain Ankerkrone, whom he counted as his friend and whose nobility had made the strongest impression on him, must in some way have come into contact with the woman whose body he had seen dragged from the lonely forest lake in a foreign country. Given his knowledge of Ankerkrone, Holst was most inclined to conclude that he hadn't recognised the young woman when her body was dragged up from where it had been hidden. It was not a matter of course that the deceased's petrified features would awaken the memory of a beautiful, smiling woman.

It was though a possibility, in which case it might seem strange that the Captain had never with a single word revealed his acquaintance with the murdered woman, so much more so since he had had a wealth of opportunity to do so during his frequent private talks with Holst. Holst had to admit to himself that the great interest Ankerkrone had shown in this case might have its basis in the fact that he knew more about the victim than he wished to tell, and gradually, the more Holst thought about the case, and about the Captain's attitude and observations,

Sjöström's gossip and Captain Kurk's serious account, the more it became clear to him that Captain Ankerkrone had to be the man who, if his efforts in Småland came to nothing, could solve the mystery for him.

Whether he would be willing was another matter. It was clear he had no part in the murder. Captain Ankerkrone, despite having had to withstand gossip of the most malignant nature in his home region, was surely raised above such a suspicion. It was beyond any possibility that he, whatever his domestic circumstances might have been, could be suspected of having deprived a loose woman of her life. Holst pushed the thought away like a hideous bug. But the fact that there could be a hidden connection between Captain Kurk's and Sjöström's narratives was another matter entirely, one on which Ankerkrone, if he so desired, could shed light.

Cedersköld, Annie's first lover, was probably Ankerkrone's friend and Ankerkrone had been the third person in the alliance of friends, which at some point had been annulled by a sad event. Sjöström was probably quite right, too, when he linked Mrs Ankerkrone's death to the departures of both Cedersköld and her husband; even a duel in Italy wasn't out of the question. In a way, Annie Cederlund's name brought up the bitterest memories for Captain Ankerkrone and, even though he may have recognised her, it would hardly have tallied with his reserved nature to give a complete stranger information about events that would only evoke the most onerous days and events in his life. No, he would never do such a thing.

Through these thoughts, and while the Småland forests slipped past his eyes, Holst arrived at an increased understanding of Ankerkrone's behaviour. He felt confident that, when he returned equipped with all the information he could gather here, the Captain would meet him as an honest, sincere friend and help him through the last difficulties. And while he was thinking about this, Ankerkrone's own words came to mind and it became clear to him that the Captain must have known far more than Holst had realised, but at the same time, he had been completely within his rights to wait and see if Holst could acquire, through his own efforts, the knowledge that he couldn't have given him without disclosing what hardly anyone could get him to disclose without a deep and compelling reason.

What remained was to follow Annie's journey from the day she left Kristianstad with Hugold Sjöström. It was natural to assume that her relatives must have known something about her and it was possible that they would be willing to help someone who had come to see them with a message and a purpose like the one which had led Holst to Bäckaryd.

The only thing that seemed inexplicable to Holst was Captain Kurk's position on the question of Annie's final year. It was possible he had held back out of consideration for Hugold Sjöström, yet he had expressed himself with great openness about the irresponsible officer whose career Annie had cut short and it was hardly conceivable that Sjöström would have committed the murder. Judging by Captain Kurk's statements, he would be more inclined to be interested in preserving what was, for him, his lover's rather precious life. It was more probable that the young man Kurk had seen in the couple's company in Paris could be linked to Annie's final drama.

In this case, it couldn't be out of consideration for Ankerkrone that Kurk was holding back, because there was no doubt at all that Ankerkrone had had no relationship with Annie either before Paris or after, but at this point the case was still extremely enigmatic, and it was unlikely that the solution to the riddle could be obtained from anyone other than Sjöström. The aim of the trip to Småland was thus more to find the path that led

93

to him and to get more clarity about the relationship that had existed between Annie and him.

There were some incidental obscure matters remaining, leaving Holst feeling like a rambler walking past the rocks by the sea and at every rock he reaches, he sees a new one in front of him that he has to go round, only to find himself face to face with a third that blocks his passage and view.

But that didn't prevent him from eating a good, tasty dinner in Vislanda.

VI

A BRANCH LINE CUTS WESTWARD through the country from Vislanda to Halmstad. It passes through an authentic Småland forest landscape with weeping birches and small friendly water meadows between slopes covered with heather, past Lake Bolmen, over the Skedala Heath military exercise grounds, to the mouth of the River Nissa. But even before Bolmen, by the little, friendly, one-horse town of Ljungby by the Laga, Holst left the train to take a small steamer along the river to Bäckaryd and the little cottage where Annie Bengtson's cradle had once stood.

It was not at all a simple journey, for even though the old corporal's widow was still alive, there was no certainty that she would be very communicative to a stranger who spoke a different language and came in through her door to talk to her about things that might recall the heaviest memories, as well as bringing her news which would have the effect of a heavy, perhaps conclusive, blow. Holst decided to proceed with the greatest caution.

He learnt from the boatmen that the magistrate in Bäckaryd lived close to the river on a large estate and that he was an influential, stately man, regarded as the richest farmer for miles around. Holst set off to his estate and met him in a large, well-built wooden house, the entire appointments of which clearly revealed that one of the important people of the district lived here. The house lay in a splendid little grove with beautiful, well-kept lawns and borders with stocks and wallflowers, and the magistrate himself stood in the entrance to a small vine-covered veranda, as strong, broad and clean-shaven as the chairman of a Zealand parish council, and dressed according to the fashions of a market town.

He was startled at the appearance of this stranger, and Holst considered it best to come straight to the point. He was soon seated in the magistrate's living room, where neat curtains gave shade at the windows, and numerous woodcuts of Sweden's kings decorated the walls, grouped around a large picture of Karl XV of Sweden and Frederik VII of Denmark united in brotherly friendship.

The magistrate was slightly reserved, clearly manifesting the solemn civil servant, the importance of whose duties often resulted in visits of a similar official nature. He regretted that, as a Good Templar, he wasn't able to offer any other refreshment than a soft drink, and formally presented his small, plump, friendly-looking wife with her starched bonnet ribbons, behind whom some young girls with golden locks peered out inquisitively. Holst bowed and moistened his tongue – he was thirsty and it was very hot outside.

He deliberately spoke a bit slowly so as to be better understood, but the magistrate explained that he was very familiar with the Danish language as he had for a number of years been having Danish hunting guests, reeling off some names which resonated with Holst. Among these there happened to be one of his brother officers and by this neutral path the conversation quickly flowed more easily.

'So the gentleman is employed by the police,' said the magistrate after some small talk. 'And what would you like from me?'

'It's a serious matter,' Holst said with a glance at the door, 'a case which shouldn't be discussed openly.'

The magistrate stood up and closed the door on the small, curious heads. The children flew into the yard like chicks flapping their wings and chirping eagerly.

'I'm at your service,' he continued, looking extremely official.

'I'm sure you know a girl with the name Annie Bengtson or Cederlund, born here in the parish,' began Holst.

The magistrate nodded seriously.

'Yes, indeed, I know her. She's brought sorrow enough to several people here in the parish, including my own family.'

'Yes, so I've been told,' said Holst.

The magistrate looked up in surprise.

'Does the gentleman know the story of my poor brother Erik?'

'I do indeed,' said Holst.

'In that case, the gentleman surely knows even more, I suspect. Well now, has Annie really ended up in the hands of the Danish police? Yes, one might expect something to go wrong, the way she lived. She has been wicked ever since childhood and has caused her parents great sorrow – the father, Corporal Bengt…'

'Yes, I know his sad story too – it was the mother…' interrupted Holst.

'She still lives here, just a few steps from my house. She's a very beautiful old woman but alone and despondent. She hasn't heard anything from her daughter for over three months, yet she loves her very much, despite everything, and the rest of us don't have the heart to speak ill of her. Because, you see, Annie is one of our parish's blackest sheep, whom we discuss now and then, of course, but now, as I said, it's been over three months since we last heard from her. I usually read her letters for old Mrs Bengtson – one doesn't have the heart to refuse and her sight is weak. But Annie's relationship with her mother is probably the only good thing about her. She sends money sometimes, quite a lot, too, and the old lady accepts it. What can I say? Money is money, isn't it, and the old lady has to survive – she isn't able to work. It's been a bit of a squeeze for her recently, but the rest of us help out as much as we can. We have to support each other here in life. It's incumbent on us…yes, indeed.'

The magistrate spoke seriously, in a rather preachy manner, like a man used to being the most important person around and the one whose word has most weight.

Holst sat pondering about how much he should say, but decided to tell him everything.

'I regret to say that Annie was murdered in Denmark this spring,' he said, a little slowly again, emphasising the words strongly with a subdued voice. 'We found her body in a forest lake in North Zealand, naked, without any clues that could lead to the discovery of who may have killed her and it's the investigation of this that brings me up here.'

The magistrate leant back in his chair, a little pale in the cheeks, and shook his head.

'So that's the way it's gone for Annie – poor thing, after all, she was such a grand sight.'

'I'm telling you,' continued Holst, 'because I think it would be easier for her mother coming from you. Moreover, it's important to me to learn everything that can provide us with clues, and it seems that Annie has maintained contact with her home.'

The magistrate was overwhelmed yet again, until it struck him that this was a serious official matter so he pulled himself together.

'How do I know that the gentleman…' he began a little awkwardly, 'you understand… I'm not doubting you, but this is a serious matter.'

Holst smiled and took out the necessary credentials, as issued by his superiors and provided with the appropriate endorsements by the representative of the Swedish state in Copenhagen.

The magistrate bowed deferentially before the seal and the important-sounding name. That matter had been dealt with.

'I'd be reluctant for this case to have to go the official way through the civil servants in the local jurisdiction,' Holst resumed. 'It's a private investigation and I've managed to keep the matter entirely secret in Denmark. The day will in all probability come when it becomes official, but before I can point to a particular man, I'm reluctant for the case to be made public. I therefore ask you to treat it with the utmost discretion.'

The magistrate looked like a man who could hold his tongue – and he could, too. He nodded.

'Not even my own wife will come to hear anything about this – it's probably also right, besides being compassionate, that old Mrs Bengtson doesn't learn how poor Annie has met her end.'

'That is perhaps – or rather, certainly – so,' said Holst. 'You have access to the correspondence and you will perhaps permit me to see the letters here in your presence.'

The magistrate rose and went over to the writing desk at the far end of the living room.

'They're here – Mrs Bengtson has asked me to keep them, to prevent the neighbours' wives and maids running off with them. She's been expecting Annie to come by with her husband at some point and bring her glory and joy… Poor thing… This will be completely different…completely.'

The magistrate stood with a pack of letters in his hand, neatly wrapped in a newspaper and bound with a pale red ribbon.

'You mentioned a husband,' said Holst. 'Was Annie married then?'

'Hardly, but she wouldn't admit to her mother that she wasn't married. Besides, she was still travelling with this Sjöström, the lieutenant from Kristianstad, and it's possible they'd got married, although in that case he would surely have written to Annie's mother.'

'So Sjöström,' repeated Holst, 'hasn't written since her death?'

'He's never written,' said the magistrate, 'but she referred to him as her husband. Could he…? No, it isn't credible…he probably hasn't had any reason to.'

Holst now told the magistrate in brief what he had learnt in Kristianstad about Annie – there was little new in it for him; he already knew most of it from her letters, albeit in a somewhat different light from the one Captain Kurk had cast over it.

Annie had been home for about six months before going to Kristianstad, after her long trip abroad during which her mother had only heard from her a few times. That was before the magistrate's time; his father had still been alive then, and he had never forgiven Annie for her part in his son's death and had never spoken to Mrs Bengtson. But he died shortly before Annie returned and the letters which the magistrate had were all from the time after her departure to Kristianstad. They were brief, but quite specific in content and form. Holst took them with him to peruse them and become thoroughly familiar with their content – to read them one by one to get to know Annie through her own words. But before he tackled this task, he had to join in with the family meal and accept the magistrate's hospitable offer of shelter.

Not a word was spoken of the case at the well-filled table in the happy circle of healthy and cheerful children, but Holst settled in well with his hosts, who offered him every delight – just not alcohol, and he could manage without that.

It was clear that the magistrate found the stranger to be a very respectable man, someone he could use; a man of few words and yet very straightforward.

Holst thought the same of the magistrate.

VII

THIRTY PACES FROM THE MAGISTRATE'S fence lay a small mud-built hovel, thatched with wood chips. The door frame had previously been painted red, but the colour had bleached and the clay was full of cracks. The windows were quite small and the door was at an angle and couldn't close properly. There was only a living room with a deep alcove and a small oven at one end by a crooked chimney. The floor consisted of stamped clay and the household effects were old and worn. In the door stood an old wicker chair, which at one time had adorned the magistrate's large hall, and in the chair sat a little, shrunken, shaking old woman spinning at her wheel, while an old half-blind cat was purring and brushing itself up against the bent legs of the chair and two small flaxen-haired neighbour children were messing around in a puddle right next to the door.

The old woman's small face was furrowed with wrinkles and yellow like parchment. Her greenish-grey hair lay divided over her forehead, sparingly covering her waxy yellow crown, and an old faded cloak shrouded the back of her head where her hair had completely fallen out. The only things living in this old face were her two big blue eyes, which despite her age and weakened sight were watching the youngsters playing as trustingly as a child; a kindly old-woman-look in eyes that had cried often and long, that had seen a great deal of wickedness yet always looked beyond evil towards something that was high above the clouds and wasn't of this world.

This was old Mrs Bengtson, sitting in the door of her shack, waiting for Annie to come home with her husband and carry her off to a glorious life in her last days.

The magistrate went over to her after they had eaten dinner, while his guest relaxed in the garden. He thought he had better prepare the old lady for the truth, no matter how heavy it might be. It feels so strangely difficult for people whose heart is dedicated to helping others to put their trust and faith in something that isn't true, even though the concealment of the truth might mean happiness. He walked slowly, sensing how heavy his steps were, yet feeling that it was his duty.

'Good evening, Mrs Bengtson,' he said with a nod.

The old lady nodded back. 'Good evening, Magistrate.'

The magistrate paused for thought.

'At last we've got some warm weather.'

'What did you say?' asked the old lady.

'I said, at last we've got some warm weather.'

'We have indeed…' said the old lady, her spindle spinning.

'A man from the south arrived here this evening – all the way from Denmark. He says it's much worse with the heat down there.'

'Does he now?' replied Mrs Bengtson.

'Yes,' said the magistrate, 'it's quite a bit hotter than here, he said. Annie wrote that last year too when she was down there.'

'Yes, she did indeed, she certainly did…' the old lady sighed.

She went silent briefly while the spindle spun.

'It's about time she wrote again, don't you think? Let me see, how long is it now since we last heard from her?'

'Four months, I'd say,' said the magistrate; now he was getting close.

'Yes, it's about time she wrote. She's always been so good before in writing to her old mother, Annie has.'

'She could of course be ill,' said the magistrate.

'She could indeed,' said the old lady, 'though she's always been healthy and strong, but it can easily happen.'

'Indeed it can,' said the magistrate, clearing his throat.

The old woman was silent for a while, then it was as if her thoughts had converged on what the magistrate had said about the stranger from Denmark. She seemed to be searching for words.

'I think the magistrate said that a foreigner had arrived from Denmark,' she said hesitantly. 'Well now, Denmark isn't all that small a country, so I don't suppose he's seen anything of Annie if she should be down there.'

'Yes,' said the magistrate, 'he has in fact; he has seen something of Annie.'

'How is she then?' asked old Mrs Bengtson. 'Is she well?'

'No,' said the magistrate, 'I'm afraid not. She had become very ill and was in the hospital down there in a city called Copenhagen.'

'Oh dear, and what about her husband then, that Sjöström feller, isn't he looking after her?'

'He's gone south to Italy on business, I think.'

'But surely he's coming back to Annie if she's ill. Is she very ill?' exclaimed Mrs Bengtson. The old lady looked at the magistrate, so unmistakeably apprehensive that it cut him right into the heart.

'Yes,' he said, 'she's quite ill, not just a little.'

'Oh my God,' sighed the old woman, 'so Annie is ill... Yes, I thought that's why she hadn't written. But now I'll pray to Our Lord that little Annie might regain her health and maybe even come up here once more before I close my eyes. I'll pray to Our Lord for that, I will.'

'Yes, goodnight, Mrs Bengtson,' said the magistrate, 'you just pray to Our Lord for Annie.'

He didn't feel up to saying the rest and thought it was a good thing he hadn't mentioned it.

He went home, leaving old Mrs Bengtson sitting at the spinning wheel, sighing and thinking of little Annie.

VIII

HOLST RETIRED EARLY TO A BRIGHT, beautifully furnished
gable room, in which the broad, comfortable furniture, in the
same style as can be found in a first-class provincial hotel, could
be attributed to the host's consideration for the comfort of his
distinguished hunting guests. He sat down at a large mahogany
desk in order to immediately and eagerly cast himself over
Annie's letters. It was getting dark, so he lit the lamp and read
through the night; it was light before he finished reading and
he went to bed under the strong influence of what he had
read, while the birds in the trees outside were beginning their
morning chorus. But by then he felt he had learnt all he could
from the letters. In all, there were over sixty of them, spread
over a period extending from Christmas 1897 to March 1902.
Some of them were without interest; they were almost all short,
quite well-written and contained small pieces of information
about Annie's life or short greetings accompanied by small

contributions of money. They were completely chronologically arranged, in line with the magistrate's highly pronounced sense of order, according to which he was also accustomed to arranging discharge papers and servant references, numbered consecutively so that he could quickly find the most important ones. It was apparent that some of the more significant letters had been read out frequently to old Mrs Bengtson; it was very clear that these bore traces of often being taken out to comfort the old woman in the long winter evenings when she needed to hear something from her only child. There was a small note on the top of the package, where the magistrate had written numbers, such as: no. 16, letter about Little Elsa's death; no. 30, Christmas celebration in Paris; no. 43, about Annie's husband – and so on.

The most important letters gave excellent, sequential information about Annie's eventful life and Holst decided to make copies of them for use in the investigation. The individual ones of the greatest significance read thus:

Kristianstad, Christmas 1897

Dear Ma,

I hope you have a merry Christmas if you're healthy enough.

Little Elsa and I are going to spend Christmas with Mrs Karlkvist in Västragatan. Elsa has sewn a warm cloak for you, which I hope will arrive with the post, along with a shawl I bought for you. I have sent 10 kroner to the magistrate. It isn't much, but I'm not earning very much. The money that the Captain pays for Elsa goes mostly to her clothes and schooling, because she needs a good upbringing, which as you already know has been decided. She's very bright and quite healthy, although a bit on the weak side, but that's probably something to do with her upbringing and will no doubt get better on its own. It's very lonely here, because I don't really want to see people, and I don't think many people know me here, which can only be a good thing. There have been some orders up to Christmas but people don't come to me much and I'm not one for going round to customers, as you probably know. When I get more money, I'll send you more, my dear Ma.

So have a merry Christmas,

From Elsa and your loving daughter Annie.

6th March, 1898

Dear Ma,

Elsa has been pretty poorly and can hardly go to school. The doctor says there's something wrong with her chest, but we're hoping for the best. So I can't send any money, because medicine and the doctor are expensive and have to be paid. The Captain came by yesterday, you know him, the one who sends the money for Elsa, but I didn't talk to him because as you know I don't want to. I heard him asking Mrs Karlkvist if I was behaving properly and that she said yes, which is true, though God knows that you don't get much for that, but I will do what you said for Elsa's sake, so that she can be well brought-up and get herself a good man when that time comes. For myself, I don't think there's going to be any more, and that doesn't really matter because I know men and I don't expect anything good from them. However, he did seem to want to do something to make Elsa well, whether it was because he had a *twinge of conscience about Cedersköld, or thought that Cedersköld had been hard on us, I don't know. Now I have to go in to Elsa and can't write any more.*

18th March, 1898

Dear Ma,

 Elsa is very ill – the doctor says it's very dangerous, but I can't believe it because if Elsa should die, then nothing would matter any more and what would be the point of it all? The Captain hasn't been here since last time, so I went to him but didn't meet him because he didn't want to. He has a young lieutenant called Sjöström, who is very kind to me. I don't think he knows anything about it, but he received me well and gave me twenty kroner so I can send you ten. I am totally in despair and can't do any sewing at all. And I had thought that since I just wanted to live a decent life, everything would go well, but it doesn't. I'm very distressed and can't write any more.

25th March, 1898

Dear Ma,

 Elsa will never recover, the doctor has said so. She is so sweet and good and lies so quietly and says her prayers, but I can see from looking at her that she probably knows she's going to die, because sometimes she looks at me with such big eyes and says, Ma! Do you think it's so bad to die and do you think you just come to Our Lord? And what should I answer, because I'm sure I don't know anything about it, but there's a nurse that the Captain has sent and she knows better because I'm at my wits' end and only know two old hymns, which I sometimes sing to her. But it's very sad. Yesterday I wrote to ask him if he would come by because Elsa was probably dying. But he probably won't. The Captain neither. Well, it isn't his child either, even though he has promised the other one to be there for her instead of the father, but people are cruel, and the eternal God knows it. That time, I couldn't help it, because I didn't want to harm anyone, and it was his own fault anyway, but now it's no use.

1st April, 1898

Dear Ma,

Elsa died tonight. She had become so little and so thin and so transparent, and when she died it was like when a light goes out. I sat alone with her, she couldn't say anything but just looked at me with such big eyes, and then she looked like her father, so I thought of him, I never usually think of him nowadays. Because I still firmly believe that it was his child, and not Cederskölds's, as I have said. But now that Elsa is dead, I will testify to God, as I testified when I tried to pray to Him that she may live and I die if it had to be, that I was innocent and that it was him who misled me and caused me such pain so that everything else followed. And now God has taken his child as he took his wife, if it was God who did it, because God couldn't be part of such an act as the one which certainly took place there. God knows everything, they say, but although it's a sin to say it, Ma, I don't believe in God, because he wouldn't be so cruel and evil to us poor people. I wish I was dead, but I have to live, because I'm no use to anyone, and we were all so happy for Elsa, but she had to die. Oh Ma, I'm so unhappy that I could walk out into the lake, but it's as if Pa appears to me and it's so terrifying if it should be true about the hereafter. Because Elsa believed she'd come to Our Lord, which she must do, as good and loving as she was, if there was any justice. I cry and cry and can only cry...

There was a long gap between this letter and the next. It was dated 8th June, 1898, and read as follows:

Dear Ma

So that was that birthday. Yes, you haven't heard from me for such a long time, because at first, I was sick after Elsa's death, and then so much happened which there's no point in writing about. But I'm well and earning a lot of money in my work for some good customers. I grieved so much, you know, but then I was still young, and God's will must be done. People are evil enough, but there are good ones in amongst them, and Lieutenant Sjöström is good to me. Not in that way, I'll never do that again, because now I want to be a good girl, and now I have no child any more for people to talk about. I haven't heard any more from him, but I get the money anyway. It's not much – if I wasn't earning well, it wouldn't actually be any help whatsoever, but now I'm sending you 50 kroner so you can buy something nice for yourself, my sweet Ma.

Your own Annie.

30th July, 1898

Dear Ma,

You mustn't believe any of the evil things that people are saying about me, because it's not true. For God's sake, a girl is allowed to get herself a fiancé, and Sjöström says I don't look more than 21 and now we have to exchange rings and then you'll hear more from us...

October, 1898

Dear Ma,

There's no truth in what is being said in that magazine the magistrate sent me, it's all slander by the evil newspaper people who need something to write about. Sjöström has absolutely not stolen from the cash box like they write, and has absolutely not been dismissed, but they don't want him to marry me, and he does, so we're going away. And all that about my wild life isn't true either, because, for God's sake, you're surely allowed to have fun when you're young and it's God's fault, because he could have let me keep Elsa, then it wouldn't have gone like this, but I'm sure It will be good again, because Hugold is very clever. And what's in the magazines isn't true – in the larger, good magazines there's nothing at all, it's just the gutter rags that have to write about something to earn their money...

Berlin, November 1898

Dear Ma

Now we're in Berlin, and I know the place of course. It's very cold here, but it was best that we left and

Hugold will get something going down here where he knows many people. Now we're married, we did it here at the consul, and I'm going to send the magistrate a copy of the papers, so that you can see that it's all done correctly. We don't have much money right now, but we'll get more, I'm sure. I promise you'll hear from me again soon.

There seemed to be a long time when Annie and her 'husband' were wandering around Germany and suffering badly. The first letter of any real interest in the large number of them was dated Paris, 28th December, 1899 and read as follows:

Dear Ma

It's been a hard Christmas, I've been here alone, you know, because Sjöström had left me and I was totally on my own. And it was like when Elsa died, that I thought now my time is also over, because God must know that I have perhaps sinned a lot and done much that wasn't right in my time, but God has not been good to me. Because I loved him then, when I was sixteen years old, and since then I haven't loved anyone even if I haven't behaved as I should have done, but men are evil. So I wanted to die because I'm ill and poor and have felt ashamed and I don't want to be poor and nasty and they will look down on me, because I'm young, only in my thirties, and that's not old. But something happened when I was walking down the street, because it was so scary and cold in the attic where I was living. I followed the lights and the places where we used to go before when we had money, but I was ashamed of my clothes because they aren't very nice any more. Then I happened to see him, so I went over and he looked at me. He has become very old now, he must be fifty and is white-haired, I haven't seen him since it happened. But he was sort of touched at seeing how unhappy I was, and I didn't think he was capable of that, but he was. And so we spent Christmas together. But since you have to let the magistrate read what I'm writing, I can't tell you what happened between us – but it was the most awful experience of my life, and it even took place on a sacred Christmas Eve. Now I've moved and am well, because he has given me so much money that I can now easily manage with money, but I will never forget the other stuff...

Venice, May 1900

Dear Ma

So you got the money. It's really lovely now down here in this town, where there are no proper streets, but only canals where we're ferried around in small black boats called gondolas. We live in a house on the grandest canal of all and Sjöström likes it very much. We're very good friends once again now, because basically he is a good man, but we didn't love each other, but there are many married people who don't and for me it's a great pleasure to have a man who has a nice name. Many people come here, mostly gentlemen, but also some ladies, and it's great fun down here in Italy where everything is free and easy and especially where they sail around in the streets in the evening and sing as beautifully as at home down by the Laga in Bäckaryd in the summer evenings. I've become really young again and everyone says I'm so beautiful, the most beautiful of them all. And I've got a lot of rings and stones and the sort of things that the gentlemen give you down here. You got the 100 kroner I sent to the magistrate, didn't you?

Venice, Aug. 1900

...Now we're back in Venice. Guess who I've met – that is, not to talk to, but she lives right next door to me. Her sister, and she looks like her, like one drop of water looks like another. You mustn't tell the magistrate anything about her or him under any circumstances, otherwise I'll be eternally unhappy, but I'll tell you about it at some point. And you won't believe who else I've met – his son. It's really strange, because it makes me feel I'm getting old and I'm not at all, but he's married to a very ugly wife, and they're living with his aunt right next door to me. He came in here a few days ago, but his wife wasn't with him. She doesn't know anything at all about it. I don't like him – he's not like he used to be. But he liked me – I could see that. We'll meet again, I'm sure – I've taken in a young girl named Johanna Ljunggren, whose father used to be the captain of the guard in his squadron. It's nice to have someone here with me and she's been through a lot just like me.

Paris, May 1901

...Now Sjöström has left again. He wanted to divorce me, but I don't want that because here in these countries it's good to have a husband, because otherwise you

don't count for anything and there are so many loose women and that kind of thing. But I think he'll be back, he's still the best when all's said and done, even though he often gets worked up and hits me and he threatened to shoot me once in Monte Carlo, where there are gambling tables, because I wouldn't give him more money because I think it's stupid to gamble it away and I'd really like to save as much as possible so that we can come home to Sweden to live when we grow older and to see you again, Ma, because I miss you. I have some money and papers, because now I'm sensible and put money aside, and I have quite a lot, but this time I want lots and lots of money, because it's not good when you get older. But Sjöström spends so much and sometimes is quite impossible...

Nice, Feb. 1902

...It's almost a year since I thought we were coming home, but we haven't arrived yet. I can't get away from here and I can't tell you why, but I might be coming to Sweden this spring. But you remember I wrote about his son who is terribly rich and who gives me all the money I want and now I spend a lot because I want to live now while I'm young. I have four horses and a coachman and a servant, and Sjöström is happy with that. I don't like him any more – I've never really loved him, but you have to have a husband. I think he liked me a lot before, then there was a while when he didn't care about me, but now I think he's started again. And that's not very good, because I don't like him hanging around me, and everything's mine, of course, but I

116

can't explain that in more detail. If I could, I'd divorce
him, but that's not good either, and it'll stay the same
as it was, I suppose. The other man, the one I talked
about, loves me a lot and will do anything for me, but
I don't like him because he's his son. But I realised that
I can get him to do whatever I want, and take revenge
for everything that he put me through, both long ago
and that terrible Christmas in Paris, and so I set out to
be really nasty, and I can be because people have made
me into that sort of person, and, as you know, Ma, I
was good once. But it's all God's fault, and that's how it
should be. Now I'll send some money home to the bank
in Kristianstad, and Madam Karlkvist's son, him the
lawyer, will look after it because it's a lot of money and
I have more so you won't want for anything in your old
age, Ma…

The rest of the letters were shorter, but still contained messages about the large amount of money Annie had and would send home. The last two were quite short and the most important of them all. The penultimate was dated Copenhagen 21st March, 1902, and read as follows:

Dear Ma,

Now I'm in Copenhagen and you'll see me soon.
Sjöström won't be coming with me, because now I've
finished with him and we're going to get divorced. He
has begun drinking and he and Johanna, who I don't
like any more, are now together, and he's often quite
wild and wants to harm me and I won't put up with it.
I don't need any more men, for now I'm certainly going
to take my revenge on him as I've promised, and now

117

I know where to hit him, but I don't really care any more. I can't write what it is, but I'll tell you all that later. In eight days, it's done and then I'll come...

The last letter was dated Elsinore, 27th March, 1902, and read as follows:

Dear Ma,
If Sjöström writes or comes, don't tell him where I am, because I don't want to see him any more, he's got what was coming to him and more. I'll send 200 kroner so that you're OK, or if the magistrate can get a house, because I'm rich and can pay and have a lot of money in the bank. I have to wait here, but it won't be for long. Finally, remember about Sjöström, because he'll probably write...

The money hadn't arrived. This last letter was written on a closed postcard and sent from Elsinore, probably on Annie's last day alive. Most of her life story was told in these letters, but what seemed to be her evil destiny was hidden for an ordinary reader. However, it was possible that the magistrate knew something about this. In any case, the old woman had to know who the person was whose name Annie didn't dare mention, and who seemed to have played such a big part in her life. With regard to the actual murder, it was simple to conclude what the accompanying circumstances were and especially who the killer was. It was Sjöström, strange that the magistrate hadn't thought so, but the individual circumstances could hardly have been clear to him. Another important point was that Annie had eventually left a considerable fortune, which could probably be traced, even though the killer had most probably taken

118

possession of it, although it was possible of course that he didn't know where it had been deposited. But it was clear that the case, as it now stood, had become considerably more interesting and Holst couldn't deny that the spoils looked considerable and this factor was important for him now.

However, now he wanted to rest – to sleep on it and get cracking for all he was worth immediately the next morning, because there was something to get cracking on.

IX

IMMEDIATELY AFTER THEIR FIRST MEAL together, the magistrate and Holst set about considering what they already knew. It soon became apparent that the magistrate didn't know anything more than what could be deduced from the letters and his personal knowledge of Annie and her mother. The old woman had read the early letters herself, but in the autumn of 1899 her eyesight had become so weak that she couldn't read any more, so the magistrate had stepped in. He had often asked her about the vague allusions to 'him' and the old woman had always answered that she wasn't at liberty to say. He had thought about it, but as he was a person of sober mind and not romantic in the slightest, he had gradually got used to these allusions without thinking any more about them. He didn't understand how Annie had come into the money that she clearly had. He didn't believe in the marriage to Sjöström and was inclined to share Holst's suspicion about this. Everything seemed quite natural and it would in particular be important to learn where Annie's money had been deposited and how much of it was left, or if, after her death, Sjöström had taken possession of it all. Information about this could be obtained from the lawyer, Karlkvist, in Kristianstad, so that would be the next place to which Holst would have to turn.

Holst didn't say a word to the magistrate about knowing Ankerkrone and Kurk, or of his suspicions about any connection that could possibly exist between Annie and Ankerkrone. In any case, it didn't have any relevance to the case and in the years the three friends had visited Bäckaryd, the magistrate had been away so he couldn't personally know anything about what may have happened. On the other hand, it was possible Holst would be able to find out something from old Mrs Bengtson. He now knew that what was most important was the content of Annie's last two letters. It was particularly strange that Sjöström hadn't ever contacted Annie's mother in writing or in person, as Annie had assumed he would. It clearly implied that it was he who had committed the murder and his motive, quite understandably, had been to get hold of his lover's money. Holst didn't believe that Sjöström had been married to Annie; it was a possibility, of course, but since she had alluded to a divorce and had written that the matter had now been settled, it must be possible to obtain information about this matter from her legal adviser in Kristianstad.

It turned out that what Mrs Bengtson would tell them was really only about Annie's relationship with the unnamed man and, even then, just the favourable aspects of who he was. Holst had to admit that his motive for looking for clarification on this question was purely personal and that he had no serious doubts about who he was. He also had to admit that it would be heartless of him, in order to get an answer to this question, to reveal to the old woman the terrible fate that had met her daughter. After the manner in which the magistrate had laid the ground, the notification of Annie's death would come to her smoothly and naturally and find her fairly well prepared. It was even possible that the investigation of the daughter's fortune could lead to the old woman, although receiving the information about Annie's death, at the same time feeling comforted by the news that she wouldn't have to suffer hardship in her old age. Holst therefore decided to refrain from any attempt to learn anything from the old woman about the strange and sinister connection that undoubtedly had to exist between Annie's fate and that of his friend, Captain Ankerkrone. There was basically nothing else for him to do than to make the necessary copies of Annie's letters and then go to Kristianstad to follow the trail that might lead to the apprehension of the murderer.

Holst's familiarity with written work meant that the copying went smoothly, but it still took time and a few days went by while he worked conscientiously and at full speed while, to be on the safe side, making sure he had copies of all the letters, even those that seemed unimportant.

At midday on the third day, the magistrate came in to him just as he was finishing the copy of the last letter. He looked very solemn, which instinctively startled Holst, who thus expected a message of great importance.

'Lieutenant,' said the magistrate, 'I'm afraid old Mrs Bengtson has fallen seriously ill. She has sent for the priest and for me. I thought it possible that the Lieutenant would like to come with me, in case something was said that might be of some importance.'

Holst got up quickly to accompany him. It was obvious that it might be very important for him if the old woman had something to say in her last moments – because there could be no doubt that she was in her final hours.

They went to the house together and entered the small living room where the old woman was lying in bed, supported by pillows, weak and dying, while the priest bent over her and delivered the holy sacraments. Holst and the magistrate stood silently by until the holy act was over, then the old woman nodded to the magistrate and looked up at him with a faint smile.

'Yes, Magistrate, now I have to go,' she said. 'Perhaps I'll meet my little Annie before you, because I dreamt so clearly that night you told me about the stranger from Denmark that little Annie had passed on before me.'

Her voice sounded quite strong as she turned her eyes on Holst.

'Well, now,' she continued, 'perhaps this is the stranger, the one who had heard about little Annie.'

The magistrate nodded, while the dying woman seemed to look at Holst but didn't say anything. She gestured to the magistrate to come closer; as he approached her, she didn't appear to be concerned about the others.

'Magistrate,' she said in a whisper, 'when I die, would you take the letter lying in the drawer over there and make sure it gets to the person who should have it. It's written on the outside.'

She waved the magistrate even closer and whispered to him in a scarcely audible voice, 'The name of the man the magistrate has asked about so often is Arvid Ankerkrone, but the magistrate may not tell anyone else in the whole world and the letters should be passed on to him.'

Holst heard every word clearly, but he didn't bat an eyelid.

The old woman's voice became weaker; she sank into a drowsiness, and when the doctor arrived a quarter of an hour later, she was dead.

Holst and the magistrate went home together. Holst asked if the old woman had given any message, but it was clear that the magistrate was reluctant to answer and they didn't discuss it any more.

Holst had planned to leave in the evening. He thanked his host for his hospitality and wanted to pay for his stay, but the magistrate would on no account accept any reimbursement. On the other hand, he was very troubled, thought Holst, and after a while he understood that the magistrate was very uncertain as to what to do with the letter he had taken from the old woman's corner cupboard. He didn't think he could refrain from informing Holst and it was of course an official matter that could bring him an official reprimand from his superior if he dealt with it incorrectly. On the other hand, he didn't want to ignore the wish of a dying woman.

Holst was very conscious of his turmoil and he understood the reason for it. This put Holst in a strong position that brought exactly the result he had wished for.

'Remember to forward the letter the old lady gave you,' said Holst as they were saying their farewells.

The magistrate twitched.

'Does the lieutenant want me to give it to the district governor or perhaps…'

'No,' Holst said calmly, 'you must send it to Captain Ankerkrone and remain silent about Annie until you hear from me.'

The magistrate looked startled.

Holst repeated, 'Yes, indeed – send it to him.'

He hesitated a little, then took a piece of paper off the desk and wrote with firm strokes:

Backeryd,
16th June, 1902
Dear friend, my greetings with this letter from beyond the grave – we two will no doubt meet soon, but farewell for now.
Your friend,
Eigil Holst.

He handed the letter to the magistrate, who read it and stood staring at the scrap of paper with an uncomprehending look. Holst smiled and asked for an official envelope, on which he wrote Captain Ankerkrone's address in bold letters.

'Send the letter to this address and thank you for your hospitality on this occasion,' said Holst cheerfully.

The carriage was brought to the door and shortly afterwards it was bumping its way over the heath towards Ljungby.

But the magistrate stood for a long time looking in the direction the carriage had gone and then went indoors shaking his head. The letter was put in the post, but the magistrate didn't say a word to anyone about the detective and Annie.

X

THE LAWYER, KARLKVIST, lived in Kristianstad and was what the Swedes call a 'schnapps lawyer'. He hadn't passed any exams, but he was a sly and clever man who had a large clientele of farmers and tradesmen, whose cases he conducted successfully and he recovered their money. The lawyers in town looked down on him, but he earnt well and since he was said to be a rather talented man, there was nothing to be done about him running his business openly as a 'self-proclaimed lawyer'.

Holst caught him in his office, which looked more like a type of registration office than a lawyer's office, and the man's completely unauthorised position meant that Holst was somewhat in doubt as to how to deal with him.

They sat opposite each other a while. Karlkvist was a man in his forties, smoothly shaven, with small blinking eyes, small of stature and looked like a wealthy farmer dressed in his town clothes.

'I'd like to talk to you about a Miss Annie Cederlund,' said Holst.

The lawyer's eyes narrowed.

'Annie Cederlund?' he repeated. 'I'm not familiar with the name.'

'Annie Bengtson,' continued Holst calmly, 'perhaps Mr Karlkvist knows her by that name.'

The lawyer shook his head.

Holst didn't allow himself to be put off, but continued in the same courteous manner.

'If Mr Karlkvist would rather call her Mrs Annie Sjöström, that's fine by me.'

'I don't know any lady by that name either,' said the lawyer, but there was a subtle change in his voice that revealed to Holst that the man was lying.

'Yes, well, since Mr Karlkvist doesn't recognise her,' continued Holst equably, 'it's possibly because the lady has had more names than these three, but since I know her, and know from her that Mr Karlkvist knows her, it doesn't really matter about names.'

Karlkvist looked at both sides of the card Holst had given him.

'The gentlemen's name is Lieutenant Holst and he's from Copenhagen. May I ask what the gentleman wants with me?'

Holst smiled.

'I've already told you that – to talk to you about the young lady whose name I have mentioned and whose money you are managing.'

The lawyer started.

'There now,' Holst smiled, 'you do know her after all.'

The lawyer shifted uncertainly, then got to his feet.

'Even if that were true,' he said very politely, 'there is nothing that entitles you to ask me about her affairs, and nothing that justifies my answering, even more so since I don't know who you are.'

'You may be right in that,' replied Holst, maintaining his calm, 'but I have important reasons to hide the purpose of my visit to you, because I don't know you and don't know how much I may confide in you.'

'Then you shouldn't have looked me up,' said the lawyer drily. 'I didn't ask you to come. Well, if that was all, there are people waiting in reception.'

Holst looked sharply at the little man, then smiled.

'You mustn't be angry, sir,' he said softly, 'but it was possible that what I wanted to ask you about was no more than you felt able to answer.'

'Not until I know who you are,' said the other determinedly.

'Yes, then you had better not answer.'

'Exactly,' answered the lawyer and bowed.

Holst stood uncertainly.

'Old Mrs Bengtson died yesterday. I was with her in her last moments,' he said in a friendly tone.

The little man grabbed him by the arm.

'What are you saying – old Mrs Bengtson dead, and Annie, where is she then?'

Holst thought for a moment, then slowly said, 'Annie's dead too.'

The little man went deathly pale.

'What do you mean – dead – is Annie Cederlund dead?'

Holst noticed the name – so Annie wasn't married, otherwise the lawyer would have called her by her husband's name.

The lawyer pulled himself together before asking,

'When?'

'The 27th of March this year.'

'The very day I spoke to her in Helsingborg – and you don't say this until now. Who on earth are you? In the name of Jesus, tell me, since you know all this!'

'Calm down a little and I'll tell you everything,' replied Holst with a friendly smile.

The lawyer sipped at a glass of water standing on the table and sank down in his chair.

Holst sat down again opposite him.

'My my, that was a bit of a shock, Mr Karlkvist, wasn't it just? Ah well, it's not as bad as all that. Annie is still alive and is in the best of health in Paris. But Sjöström has had a small difference of opinion with the Danish police, which is why I've come to you.'

The lawyer looked Holst up and down; his teeth were clenched and his eyes were glaring peevishly.

'The gentleman is having a bit of fun, I gather?'

'Not at all,' said Holst kindly. 'If Mr Karlkvist wants to see my credentials, go ahead – here they are.' He unfolded his papers for the lawyer. 'We could of course negotiate at the office of the chief constable, but I thought Mr Karlkvist would find it more comfortable if we could converse here in a friendly fashion.'

Karlkvist's jaw clenched once again and he glanced irritatedly up at Holst. He knew he had been outwitted.

'What does the detective wish to know?' he asked reluctantly.

'Very little in fact,' said Holst. 'When did you last receive a payment from Mrs Cederlund? Yes, now you know you can postpone the answer to another time, but you are going to answer.'

The lawyer scowled.

'I'll have to look it up in my records.'

He went over to the cabinet. Holst followed his movements acutely; he had a sense he might try to escape. Holst stood up.

129

'Mr Karlkvist,' he said, 'you must tread carefully – this doesn't work with me. Your conscience is not clear, I can see that, and there's only one way for you – full openness with me and I will cover you where I can. If you don't do that, we will have to go to the chief constable. I have been so prudent as to call in there and I have the right to arrest you on the spot.'

This was, to put it mildly, not true, but Holst's tone was very convincing and he had already injected a considerable fear into the schnapps lawyer through the surprise attack whereby he had forced him to show his true colours. However, it was possible that Karlkvist was colluding with Sjöström and it was therefore necessary for Holst to be very careful.

Karlkvist eventually produced his records. It turned out that Annie had been making deposits for a long time at Enskilda Bank, albeit directly, but had always informed Karlkvist about them and that Karlkvist had assisted her in buying a house in Kristianstad, on which occasion it looked as if her legal counsel had cheated her significantly, though this was forgivable. There was however undeniably more interest in the relationship with the bank and the visit to Helsingborg.

Karlkvist's account, forced out of him by a very sharp interrogation, was to the effect that Sjöström, whom he had known well and, in his lieutenant days, had often advanced money, had created a legal document with Annie, according to which he was to have ten thousand kroner and vanish, and the furniture and fittings which the couple owned in Cannes would likewise be allotted to Sjöström. They hadn't been married, but Annie apparently wanted to marry someone else who was already married and Karlkvist was to have taken care of this person's divorce the following day. However, he hadn't heard anything more about this. On the other hand, he had received an enquiry from the bank as to whether he could come in there the next day, as a gentleman had wanted to withdraw a large amount and the bank wanted to know if he knew anything about the matter. The gentleman had been Sjöström, whom the bank staff knew well, but whose reputation had of course been poor. He was in possession of a cheque issued by Annie for 90,000 kroner. Karlkvist had been surprised by the large amount, but since he knew that Annie had 130,000 kroner in money and papers at the bank, he thought the couple might have made another agreement and, based on his testimony, Sjöström had been paid the amount.

He hadn't heard from Annie since. He presumed that she had changed her plans and gone back to France. He was, besides, a sort of cousin of Annie and this strange coincidence meant that he and a sister living in Vislanda were probably Annie's heirs.

Although Holst had retracted the truth about Annie's death, he decided to keep an eye on Karlkvist, even more so as he had a strong suspicion that Sjöström had paid him generously for his so-called testimony. It turned into a long conversation and the lawyer had surrendered unconditionally. Holst treated him kindly and promised to hold a protective hand over him if Annie should demand that he account for himself; he even gave a definite promise in this regard, which he was able to do with great peace of mind and would never be tempted to break.

He didn't want to say anything about Annie's present place of residence, but told the lawyer that Sjöström was under arrest in Hamburg and would be brought to Copenhagen. He had falsified the cheque and Annie's new husband had reported the falsification. Holst was equally silent regarding this person's name.

It became clear to him, however, that there could be no question of complicity from the lawyer's side in anything other than the falsification, which, strangely enough, would probably affect himself, and since it was primarily a question of getting hold of Sjöström and Karlkvist would no doubt keep quiet about what he knew, Holst left him with his kind regards and a promise to visit him again soon.

Karlkvist was not exactly delighted at the thought, and the good people of Kristianstad became aware that something very unpleasant must have happened to Mr Karlkvist, because it was evident how seriously thin he had become in the space of a few days. He was not particularly comfortable with the situation either, because there were things that could interrupt the operation of his business in an unfortunate way if people were inclined to investigate them. That damned Danish devil of a detective!

Holst didn't visit anyone in Kristianstad, but took the train directly to Helsingborg, very satisfied with the relocation of Enskilda Bank from Kristianstad to Helsingborg, which in 1898 had so directly saddened the former town.

XI

HOLST WAS RECEIVED WITH GREAT COURTESY in the bank in Helsingborg. He didn't go into his suppositions in great depth but restricted himself to disclosing the suspicions of the Copenhagen police that an international swindler, whose numerous frauds had affected several Danish citizens, had made a big coup in the bank at the end of March 1902.

The investigation showed that Karlkvist's confession had been essentially true. On 28th March, by instructions to the bank's Berlin and Paris correspondents, Lieutenant Hugold Sjöström was paid 90,000 kroner to be charged to the account of Annie Cederlund of Kristianstad, following an instruction dated 27th March 1902 in Elsinore.

There was nothing unusual about the cheque. Now that falsification was suspected, it appeared that ten thousand had been changed to ninety thousand, a formal change, the likes of which at one time in Stockholm had cost the National Bank a round sum, but on a normal consideration, everything had seemed to be as it should be.

After a good deal of formality, Holst succeeded in borrowing the original cheque, in particular using the fact that the falsification had probably been committed in Elsinore, where the cheque had been issued. At the same time, Holst achieved the great benefit that his investigation had produced a factually-based charge of falsification, which offered several advantages over a dubious assassination for murder and was far less sensational, a point that, for a policeman who works in an age in which a public thirsty for news from its press is constantly at his heels, was of the utmost importance.

In addition, Holst conducted enquiries in Helsingborg, which could lead to further information about the actual murder case. Sjöström had lived under his own name at the Hotel Mollberg from 25th to 28th March. He had been alone on the first day, but on the second had been visited by an officer well-known in the town, Lieutenant Claes Ankerkrone, who had stayed at the hotel from the 26th to the 27th, but after that had sailed with the ferry to Elsinore along with Sjöström. On the 28th, Sjöström had returned and had left Helsingborg via Lund, probably heading for Copenhagen via Malmö, since he had told the concierge that letters should be forwarded to the Hotel Kongen af Danmark, Copenhagen. However, the concierge didn't recall that any letters had been sent, but the day after Sjöström had left, his brother, Equerry Bror Sjöström, also well-known in Helsingborg, had turned up and asked for him.

It turned out that a rumour about the money Hugold had withdrawn had leaked out and that some aggrieved creditors had decided to act against him, which had manifested itself in a referral to the local police who had immediately advised the brother about the matter, with the result that the worthy man had immediately presented himself at the hotel. However, the case had died down. Some people believed that the equerry had had to scatter some crumbs to the hungry creditors.

That was everything that was known in Helsingborg and Holst thus had to follow the trail, partly by contacting Bror Sjöström – a very delicate matter – and partly by seeking further information in Elsinore. He decided to visit Hamlet's town first and took the ferry across the Sound, where he found himself once more on Danish soil after his eventful foreign travels.

Sjöström wasn't known in Elsinore and it turned out from examining the guest books at the local hotels that he hadn't stayed there, at least not under his own name. On the other hand, something else of the utmost importance emerged.

At the railway hotel by the harbour, diagonally opposite the beautiful new railway station, a lady whose description matched that of the deceased had stayed from 25th to 27th March. This hadn't come to light during the first investigation because the hotel's concierge had gone away on other business, but had now been engaged at the large Marienlyst establishment and it therefore became possible to obtain more accurate information. The current waiter and maid were new in their jobs and the hotel-keeper had been on a trip to Copenhagen.

In the hotel's guest book, the person in question was listed as Mrs Gorin, Nice, and it was determined that her luggage had been sent to the Hotel Kongen af Danmark, Copenhagen, as express goods. She had been in the company of two gentlemen, at least for one day, but the concierge had no information about who these gentlemen had been. She had also been visited by a young lady, who, however, had immediately returned to Copenhagen.

However, the concierge was certain that one of the waiters, now employed at the Marienlyst and married and living in

Elsinore, personally knew one of the gentlemen. In the hotel guest book, he was listed under the name Lundkvist, rentier, but it was certainly an assumed name – the young gentleman was a Swedish officer from a noble family. The waiter couldn't reveal his real name to the concierge. He had probably received a generous tip for remaining silent.

Holst wasted no time in giving the waiter a good talking to and, by questioning him appropriately, he succeeded in discovering that the young gentleman was a lieutenant in the Crown Prince's Hussars, probably a landowner, immensely rich and very handsome – his name was Claes Ankerkrone.

That information startled Holst. There was no doubt about it; Claes Ankerkrone was strongly implicated in the whole matter, and it struck Holst how carelessly he had behaved in sending Annie's letter to Captain Ankerkrone. He had to admit that he had acted very unwisely. Demonstrating his trust in the Captain was understandable and natural. But Bror Sjöström's story should have alerted his vigilance earlier and, after the conversation with Kurk, he ought to have been even more suspicious of his friend, the Captain.

Annie's correspondence had further revealed to him that the Captain had hardly been completely honest with him, and now it could certainly be said that Claes Ankerkrone, the Captain's son, was severely compromised by the whole case, even though there was no justification for assuming that he was an accomplice in, or even aware of, the murder.

Even so, the unexplained fact remained that, in his conversation with Holst, Captain Ankerkrone had dropped a hint about helping, and that Holst might come to need him.

Holst immediately decided to visit the Captain and, putting all due consideration aside, force him to put his cards on the table and reveal everything he knew.

XII

WHEN HOLST ARRIVED at the district magistrate's home late in the evening, he was received by his housekeeper with the announcement that the magistrate had gone on leave the previous day accompanied by Captain Ankerkrone and the young Swedish lady. It had been decided a few days before and their destination was the Tyrol.

Holst felt extremely disturbed by this news. That the district magistrate had taken leave while such an important case was in progress was his business. He had to admit that the prospect of a speedy resolution of the case was very small. That he had travelled together with the Ankerkrones was very unfortunate but also very natural; the friendship between the Captain and the district magistrate had become very close.

But now Holst stood there. His superior was away; he didn't want to decide the case with the chief clerk, an industrious Danish lawyer whose life was exclusively engaged in private business. He was thus forced to temporarily let that aspect of the case rest and, by visiting the equerry, Bror Sjöström, see if he could follow Lieutenant Sjöström's tracks.

In very low spirits, he was about to return to Elsinore after refusing the housekeeper's hospitable invitation to stay in the magistrate's house, when it suddenly occurred to him to go down to the farmer with whom the Captain had been staying, and where he himself had stayed, to see if he could find out anything about the sudden departure.

His former host received him with great joy and, despite the fact it was late, he had a well-filled dinner table laid, to which Holst did great justice, before afterwards, equipped with a large toddy, talking about the old days.

Holst only told him a little about himself; he didn't have any experiences out of the ordinary to relate, he said, but he asked questions and it struck him how strangely circumstances had changed. Now he was sitting here, where he had so often been Ankerkrone's guest, conducting the most painstaking enquiry into his 'uncle's' life and times recently.

It went very easily; the farmer admired the Captain and talked about him with the utmost enthusiasm.

'Yes,' he said, 'he's a nobleman in the full sense of the word, a splendid fellow. Since I first met him, and until he left yesterday, there was not a bad word between us. He paid well, but he made no demands. He is unconditionally the best man I've met in my life. And the daughter – how lovely she is.'

Holst thought of Ulla – yes, she was lovely and her father was a man of honour, beyond all doubt, but why hadn't he been honest – or had he been honest? No – he had known that the murdered woman was Annie Cederlund; he had concealed it from the authorities; and he had had his reasons for concealing it. However, Holst thought that Ankerkrone should have shown greater trust in him.

And he began to ask questions to find out when Ankerkrone had first set foot in the district.

The farmer rubbed his neck.

'Yes, I really shouldn't tell you that,' he said, 'but you're a friend of the Captain, and it was a long time ago, so now I can talk about it. It'll be some time before he comes here again, if he ever comes. His health was not at all good. He has had a couple of fainting attacks recently, after you left. The young lady was completely beside herself, and he bid me such a strange farewell. But we never know when we will depart this life. Yes, Captain Ankerkrone is an old acquaintance.'

'So…' Holst began – it struck him that he should have known before, but in his relationship with Ankerkrone he hadn't been on his guard; it wouldn't happen any more. 'When was it then?' he asked.

The farmer blinked a little while reflecting on it.

'It could have been back in the early eighties. I'd taken over the farm from my father, who lived in retirement down in the little house where my daughter and her husband now have their business. It was around summertime, then one lovely day, a Swedish gentleman came by with a lovely lady and requested accommodation for a couple of days. She was uncommonly beautiful, a little weak – I suppose there were reasons for that. What sort of person she was, I can't say, but she was outrageously lovely, and he, by the way, was a charming person. They lived here for a month, went for walks, billed and cooed and were happy for each other. They weren't married, but that was none of our business. He called himself Cederlund and her name was Annie. The loveliest little female anyone could imagine and, goodness, how much in love she was.'

Holst drummed his fingers on the table.

'All right…and then?'

'Yes, well, they stayed a month and then they left.'

'And then?'

The farmer looked up at Holst with a wide, roguish smile.

'When I saw him again this year, he was no longer called Cederlund, but Ankerkrone. I suppose he felt a little embarrassed by it, but he would surely have understood that I wouldn't talk about it. And I wouldn't have done either, by the way, even though those gentlemen from the police are so used to hearing all sorts of secret stories. And it was a long time ago now.'

Holst had gone pale – he poured down a generous gulp of cognac toddy and leant back in his chair. He was extremely fascinated with what he had heard, even though Annie's letters had clearly revealed her relationship with him. He knew who this 'him' was; it was Ankerkrone, and now here in this place where Ankerkrone had once more seen the woman who had been his mistress 20 years ago as a corpse – murdered and immersed in the deep marl quarry – he had been capable of implementing a complete charade with the man who had to bring the evil deed to light.

Holst had arrived a day too late. The blood was pulsing in his temples as he instinctively got to his feet.

'It's warm in here,' he said.

The farmer raised his glass.

'Your health, Lieutenant – shall we drink a glass to our good friend the Captain and his lovely daughter, who has fallen rather heavily for you, believe you me.'

Holst blushed, but drank the toast.

'How did it actually come about that the Captain once again became a guest in your house?' he asked a little absent-mindedly.

140

'It happened quite naturally,' said his host. 'I had travelled down to Elsinore one day in early May, and then I bumped into the Captain and his daughter in the Railway Hotel. We began talking, they said they were heading south, and then I asked if they would like to pay us a visit. They did so and it resulted in them staying here for three months.'

'And you recognised him right away?' asked Holst. 'That sounds strange, given that you hadn't seen him for twenty years.'

The farmer laughed.

'No, my memory isn't that good, although when I think about, it's not that bad either. But anyway, I wouldn't have been able to recognise the Captain. I'd been at the Hotel Øresund – there was a meeting about some county business at the horse group I'm very involved in, sometime back in the spring. I'm just sitting there having a drink with a couple of friends, when I see a gentleman sitting looking straight at me at a table opposite. I thought I ought to know the face, but I had absolutely no idea who it could be. Then he gets up and comes over to me and asks if I'm Anders Mortensen from this town.

'Yes, I am, I say. Did I recognise him? But no, I didn't. Then he laughed and said, surely I remembered Mr Cederlund, and then I was immediately with it. But then I thought he became a little abrupt just as the young man he was with came over to him. He blurted out: This is my son. At that time, I didn't get to know his name and a month later I met him with his daughter, and that was when we became very good friends. He probably thought he had been a little brusque with me last time.'

Holst had been leaning back and listening with great attention to the long account.

'When was the horse group meeting?' he asked, when the farmer paused for breath.

'Well, I don't know the exact date, but it was in late March.'

'Can't you look up the date?'

'Yes, just a moment – it's in my desk diary. I have it organised on a sort of blotting paper, where I make a note of everything of that kind. Nowadays you can find yourself involved in no end of meetings and that sort of thing.'

Anders Mortensen rummaged around in his papers and found the date.

'It was on the 26th of March precisely this year. Yes, it was indeed and it was lovely spring weather; I remember I was driving in to town with my wife's sister and we hardly had any extra clothing with us. Yes, now I'm sure, it was on the 26th of March this year that I saw the magistrate once more after a break of 20 years. It's rather odd that it wasn't until he came back that I found out his real name. My wife and I talked about it often – that it was a strange coincidence. We never talked about her, the young woman, him neither – it was probably just a floozy he had that time, but she was outrageously lovely too.'

They talked for a while about the Captain's health, which was bad according to the farmer. They hadn't really noticed anything, but eight days ago, round about midday, the Captain had been out to fetch the post; he came home and became extremely ill. The daughter thought he had been walking too briskly, and that was possible because it was very hot.

'They sent a message for the doctor, but then it had just seemed to get better by itself. The Captain took it easy for a few days, then a friend of his came from Sweden, a tall, stately captain, a baron whom they called Uncle Holger – Kruk was his name, or something like that. He stayed a couple of days and then they decided to leave. They said they wanted to go to the Tyrol and the doctor thought it was a good idea to go up in the mountains where the air was supposed to be so light. Yes, we were sad to lose them. They were lovely people.'

Holst went to bed late; he carefully read Annie's letters and blamed himself bitterly for missing the most important clues. That was an unforgivable mistake.

The next day he left for Scania to visit Equerry Sjöström at Riddartofte.

XIII

RIDDARTOFTE LIES ABOUT A MILE from Bjärsjöladugård
station on the Eslöv-Ystad line, placed high up, surrounded by
inviting beech forests overlooking Vomb Lake and the Romele
escarpment across the plain surrounding Lund. A splendid
gentleman's seat with large buildings in the Dutch Renaissance
style and numerous extensions. In a small pavilion, not unlike
the bathhouse at Frederiksborg, the equerry Bror Sjöström
lived in a neat little bachelor flat, which was taken care of by
frequently changing housekeepers, who invariably allowed the
old soldier to attack them, relatively quickly laying down their
arms in the hope of winning the day, but who, not long after
their defeat, were removed in pain and a great deal of sorrow
and were found a place elsewhere at the expense of the estate, at
least for the time being.

The Count of Riddartofte, Tage Falkenberg, a friendly and
pleasant Scania tycoon with an awful lot of inherited gold

stashed away, had suggested admitting Sjöström to the main household. There was a trial run, but the Countess never allowed it to be repeated. And the compensation sum was transferred as a fixed component of the equerry's already quite significant remuneration.

Holst had let the equerry know that he was coming and he was picked up at the station in a smart little dogcart, harnessed to a pair of well-groomed Hungarian half-breeds and driven by a young, flaxen-haired coachman.

In the door of the pavilion, known to the neighbours as 'Arcadia', he was received by an attractive, buxom Jewess, still in the initial stages of surrender, who smiled in a free and easy Swedish way with a pair of inquisitive eyes.

It was 'damnably stylish' in Arcadia.

The equerry appeared in an elegant dinner jacket and did the honours like a feudal vassal king at an enchanting party. It didn't occur to him to ask the nature of Holst's visit; he was the unsurpassed, dapper Swedish host, the born Scanian nobleman and warrior who is unique in this world.

It was a little difficult for Holst to present his errand so he had to take a considerable detour. He had to admit that it was concerning Hugold, and Bror Sjöström shivered at the thought. Hugold always meant paying out money; admittedly the estate financed it, but it always annoyed the equerry to have to draw on this limitless resource for that reason. The Count of Riddartofte had on one such occasion had words with his equerry in more serious terms than usual.

'Dear Bror – I pay for your women with pleasure and joy. I have no one other than my dear wife myself, and the poor women have to live; to give to them is a noble duty, which you are also performing at Riddartofte, my dear Bror. As for your children, I pay for them too, for I have faith in your offspring, but that idler, your brother Hugold! No, now it's enough.'

The equerry knew that the Count invariably paid up, but he didn't like it. Holst thus brought the matter up extremely carefully and said that he and a friend employed by the General Staff had met Hugold in Nice and made a deal with him there, which admittedly was insignificant, but a paper had been created that was waiting upon Hugold, and he wouldn't deliver. It was only a trifling matter and it didn't concern money, but Holst's friend wanted the paper delivered and it was impossible to find out Hugold's address.

He wasn't in Nice any longer – Holst had found that out through enquiries – and that was true enough. When the equerry realised that it wasn't about money, he calmed down somewhat and told Holst that he didn't know the whereabouts of his brother, who was regrettably drifting off course, but that he had met a neighbour at Eslöv Station who had opportunely told him that Hugold was now living in Venice with a charming girl, a little jewel, whom he was struggling to hold on to.

The equerry shrugged.

'Hugold is an idler – but he's my brother. I've done what I can for him – I can't do any more. Just as long as he stays away from Sweden and dies as a reasonably decent nobleman. I daren't hope for more than that.'

Holst stayed silent.

'So, you know my brother Hugold,' continued Sjöström.

'No,' said Holst, 'not personally.'

Sjöström took a picture off his desk; a tall, erect soldier, with handsome, regular features and a large blond moustache.

'He was a bright lad,' he said with a sigh. 'It's these women who have spoiled him and especially that devil, Annie Bengtson, wherever in the world she may be.'

Holst asked airily who Annie Bengtson was and learnt about

the same as Kurk had told him.

'Do you think it's now over between them?' he asked cautiously.

'I think so,' said the equerry. 'In March this year, Hugold wrote to me that it was all over between them. He promised to come back here; he was in Helsingborg on some kind of business, but when I got there he had left. Since then, I haven't heard from him, but my understanding was that the affair with Annie was over. Well now – so he's found another one. These devilish women are the ruin of us men.'

Holst smiled; at that moment, the house nymph showed up with the pousse-café; she looked like a hostess and moved around with a seductive lack of constraint in a demure outfit that had been adjusted in a suitably appealing way.

The equerry nodded and lit a monstrously long cigar.

Holst asked him for his card with a few words to Hugold as introduction should he meet him; he was on his way to Venice, and he would be happy to bring greetings.

He was given it with a sigh and without ceremony. It was clear to him that there was not much more to learn here about Hugold, so he carefully led the conversation around to the Ankerkrones. He was particularly interested in finding out something about the young man and his relationship with Hugold.

'Wasn't Claes Ankerkrone a good friend of your brother?' he asked tentatively.

'Of Hugold…?' Bror looked completely horrified. 'That's the first time I've heard that.'

So, he didn't know anything. Holst seemed to recall that Sjöström was the first to tell him about young Ankerkrone so he touched upon this. The equerry shook his head.

'No,' he said. 'I know there is a tale about Claes gadding

147

around France for a couple of years with a lady, but I've never heard anything about Hugold being with them.'

'How did that end?' Holst asked.

'Very unromantically,' said the equerry, 'as it always does with those damn women. Claes's pappa, old Ankerkrone, had to buy the lady off with Claes's wife's money, which is alleged to be inexhaustible. It happened at some point during the winter or spring, so I understand. The lady went away to the south and the old man took his son to Italy, where there was said to have been a tender reconciliation. According to some. Others say that when it came to the pinch, the lady ran off with someone else, and old Ankerkrone kept the money for himself, which was extremely reasonable because he needed it. Anyway, it was all sorted out somewhere in Denmark and we don't talk about it. The Count here bumped into Claes in Venice a few days ago. He had just arrived with his wife and children when Tage Falkenberg was passing through the city. He was said to have been having a very nice time with his wife and yet it may be falsehood, all of it. Old Ankerkrone is extremely rarely here in Scania, yet he is a charming man and his daughter is pretty – unusually pretty.'

Holst nodded.

'I know them quite well. That is, I've met them. The Captain is a splendid man, a handsome man.'

'Well, bless me,' said the equerry, sipping at a maraschino with much devotion.

He was clearly reluctant to talk about Ankerkrone, and he had quite forgotten the indiscretion he had committed in his first meeting with Holst with regard to the Captain's earlier life – or he didn't care to be drawn into the question.

Holst looked at him a little intensely under lowered eyelids and asked in a light tone whether he believed Captain

Ankerkrone could commit any act of dishonesty.

'Bless me no,' said the equerry, emptying his glass of maraschino. 'He's a complete gentleman.'

But he didn't want to talk about him and the conversation changed tack. It essentially concerned the three things the equerry understood: horses, dogs and women. Holst was the audience, while Sjöström talked incessantly and had a royal good time. He found the lieutenant charming, and they came on intimate terms before the house nymph intervened and made sure that her strict master came to his soft bed.

The next morning the equerry had a hangover and Holst set off back to Copenhagen.

XIV

WHEN HOLST RETURNED TO HIS HOME in the capital, he found, in addition to the other post, a letter from Ankerkrone, with a package of papers attached. The letter read as follows:

Malmö, 17th June, 1902

My dear friend,

I have been considering for some time whether I should write to you or if I should wait and see if our paths would cross. Our acquaintanceship is young, but you will believe me when I tell you that I, an old man in mind if not in years, because life has bent my back and drawn furrows across my brow, have never met a young man who has warmed my heart like you have. From the first days of my youth, I have believed that the most wonderful purpose of life would be to bequeath my name, and what life has taught me, to the person who could take up the calling that I couldn't accomplish, that of living life how a human being should live it. My son cannot take this up because he is so distant from everything that is close to my heart. I have found in you so much of what I love and so much of what I miss and I am fonder of you than you could imagine.

Which is why I am writing to you. You sent me, without understanding it, a message that you called, 'from beyond the grave'. You could not have sent me a more onerous message, even though it wasn't the first time I had heard it. Holger Kurk, my old friend from my youth, has told me about his meeting with you. I now know that you know some of the events that linked my destiny to the woman whose body you found in the forest lake that day. You know far from everything, but what I am sending you here will tell you all that I am at liberty to say.

I recognised her immediately the day you found her. Perhaps you feel betrayed by my silence. But I had to hold back about all that time that had faded away, which you are going to hear about now, and you will understand why I stayed silent when there was such an uproar around me, with people wanting to know everything and spread it to thousands of unimportant and irrelevant people – wasn't that so?

I don't believe you will ever get to the bottom of this case. I advise you not to give up – you should not. Neither do I ask you for anything because I trust you. But I can't help you. I am no longer in the best of health, but should our paths cross, then accept me for who I am,

Your fatherly friend,
Arvid Ankerkrone.

151

This letter was on top of a parcel of papers, which had clearly been selected with great care from a larger collection of letters and documents, and which put on record everything that had happened between Annie and Ankerkrone.

The first in the pile was a folder with loose pages, on the cover of which was written in the Captain's firm, meticulous hand:

> *From Arvid Ankerkrone's diary.*
> *Motto: Wie man Geld und Zeit vertan, Zeigt das Büchlein lustig an.*[1]

The diary was divided into short sections, each of which was introduced by a quote from Goethe's Venetian Epigrams. In several of the passages, the master's words from these epigrams were woven into the text in translation. It was clear that Ankerkrone had been heavily influenced in his youth by this writing, and had even attempted to build his diary upon its verses. But life had strangely and jarringly intervened in this poem and bent it more and more towards serious prose, until Ankerkrone had laid his pen aside with heavy, bitter words to close his diary for ever. Its content was as follows:

> *Venice, July 1875*
> *An dem Meere ging ich und suchte mir Muscheln. In einer Fand ich ein Perlchen; es bleibt nun mir am Herzen verwahrt.*[2]
>
> *Twenty-six years old and in Venice! In truth, you great immortal poet, I didn't need you to show me the way in the whirring labyrinth. I have seen Baiae and the fish and the sea, as I have seen Venice and the pool and the frogs. I don't sleep, I'm wide awake. 'Which woman do I want?' you ask me; I have found her, just*

as I want her to be – the pearl in the mussel, which I will keep by my heart.

Giulia Cassini: 'Yes, I understand it so well; it is my body that travels, while my soul will forever rest in my lover's bosom.'

In short, I'm in love – in love and young, I'm in Venice.

It's summer and the heat is hanging heavily over St Mark's Square, while the water splashes lazily in the Grand Canal. Spending hours leaning back in the gondola, I let myself be conveyed past the house of my beloved.

'I can liken the gondola to a gently rocking cradle; the box shielding me from the sun is like a black sarcophagus. And it carries me between cradle and grave in the canal of life, carefree I dream, gliding lightly on water.'

I know she is coming and, when she arrives, she is mine.

She promised me the first kiss in Venice; Venice is her home, and I'll be looking for her there. I'll meet her there when she arrives.

She hasn't arrived yet.

Meanwhile, I will have to comfort myself with Venice and Goethe.

The waiting certainly isn't easy.

'Oh, how I would pay attention to all the seasons, Greet the embryonic spring, yearn for the autumn. But now is neither summer nor winter; for I am happy In the shelter of Cupid's wings, surrounded by eternal spring.'

Giulia has arrived.

153

'Tell me, how do you live? I am alive! And if hundreds and hundreds

Of human years are to come, I want tomorrow to be as today.'

Great master, whose lovely verse a fool like me has tried to reproduce. Thank you for what you were for me during these days.

Thank you in your own words:

'I had become tired from just looking at paintings,

Those splendid art treasures which Venice has preserved,

For these delights also demanded recreation and leisure;

My yearning eyes sought lively enticements.'

Forgive me, master – now I am trying to write poetry.

Paolo Veronese once painted a portrait of a Giulia, but no one has been able to paint that glow in your eyes – my Giulia. And your lips, Giulia – are now the reality of dreams.

On 14th July, 1875, in Venice, the noble Donna Giulia Cassini promised to marry Arvid Ankerkrone.

Småland, Aug. 1881

Oftmals hab' ich geirrt und habe mich wieder gefunden,

Aber glücklicher nie; nun ist dies Mädchen mein Glück!

Ist auch dieses ein Irrthum, so schont mich, ihr klügeren Götter,

Und benehmt mir ihn erst drüben am kalten Gestad.[3]

These four lines say everything. I have erred, and I didn't realise until here in this lovely green valley by the Laga what my error consisted of. I have loved Giulia and, in the first years of my marriage, I believed in happiness. But I have acted wrongly in wanting to plant a rose from the south in the cold ground of the north. The first puff from the merciless northern wind has turned the rose to ice. Giulia has given birth to a son, and I have baptised him with the name of Claes, which comes from my family's history. Giulia has given birth to other children, but they have died and, with them, it is as if her blood is spent. My rose has become pale.

Giulia has gone to the south, towards Venice; she didn't ask me to join her, nor did I want to because our dreams have been dreamt to their end. Five years is a long dream and the dream was sweet. Now it's over.

'I have often erred and come to my senses again, but never more happily.'

Now my happiness is called Annie. She is sixteen years old and was bathing in the river when I first saw her. She was standing naked by the bush which drinks from the creek and as I stepped forward without suspecting she was there, she lifted her eyes towards me and laughed. As beautiful as Venus rising out of the sea, she hid nothing because she had nothing to hide her, and there was laughter in her eyes while the river rippled around her feet.

Annie is the daughter of Corporal Bengt Bengtson, born in Småland among the heather, flowers and shimmering lakes. And Annie is as docile and good as she is gentle and patient.

Annie is my mistress...

Cedersköld and Kurk have been hunting today. I don't hunt any more; I've bruised my foot. The magistrate laughs, as he knows I'm going to the river to fish.

Annie is knowledgeable about casting lines and the fish comes in to her. Annie catches it easily with a playful hand.

I'm leaving tomorrow and Annie is coming with me.

There's no point in asking, and why should I? What happiness would Annie find in Småland?

Giulia has sent me a letter. She asks if I'm coming to Venice.

No, I've chosen Annie – if it's the wrong choice, may the gods spare me and let me keep on believing...

Zealand, Aug. 1882

Arm und kleiderlos war, als ich sie geworben, das Mädchen; Damals gefiel sie mir nackt, wie sie mir jetzt noch gefällt.[4]

The beech trees in the Danish forests north of Hamlet's town whisper their silent language in our ears. Annie is a good, loving woman towards me and the days pass so gently and easily beneath kisses and sunshine. It isn't the great Eros...but...

I haven't forgotten Giulia. Day after day, it seemed that her picture was becoming clearer to me...but these days belong to Annie.

Up in the fringe of the forest lies an unfrequented little lake, where we like to linger, Annie and I. Tightly bordered by the forest, it lies like a small shiny shield between flowering bird cherry trees and hawthorns.

We sit on the root of a wind-felled beech, where the lake cuts in under a bank which is stabilised by the interlacing roots. It's a place we both love.

Annie is mournful and afraid. She often leans her head against my shoulder and whispers: Arvid, I'm so afraid you'll leave me to go to her. Say that you will, and I will slide quietly into the lake with my unborn child – quite quietly so that you can go away to her; she has rights over you.

Then I answer: Annie – no one has any rights over me except the one I choose.

Then she kisses me with tears in her eyes – Annie, who came up to me that bright summer's day in Småland – and I slowly pull her back from the edge.

But at times I feel heavy of mind when the people come home from work and they squabble out in the yard.

Then I think of the master's words:

Why do people carry on so and make such a fuss? They want to be fed,

To beget children and feed them as best they can. Take note of this, traveller, and do likewise at home! No man can do more, no matter how much he wants to.

Gammalstorp, Oct. 1882

Eine Liebe hatt' ich, sie war mir lieber als Alles! Aber ich hab' sie nicht mehr! Schweig, und ertrag' den Verlust![5]

I am nevertheless a soldier. When we break camp and the signal trumpet sounds, my heart beats freely

157

and easily in my chest and I restrain my black and brown Flora, dancing under me on the sandy roads. Then I ride across country, with Ljunggren, my worthy captain of the guard, riding silently behind me until we reach the farm where his wife and his curly-headed children wave to him. Sometimes, we ride in there and drink a glass of milk while I stroke the fair hair of his little Johanna, whose clear blue eyes smile at me.

Then we continue at a fast pace.

Annie has gone – Giulia is still in Venice.

What do I care about Annie and Giulia now?

I am nevertheless a soldier and now we are approaching camp; I have no more time for thoughts of affectionate games and my friends are waiting, both Cedersköld and my good friend Kurk, whom I have neglected so shamefully because I was dreaming with Annie. Why did she leave me, I wonder?

'If I were a domesticated wife, and had what I needed, I would loyally and happily caress and kiss my man. That's what a young woman sang to me, among other bawdy songs,

In Venice, and I never heard a more devout prayer.'

Now we are on our way to camp – and who thinks about women then?

Venice, May 1883

Und so tändelt' ich mir, von allen Freunden geschieden,
In der neptunischen Stadt Tage wie Stunden hinweg.
Alles, was ich erfuhr, ich würzt' es mit süßer Erinnerung
Würtzt'es mit Hoffnung; sie sind lieblichste Würzen
der Welt.[6]

Back in Venice – but at first glance, how changed – perhaps mostly myself? Only eight years have elapsed since I last visited you, Venice – only eight years, and what has not happened since then? I'm not looking for the first bright days of my love, its brilliant nights; Giulia has asked me to come, and I come.

But I'm not expecting anything – I'm not hoping for anything – it's a pilgrimage to holy places...

I dream, but I've never dreamt a more delicious dream. Giulia is my own, and my youth lives on, lives a new life after a torpor which I thought was death. I planted the rose of the south in the cold soil of my homeland and the rose didn't flourish; its head bowed and its leaves withered. Now it has drunk the dew of its mother earth, now its petals unfold towards the sun, now it smiles redder than before, and its fragrance rises in the light air. Giulia, I love you now, love you more ardently than I have ever loved you. You are the Rose of Venice, my lovely, you are my only one. And you smile, you don't ask, you know your love is all; it doesn't doubt because it doesn't see; it doesn't ask because it doesn't hear. Now life begins again.

'You inspired love and desire in me; I feel it and I'm on fire.

Beloved, now inspire faith in me!'

From that day and hour, I am Giulia's and Giulia's alone – everything else has to be forgotten, everything else.

The name too – everything.

The memories grow out of every stone, out of every painting and whisper the same sweet story about me as in bygone days.

159

Giulia...

But we will linger in Venice – linger a long time, forever if you want to, and I'll prepare a herb garden for my rose where the wind doesn't kiss its pot with sleet, where the dew falls mildly and sweetly and the sun caresses it.

If that is your wish.

Here you shall give birth to a child who will be the child of our love, a daughter who will bear your name; or no – only you shall bear your name. No one else.

Venice for me is the city of memory and hope. The memory and hope are you.

Verona, March 1884

Widerfahre dir, was dir auch will, du wachsender Jüngling -

Liebe bildete dich; werde dir Liebe zu Theil![7]

Giulia has given me a daughter; she was baptised with her mother's name, but we have decided she should be called Ulla. Because there is only one Giulia. When Giulia is well again, we will visit Capri and Palermo, and when the summer arrives, we will return to Gammalstorp while the sun shines. The post is troubling – it has brought me letters from Annie.

Annie was a name – Annie is forgotten.

But the letters demand to be remembered. I have asked Holger Kurk to care for Annie and her child. I say her child. I have children, but they are Giulia's. A mistress shouldn't give birth to children. Children should only be bred by the hearth.

I don't wish to see Annie again, nor her child. It

surely isn't in distress; it was conceived in love – but it was a love that vanished – a jest.

Es sei, Liebchen, des Scherzes genug![8]

Gammalstorp, March 1885

Wundern kann es mich nicht, daß Menschen die Hunde so lieben,

Denn ein erbärmlicher Schuft ist, wie der Mensch, so der Hund.[9]

There were three of us, from our years as youths: Kurk, Cederсköld and I. Our fathers were friends and we spent our childhoods playing together. We grew up together and we received our education under the same roof. If anyone had asked me which one of these two was closest to my heart, I wouldn't have been able to answer, because I valued both of them equally highly.

And now. I am writing because I once committed these things to paper, so that in many years' time I would be able to see what I once felt; so that one day my boy would be able to read of the honest, true fate of his father as it confronted him in life. But every stroke of the pen is a rift in an open wound.

Annie has spoken. She had gone to Småland to stay with her father, and she wrote from there to Giulia and told her everything. Giulia will forgive me, I feel that, but we didn't discuss it, and Giulia fell ill. I was sad. Not because I felt regret – I had followed a voice in me which spoke at that time and which is now silent. But Giulia's suffering was painful for me. She didn't understand how infinitely higher my love for her was compared with my infatuation with Annie.

And I couldn't tell her, because you can talk to a woman about your love for her, but you can't, not even with a single word, touch upon a friendly feeling for another, let alone infatuation.

Autumn passed and it was heavy and dark. I wanted to head south, but Giulia didn't.

Giulia was more beautiful than ever before, but she didn't want to see me.

Winter arrived and, with winter, parties, where Giulia shone like a queen among all the pretty maids.

She was friendly towards me again, but she didn't match my dream. I would wait and hope. Then it happened.

I didn't believe it – I didn't want to believe it – but I couldn't be in any doubt.

(Between the pages of the diary was a yellowed letter in Annie's handwriting.)

Kristianstad, 20th March, 1885

Arvid Ankerkrone.

You've caused me sorrow and injury more than anyone can bear, but for my child's sake I've borne it faithfully. I write my child because you say that the child isn't yours and that's a possibility because I have known other men than you, also at that time – you have said that to Cedersköld and that's also true, because I have known him too. And now I only have him to comfort me, because I don't want anything to do with your money. And Cedersköld will provide for both me and the child.

So everything is over between us because, after

all, that's what you want, you love your wife over everything in the world. And I suppose she loves you too, although I thought it was fair and right to show her how you were and how a woman can trust you in her time of need, despite your words and assurances, which you never mean. But she has nothing to say to you, because you fine people are no better than a girl like me – for we are all equal before our Lord and all of us are sinners.

But fair is fair anyway.

And I tell you that you can mock me and leave me and push me away as much as you want, because I have Cedersköld, but your fine lady, whom you love and who is so proud, shall not deprive me of the last and only one I have.

And now I know that your wife is Cedersköld's lover, and they meet in many different places, and if you don't believe me, you can get confirmation of it whenever you want.

And that, I say to you, isn't fair and right, because when a woman is married and has children, it's not the same as it is for someone who is in need.

And you have your wife as she has you – that's what I wanted to say.

Annie Bengtson.

P.S. If you don't believe me, you can come and see for yourself next Monday at 8 o'clock in the evening in Västragatan at Madam Engström's.

The diary continued:

I have killed my wife…

Not with my own hand, because I don't believe I could lift a hand against Giulia, but I'm guilty of her death and I will bear that guilt to the last day of my life – beyond it even, if anything beyond exists. I gave Giulia the letter and asked her: Is it true?

And she answered yes.

At that point, I wanted to leave – I only had one thing to do, avenge my honour and I would do that in the hour when I learnt my shame.

She asked me to stay and told me that the fault was hers and hers alone. But she had had the right to act as she had acted, the same right as I had had.

To this, I replied that this wasn't a question of right or no right. My wife's honour was my honour, my house's honour and my children's honour and I was its avenger.

Then she smiled and put her arms around my neck and said it wasn't true. She had only wanted to take her revenge, just wanted to test me, and that it had all been set up. Now I had been punished enough and now she wanted to forgive me.

I didn't believe her.

So she asked me to wait and to call the other two in to hear from their own mouths what I wouldn't believe when she said it.

Those days were the hardest time of my life, because Cedersköld was away travelling at that time and Annie was in Kristianstad.

But the day came and I let the two be called.

Cedersköld, who had been my friend for so many years, refused to say anything, and Annie laughed in bitter disdain and said everything she had written was true.

Giulia wept and I didn't believe her.

Then came the night, and she implored me to believe her, but how could I believe the person who had betrayed me? She said she would die if I doubted her.

And I doubted her anyway.

So Giulia died on 27th March, 1885 by her own hand.

I buried her, but didn't mourn for her.

I swore to live only for my children's sake, and on that day, the smile on my lips died and I became an old man.

I swore yet another oath: to avenge the dishonour that was brought upon my house and that oath I will keep.

Here ends my diary, or rather the records that were originally intended to form my diary, but which the seriousness of life has interrupted. A man cannot write down his sorrow; what's the point! Be quiet!...and speak only where word is action.

Attached were three letters to Holger Kurk, which spoke of that which the diary was silent about. They had clearly been chosen out of many, but each one threw the sharpest light on an action.

Vintschgau "Neuspondinig",
12th Aug. 1899

Dear Holger. I am writing from the Tyrol, from Stilfserjoch, where I'm staying at a guest house with the name Neuspondinig not far from the high point of

Ferdinandshöhe. You know why I came here and I'm writing this to inform you that my business has been completed.

Cedersköld is dead.

It didn't go as I had expected, and it was no doubt a higher will, if such higher will exists, that decided differently. I loved him as I have loved you; what that means, you know yourself. He broke our friendship and acted badly towards me. I swore I would find him and demand that he accepted his responsibility. I found him here in this place, dying, and he died without speaking.

He had arrived here from Trafoi, to which I had followed his trail. He wanted to take a short-cut on foot and plunged into a stream called Klammbach.

He was pitiful to see; his chest was crushed and his head badly injured. He was breathing weakly when I found him, but he died not ten minutes after my arrival.

I still think that if I had met him at Franzenshöhe where the accident happened, I would probably now have been charged at the assizes in Bozen. I could have thrown Cedersköld into any abyss in this world.

Now he is dead and I haven't killed him in a fight. I wish I had because since Giulia died, every drop of blood in my body demanded his death and I have pursued him as his malignant destiny.

Annie has left him; I see from a letter that was found in his effects that she has found a friend in Vienna. Annie was created to be a woman of pleasure and that will be her lot. She deceived me when I loved her; she also deceived Cedersköld and lied to both of us.

Poor Corporal Bengtson! He believed me, and while I was heading south to see Venice and Giulia, he tried to avenge his daughter's honour by killing Cedersköld. I don't know whether the child is mine or Cedersköld's, but it shall not suffer hardship; it has been taken care of with the provisions made. Cedersköld didn't utter a word, but I think he recognised me and that gives me some comfort. I never thought I would be able to see a human being suffering and feel comforted by that. But in this case, I did. I have had him buried. He didn't own anything, or at least only a little.

Now he is dead, and his name shouldn't be mentioned between us any more. He died on 6th August, 1886 through a fall between Ferdinandshöhe and Trafoi. The coachman who drove him didn't see how the accident happened, and no one will ever learn how it happened.

Now I am returning home to the children. Their upbringing is now what I live for. Brotherly greetings,

Your Arvid.

Malmö, 10th April, 1898

Dear Holger,

You have written to tell me that Annie's child is dead. Annie has also written to me and looked for me. I won't reply to her. I was fond of Annie when I saw her the first time. You may reproach me for this infatuation – one can do that afterwards. I think I acted right because life offers so little sunshine and we humans should seek sunshine. Well, I don't want to preach that sermon and it would also be stupid. Now I have changed a lot. If I acted wrongly, I have had to

*bear the 'punishment'. I don't believe in punishment,
but I believe in revenge. All punishment is revenge and
revenge can satisfy; I have felt that myself once in my
life.*

*It's only for the best that the child is dead. Annie
doesn't deserve a child, and I don't believe in her
repentance, as you call it. A man can love many
women and yet not be affected by his infatuations; a
woman who loves many men is, and remains, a whore.
You may well have learnt the opposite and preach your
morality or immorality just as eagerly.*

*I'm a nobleman from birth, and my morality is
the nobleman's morality – it will never be different.
It definitely isn't practical considerations, definitely
not society, I want to preserve; it is purely and simply
my soldier morality, which, when it comes to it, is
no morality. I have forgotten the whore, and I didn't
acknowledge her child when it lived, nor do I intend to
cry at its deathbed.*

*Bury it and give her some money, that's probably
what she has most need for.*

Your Arvid.

Paris, 25th December, 1899

Dear Holger.

*Merry Christmas – you are probably surprised that
I'm not spending Christmas with Ulla in Lausanne. It
was chance; we had decided that she should come here
but bad weather and train cancellations thwarted our
plans. Claes and his wife are in Sicily. The honeymoon
still has 14 days to go, though Claes's marriage doesn't*

please me; she is too rich and not beautiful enough.
Thank God that Ulla is poor, so she is saved the
disappointments. Ulla will probably arrive tomorrow.

I spent Christmas Eve here in the company of a
woman – Annie. I was strolling down the boulevards
in the evening to take a look at Christmas in Paris.
I met her and recognised her immediately. It seemed
as if she was in some distress – she looked poor. You
know, I think everything in this world has its destiny,
and I stopped her and asked her if she wanted to spend
Christmas Eve with me. I don't know why I did it, but
now that has happened, I don't regret it. It was the
strangest Christmas Eve I have ever spent.

Annie has passed from hand to hand, but she is
still very beautiful. Sjöström has left her, she says; he
is what I've always said he is – a bad sort who has
probably lived off Annie's friends. We didn't talk about
the child – she tried to, but I refused. I didn't recognise
that child as mine. I have loved her. At that time, I
had no idea she was his mistress as well as mine. But
she was hungry and I gave her a princely meal at the
Cafe de la Paix. I really think she began to hope that
the old days would begin again and I won't deny that
I reinforced her belief and hope. I wanted her to talk
about the only thing that still today, out of everything
hidden in the past, is close to my heart.

About Giulia. She spoke, but she only said what she
said that time, and I'll probably have to believe her.
She says she hated Giulia because I loved her. That's
no doubt true. She says she hated Cedersköld and that
she only became his mistress because I betrayed her. It's
obviously untrue, but women who lie, lie with all their

soul and believe their own lies. I rarely lie myself – I have only lied to you once, as you will read here. It was late and I accompanied Annie to her home, a humble garret in a neighbourhood I'm not familiar with.

Why I did that, I don't know, but something of the devil had taken hold of me that holy Christmas night. I can be evil and I was. I told Annie while she was resting in my arms how a man died on 6th August, 1886 while taking the path over Stilfserjoch from Trafoi.

You, I and Annie are the only ones who still remember the man whose bones are crumbling in a small cemetery in the Tyrol. I told Annie somewhat more than I've told anyone else and than I ever wished to tell anyone else. She stiffened in horror, and I won't forget her look for a long time. She only talked a little, and I think her hopes of a renewal of the old days waned during my account.

If Giulia's death is my responsibility, I don't know; Cedersköld's is his own and no one else's. If I were standing on the road at Ferdinandshöhe today, I would still force him to dare to jump and ask for the divine judgement that would say whether he was guilty or innocent. I said that to Annie that Christmas night. Now you also know what happened. Put it to one side and forget it.

Your Arvid.

Finally, attached to the letters was a document which Holst recognised – it was Annie's letter to Ankerkrone, which Holst had had forwarded to him. Holst's note was attached. A greeting from beyond the grave. Annie's letter went as follows:

Venice, 10th February, 1900

My only friend,

You can believe me or not, but I've never loved anyone but you; I will swear directly to God the Father if I die this night, which I think I will because I'm very ill. But if I live, this letter will be kept in a safe place, and my old mother will keep it and send it to you if I die before her. I have never loved anyone but you – never. Cedersköld's seduction of me is proven and true, but I was young and didn't love him, but I loved you and the child was yours. It was, because it was born while we were together and had been together for a long time for the happiest days of my life and you know that too.

It was yours. But you turned nasty towards me and didn't want to divorce your wife, whom you didn't love at that time, and so I left you to see if you would return, but you wouldn't and you went to your wife whom you had no right to because you had left her, and it was me who was your beloved and had given birth in pain to your child.

I wrote to your wife and spoke with her and said you had loved me before now and she went pale and would not believe it, but I had the child with me and she could see that it looked like you, which proves that it was your child. And she talked so much to me and was sad because she was no doubt a good woman, but I hated her because she loved you and because you had deserted me. But she didn't want to leave you, and then some time after she called me in and told me she would punish you because I had seemed sad and she was good to me, but that only caused me pain because

171

I could see she was afraid of me.

And then I told her she should say that stuff about Cedersköld, and he did what I wanted, because he was a fool for me, but I didn't care about him.

And then I wrote to you.

But afterwards, I said that I had told the truth, and it wasn't true, because Cedersköld has never been your wife's lover, but I did it to get my revenge. I would have told you that in Paris, but you told me you had killed Cedersköld, and I was afraid you'd kill me, so I didn't dare tell you the truth.

But it is the truth and if you have killed both your wife and Cedersköld, then it is God's punishment for deceiving me and leaving our child, whom our Lord has taken and whom you wouldn't even reply to me about, when I wrote so touchingly to you about it when she died. That's what I wanted to write to you and you have to know this, if I die, so that your evil deeds may be known to you and it is all punishment from our Lord.

Now I don't want to write any more, because I'm very ill, but now you know everything and that I have never loved anyone other than you, Arvid Ankerkrone.

Your unhappy beloved, Annie.

XV

IN ADDITION TO THE IMPORTANT POST from Ankerkrone, Holst found a short letter from Elsinore, which read as follows:

Lieutenant Eigil Holst, Copenhagen police

After the lieutenant's departure, I have obtained information that the gentleman, who on 27th March this year stayed at the railway hotel together with the lady who called herself Mrs Gorin, was a Swedish officer of bad reputation named Hugold Sjöström. I have also learnt that at midday the same day, he hired a carriage from the carter Larsen of Stengade and was driven to Esrum, and the coachman and carter were both surprised that he let the carriage return empty. I have not been able to find out anything else.

Respectfully yours,

Jens Petersen Stub, waiter.

This letter gave Holst a reason to make yet another reconnaissance trip to the place where the body was found and the area around it, as well as a further visit to Elsinore. There was, however, apart from the carter's statement, nothing significantly new that came out of it; in particular, there was no one at all in the area around Esrum who had noticed the couple at all.

Holst decided to meet up with his immediate superior in the capital and provide a detailed report on what was known, though without touching upon the individual circumstances which had connections to the Ankerkrone family. He emphasised that the search for and arrest of Sjöström was based on the falsification and that the charge of murder would be the subsidiary one, thereby making it easier to keep the case from the public eye. The murder and the discovery of the corpse in the quarry were both forgotten, in the way that all newspaper copy is forgotten quickly and completely.

Holst was not one of those policemen who immediately fashion an opportunity for a compromising charge. He didn't seek recognition as the one who hastily jumps in, and he calmly allowed his colleagues to say that it was luck and chance that stood by him, but his superior knew that it was his persistent, unobtrusive use of chance that was his strength, and that he was among the few who understood how to quietly follow a trail.

Holst quickly prepared for his journey; he wanted to look for Sjöström in Venice, bring about his arrest and transport him to Denmark, but subsequently he wanted to find Ankerkrone, and then the Captain was going tell the whole story of what he knew.

PART THREE
Venice

I

AT THE BEGINNING OF JULY, Eigil Holst arrived in the city of lagoons, the Queen of the Adriatic, the one and only Venice. It was eleven o'clock in the evening, in moonlight with a clear, starry sky and fairly quiet. The train rolled over the long, stone causeway connecting the lagoon city with the mainland. Holst leant out of the window. In the distance, he could see lights flickering, but they disappeared and as far as the eye could see, there was only the clear surface of the sea, in which the sky was reflected, shiny and blue. The train stopped with a jolt. The carriage doors were thrown open, a confused yelling and commotion reverberated around the covered terminus hall, and Holst leapt out, accompanied by a young travelling companion, a German doctor named Braun, with whom he had become acquainted on the journey from Munich.

They walked together, defending themselves manfully against the numerous porters who offered their services. The German was familiar with the situation; he strode determinedly in front of Holst, and they were soon standing outside the station building, where the lamps were burning in a strangely subdued way and it was much more peaceful.

Venice receives its guests differently from any other European city. Here there are no shouting coachmen, no rolling omnibuses, no electric trams that slide like moving lakes of light over a crowded square. Here there are no bright cafés, no illuminated shop windows, no undulating life, no puffs of air from the big city blowing gently at night with candles flickering from every nook and cranny.

It is so strangely still; not a single sound of a rolling carriage, no noise of wheezing machines, only the lapping of the water against the quayside and subdued oar strokes from the slender black gondolas, gliding out of the night bearing a yellowish flame, silent, with a flickering wake behind.

Holst and Braun sat themselves in a gondola and Braun gave the name of the hotel – the Bauer-Grünewald, the place which most Germans head for. The gondola glided silently from the quayside across the Grand Canal into a network of crooked canal streets, between white and yellow houses with closed shutters. The deepest stillness descended over their journey. The two travellers sat in silence, their eyes searching over the water towards the damp walls where the wake murmured. They slipped silently past the houses. Then the gondola turned sharply round a corner; the gondolier uttered a short, muffled, monosyllabic word and past them glided another gondola, the yellow lamp of which for a second threw its faint gleam over the water to light up the black bow of their boat, which with its broad, serrated nose pointed forward like the prow of a Viking ship. The gondola listed over slightly, then picked up speed once more down a new street, still and desolate like the first. The nocturnal journey took a powerful hold on Holst. He looked ahead – it was like an adventure in an unknown country, where the waves whispered the most mysterious fairy tales, telling of hundreds of years, of a city whose power was great, but whose streets were silent, whose strange legends grew forth not out of soil, not rooted in the solid land, but like creepers and strange species of seaweed from a deep where the water wiped out every track, and where everything was wrapped in the deepest cover of silence.

Then the gondola glided out into Grand Canal. It became livelier; boat after boat met them as they glided past the tall, dark palaces with their solid pales, embossed with shapes like dragons' heads which told of the greatness of their owners, and on the wide marble stairways of which Venice's great men had trod, where the destiny of kingdoms had been decided, where festoons of flowers had once waved in the sea breeze and flaming torches flickered in the night, when the young slept and the old had kept vigil and spun their schemes.

Here and there a window was open; figures dressed in light colours bent out over the marble balconies, and music rang from high-ceilinged halls, where lights flashed in cut-glass chandeliers and cast a shiny glitter over the canal. There came a sharp whistle as a wheezing steamer worked its way up the undulating street, lacerating the dreams of vanished times and striking the quiet water with its paddles, so that the gondola swayed from side to side as the frothing wake struck its bow.

They swung once more into the narrow canals; the same muted shout sounded, the same quiet meeting, the same dead houses and the same dull slap of the oar in the dark water. They journeyed softly, slipping through the night, gently lifting the veil over the sleeping city, then the gondola stopped with a jolt by narrow steps. A sharp voice ripped Holst and his companion out of their dreams.

'Zwei Zimmer – vierter Stock.'

Two rooms, fourth floor.

And they found themselves standing once again in the caravanserai, in the middle of one of the 20th century's great hotels, between suitcases, boxes, gas and telephones, while the smell of food rushed out to greet them, bells chimed and called, and apron-clad waiters ran up and down carpeted staircases.

The Hotel Bauer-Grünewald.

Holst was shown to a room on the fourth floor and settled back into the interrupted dream. He opened the window and looked over the canal: roof after roof with strange extensions, peculiar angular chimneys, quaintly protruding walls and cornices and, deep down, the water lapping.

On the canal, a boat with music was gliding by. A guitar, a violin and male voices sang unfamiliar, pulsating melodies that rose up to him in the still of the night – heavy, subdued, at times tremulous, at times full of fire and like tolling bells, messages from alien lands, singing about love, about sighing and sadness, while the oars splashed.

He looked up at the sky where the stars flickered so unendingly close, as if weighing down on him with the mute, insoluble riddle of existence – who are you? Who are you?

He felt so alien to himself, gripped by an indomitable horror, while the stars kept repeating – who are you? Who are you?...

He was alive – and yet he felt it wasn't actually him. He shuddered and took a step back into the longish rectangular room, where the ceiling was very low, and where there was a sigh in every nook, as if countless generations were whispering their most clandestine secrets to the silent walls.

He was in Venice, the silent city of dreams.

Holst went down and met his travelling companion in the

restaurant. The kitchen was French, neither worse nor better than at most European hotels. The elongated dining room was abuzz with guests speaking all the languages of the world, while the service personnel, aproned and hurried, crossed the floor with steaming dishes and wine in coiled carafes and long-necked German bottles. Dr Braun raised his glass.

'Welcome to Venice and many thanks for your company on the journey.'

Holst smiled. He had been lucky with his companion. Dr Braun was a young German scholar who was studying art and had travelled widely around the world. He had spent several years in Copenhagen as the guest of a major Danish manufacturer and patron of the arts, in whose large collection he had worked on the exhibiting and cataloguing of works of art bought abroad. He was a true Bavarian, with a South German's lively nature; full of jokes, but often strangely silent. Holst had quite won his heart on their journey, when their travelling companions had consisted of a couple of Middle German commercial travellers of the dreadful, international hawker type, whose banal chatter and racy stories had irritated Holst and the doctor equally. In Bozen they had properly found their feet with each other and spent the rest of the trip in lively conversation about things beautiful and grand and about the promised land – Venice. The meal was quickly over, and they walked together through the narrow, twisting streets to the place that attracts and calls, the place to which everyone hastens – the eternal, the incomparable, St Mark's Square.

They entered the square, which appeared white as if covered with snow in the sharp, clear moonlight, through an arch in the colonnade of the procurators. Only a single wanderer slipped effortlessly across it; it belonged to the night – not the heavy, sighing night that spread itself over the silent canals, but the moonlit night, where the stones were bathed in moonbeams, where dreams take off easily in the bright silence only to tremble in the shimmering white lustre with a yearning filled with presentiment.

Nothing burdens the mind when the moon shines over St Mark's Square. It isn't the depth of this wealth of beauty that forces one to bow one's head in humble wonder; neither is there a feeling of peace, a craving for rest – it is an enticement to imbibe beauty, like emptying a crystal glass of wine, yellowish and sweet. The arms of the procurators don't extend out wide like St Peter's columns in Rome; they aren't open so as to squeeze the observer in towards the great bosom of the mother church, but lightly stroking, as a confident love strokes the hair and neck, a love that knows that its call will be followed so willingly.

The Byzantine domes of St Mark's Basilica rise up behind the rearing horses and the slender pillars as if to offer a barrier to the eyes. The Campanile reaches up to the sky as if lifting its gaze towards wide expanses where nothing stands in its way, and the beautiful doorway that leads to the Doge's Palace is firmly closed like a mouth that, if it so wished, could open up and tell about the pain which lies behind all this silent desire that captures the eyes and the thoughts.

And the feet move willingly – to the Piazzetta, where the Moorish surfaces of the Doge's Palace offer themselves to the eye, unveiled like the sultana in the fairy tale for the one she has chosen in secret, and one's gaze slides over the Piazzetta's stones across the lagoon, the wide water, to where the island lies in the distance with the domes and spires of San Giorgio Maggiore and an inkling that the chalice of beauty is still not empty, that Venice still has rich treasures hidden away for those who are willing to tread the gently rocking pathway which mirrors the sky and its light, the path which is trodden as if in a dream, without the tramp of footsteps but with the murmuring of waves.

One doesn't speak when the moon is shining over the Piazzetta in Venice, but if the peals sound muted from the clock tower at the left wing of the procurators' building, mutedly tremulous in quick succession, they build a bridge for every impression of beauty, pulling the thoughts upwards, gathering them in a uniquely blissful feeling of seeing and enjoying.

And onward it goes along the quayside, across the canal where the Bridge of Sighs stands darkly against the Doge's Palace, where all of Venice's dark legends are given life in muted speech and strange stories of death and oblivion. The water slops against the quay, and out there, like a reminder of the present, the hull of a large steamer glides forward across the mirror, anchor chain clattering and windlasses whining, while steam is breathed out of its funnels in short, hoarse snorts. The wanderer turns instinctively towards land and his eyes meet the equestrian statue of the Piemontese soldier who put the crown of Italy on his head: Il Re Galantuomo Vittore Emanuele, whose rearing horse towers over the Riva degli Schiavoni like a brutal monument to a victory won by others and written in the destiny of the losers.

Again, the wanderer is drawn to the past, towards the Piazzetta and Doge's Palace, and from the arch of the procurators he casts his last look at the beautiful St Mark's Square, as it rests, bathed in moonlight, eternally one in its silent loveliness…

Holst slept only briefly on his first night in Venice.

II

TIME WAS SCARCE AND WORK WAS WAITING. Holst knew only that Sjöström had travelled to Venice and that a countryman had bumped into him there and had brought back the message which the equerry had disclosed. It didn't sound like his financial circumstances were in the best of health and he wasn't staying at one of the big hotels. The hotel the equerry had mentioned was a small unimpressive hotel by the Riva, where sailors in particular would stay. Holst enquired there the next day, but no one was familiar with any Lieutenant Sjöström; it was probable that he had lived there under an assumed name. It was natural to assume that, if he intended to stay in Venice, he had looked for private accommodation, but it was most probable that he would be found at the Lido, where the best opportunities presented themselves for an adventurer like Sjöström who was struggling to pay board and lodging. Holst wasn't in much doubt that Sjöström had put the stolen money

184

into play in Monte Carlo; his brother had already disclosed that he had been seen there in May, eagerly involved in the roulette.

Holst spent two days on the search without discovering any clues to his whereabouts. Then one evening as he was about to go to bed, he felt an icy chill, and when night came, it was as if poisonous mists came in through the window and lay over him. His temples were pounding, his blood pumped like fire through his veins, he completely lost consciousness and he slipped into feverish imaginings so violent that they flickered around him like flames, and all his thoughts whirled around like a maelstrom. Dr Braun, whose room was close by, came to him and fetched a doctor, who shook his head and diagnosed a malignant feverish cold, the type that so often grips foreigners who succumb to Venice's alluring beauty. Holst's condition was not without danger, especially in the first days, but gradually the mist lifted and his strong constitution prevailed. It took eight days for him to overcome his indisposition and he now decided to continue the search for Sjöström with full force. When he took a light lunch with Braun in the Bauer-Grünewald, he noticed that his young friend was somewhat depressed and seemed to be plagued by a number of specific, constantly recurring thoughts. Holst questioned his friend intensely, but to start with he didn't want to discuss it.

It was an embarrassing story, he said, but Holst persisted.

Eventually, the whole tale was revealed.

While Holst had been ill, Braun had been to St Mark's Square where he had met a very beautiful young French-speaking lady, with whom he had exchanged several looks of the type which initiate an acquaintanceship. The young lady was not completely unwelcoming, but on the other hand she behaved in a perfectly ladylike manner, and Braun had decided to fasten Germania's broad sword on his loins to take up the conquest. It was begun with small courtesies, brief opportune words when the lady had taken a seat at one of the numerous tables in the arcades, and led quite quickly to small excursions to the Gallerie dell'Accademia – even a trip by steamer to the Lido. Finally, Braun decided to risk a full-frontal attack and, during a promenade in the park, he confessed his love to the beauty with as much warmth as his Bavarian nature allowed. It appeared that victory would follow his assault. He obtained permission to follow the beautiful lady back to the Riva and from there in a gondola to an unknown destination along secretive waterways.

The gondola meandered through the strangest out-of-the-way corners, without Braun being able to recognise anything other than that he twice passed along the Grand Canal and finally after this strange detour found himself near the Arsenale. The trip ended and he followed his beautiful companion up a narrow staircase to a first-floor apartment in a well-maintained old house in the usual Venetian style with many small rooms, corridors and balconies.

It was very hot and the beautiful unknown lady swiftly put a soft drink in front of her conqueror, while he continued his attack, encouraged by the generous concessions he had extracted from his beautiful enemy. The temperature rose and the lady took compassion on the greatly overheated northerner, bringing him a very fine, light dressing gown, and discreetly retired while he put the tunic on and at the same time removed a not-so-small part of his civilised clothes.

Everything was set up for a moment of dalliance when suddenly Arcadia was ravaged by a storm with violent thunderclaps. There was a thundering at the door and a powerful male voice was heard in the hallway outside the dallying couple's sanctuary. The beautiful lady shot to her feet in horror.

'My husband has come home unexpectedly,' she exclaimed

Braun was gripped by a paralysing terror and, unfamiliar with the dangers of war, he allowed himself to be hurriedly pushed aside into a kitchen-like back room, while the angry man, like a troll who has got a whiff of human flesh, came storming into the apartment's rooms.

In the murky room, a new danger popped up in the shape of an old hag who adopted a very menacing attitude and demanded a significant sum to let the unfortunate wooer escape down the back stairs, with the threat of handing him over to the rightful owner's charge if he refused. Braun chose to buy his freedom. He had a hundred and fifty lire on him, which he offered, and after he had stripped off the silk tunic and quickly dressed on the stairs, he beat the retreat in an extremely cooled-down state of mind that wasn't warmed by the discovery that he had forgotten his very valuable gold watch and an especially valuable jewel ring, probably now being valued for profit in Arcadia. The war costs thus amounted to around one thousand lire in the country's money, in addition to the loss of honour – to put it briefly, total defeat.

No wonder the young German was depressed by this experience of battle. Holst laughed, but his police instincts led him quite quickly to lay plans for an attempt to make good the losses by a new, energetic attack on the beautiful lady with other more prosaic goals than before, and since it was not out of the question that the opportunity could present itself, he subjected his friend to an incisive interview in order to draw up a report for his own pleasure. They quickly agreed that there was nothing to be gained by involving the local police in the matter; it would only lead to the German being ridiculed in the local press and the beauty quickly being given no more than a warning.

The first step was to reconnoitre the terrain and they discovered that the route from the scene of the crime to the

Riva degli Schiavone had only been three or four small alleys away from the Via Vittorio Emanuele, which heads northwards from the Riva. It was not possible to determine the house, of course, and, moreover, not wise to walk around too much in that area, which would probably attract attention, but Holst found another far safer and more convenient way to the target by sea.

Braun had an innate ability to remember faces with great certainty; he was able to recognise any person he had noticed, even a total stranger, and with their confidence in this, the friends decided to pay attention to the gondoliers by the Riva, where Braun recalled that the beauty had repeatedly used the same gondola. It proved possible to find the man once again, but approaching him directly would be unwise, as he had probably been used frequently by the lady and would therefore naturally be reluctant to give information about her. Holst therefore chose to use his gondola frequently for a few days and pay him generously for quite short trips. The man wondered at first about this, but reconciled himself with the thought that it was probably a disturbed Englishman who had conceived a certain fondness for his gondola and his small talk and he thus decided to exploit him.

It didn't take long for Holst and the gondolier to become good friends, and Holst made good use of the scraps he recalled from his studies of Lombroso. To begin with, their conversation was about a tall, blonde northerner who was supposed to be staying in Venice, and whom Holst was eagerly looking for, without any significant information coming out of it. Then Holst cautiously asked the gondolier about the beautiful lady, and he immediately saw from the man's crafty smile that he knew who Holst was talking about. However, he was reluctant to reveal what he knew, and only after Holst, who in order not to cause any suspicion, had left Braun back on the Riva during these trips, had assured him of his burning love for the lady, did the gondolier agree, in return for a substantial tip, to show Holst the house, which lay by a small canal not far from the Arsenale, and also deliver a note to the lady about an assignation on St Mark's Square at a specific time.

Holst stepped out of the gondola a few houses away from the designated place and walked up the staircase to the alley behind in order to closely inspect the lie of the house. He was now quite sure in this regard and it was now just a matter of the assignation taking place without the lady suspecting anything.

III

HOLST MET THE BEAUTIFUL UNKNOWN woman in the procurators' building opposite the Campanile. She was very beautiful, small and nimble, dressed in a tight-fitting travel suit, decent and modest to look at, with a pair of wonderful, beautiful, brown eyes and a mournful smile. When Holst approached her with a greeting and the few words he had provided as a kind of password, she looked up at him and a slight blush passed over her cheeks. It struck Holst that the last thing she resembled was a brazen adventuress, with her slightly tired face and her melancholy gaze; she awoke some compassion within him and he looked kindly at her. Her gaze rested on him as if trying to gauge him; it was apparent that she found the handsome young man attractive, almost as if her role fell more naturally to her, and it didn't take long before they were conversing freely. Holst found he could express himself easily enough, although it was a little tricky for him with the French, and the couple

190

walked together over the Piazza towards the Riva in cheerful conversation like old acquaintances.

Holst told her that he had seen her several times and felt drawn to her beauty and grace, that he had used all the tricks imaginable to find out her address, that he had acquired it through her gondolier and that he was happy for the trust she was showing him. He also said that he was a Danish officer spending his leave in Venice, studying the beautiful heritage, especially the art, and ended by paying a nice little compliment to his companion.

She called herself Jeannette Gorin; she was from Lyon, she said, and her parents were merchants whose business had fallen on hard times. She had left her home with an artist who was now living in Venice, but she felt very unhappy in this alien country. She had only dared to meet Holst because he had written so warmly and beautifully to her; she trusted his chivalry and hoped he wouldn't misunderstand why she had come.

It was apparent that there wasn't a word of truth in any of it. Her attitude would probably adjust itself according to Holst's tactics; she belonged to those women who, having gone down an insecure path, follow the flow. Confronted by a cynic, she would have stripped off her melancholy and been a fluttering butterfly; in front of a ponderous idealist like Braun, she had been a kind of Gretchen, a *noli me tangere*; and towards Holst it appeared she would go in for the same style.

Holst was curious. For him, it was a matter of bringing this adventure to an end and it was possible that a swift move from his side could speed up events. But coarseness was against his nature. He gently felt his way forward and it really did appear that he had made a certain impression on the young lady. He decided to pursue this line and smiled quietly to himself at the warmth and infatuation he displayed. He was the cold northerner melting under the looks from this southern beauty like the snow on the mountains melts under the rays of the sun, and when they were sitting in a separate cabinet in one of the Riva's restaurants after an hour's stroll, the thread between them was tied tighter, little by little. Jeannette was moved to talk about her childhood home and about her good father and mother; Holst played on the same strings.

'Have you been in love before?' asked Jeannette, giving him a semi-veiled look.

Holst looked up in a free and easy way.

'Never.'

She believed him and pressed his hand warmly.

'Yes, you probably won't believe me,' he continued, 'but it's true. I've never been in love before, even though I've met a lot of women. But we northerners are as harsh and tough as the climate in our country, where the ice covers the fjords, where the bear builds his winter lair in the great pine forests, and where the wolves howl on the steppes in the winter.'

She looked acutely at him.

'Didn't you say you're from Denmark?'

'Yes, from Denmark high up in the north, where the women are blonde and cold, like the snow covering the plains and high...'

He changed it to mountains because he thought it rang truer.

Jeannette smiled – then she gave him a kind of quizzical look.

'Why do you talk to me of bears and wolves and mountains? I know very well that Denmark is an extensively agricultural country where there are neither wolves nor bears, where the mountains aren't much higher than the houses in this town, and where the women are neither blonder nor colder to any great degree than the women here. Yes, in fact I know more than that. I know that Copenhagen is a city that looks like all other mainland cities, where the women are just as sly, the men are just as stupid as everywhere else in the world, and where the watchword is: A toast to you, a toast to me and a toast to all the beautiful girls.'

Holst blushed.

Jeannette continued in excellent Swedish.

'For that matter, I would say that if the lieutenant's feelings for me are as honest and genuine as the lieutenant's nonsense about his country of birth, well, thank you very much, but why don't we just be honest with each other. What do you want of me?'

Holst pulled himself together and took her hand.

'Miss Gorin,' he said in Danish, 'you are mistaken – what I said was calculated for a daughter of the south, but my feelings are the same. Your beauty has really captured me – totally – and my intentions are just to be where you are, to see you, talk to you, so I'm twice as happy now that I know you understand the language that I speak honestly like my native language. But you have lied to me. You aren't Jeannette Gorin and you aren't from Lyon, You're Swedish. I've told you my name – Eigil Holst, Lieutenant from Copenhagen. You have nothing to fear by telling me yours.'

Jeannette looked sharply at him for a moment, her gaze gradually becoming milder; it was as if she was struggling with herself.

'What's the point? You can't help me, can you?' she replied tiredly in a subdued voice.

Holst took her hand once more.

'Dearest Jeanette, you say I can't help you. How do you know that? Are you alone in a foreign country, far away from friends and relatives? Are you unhappy, maybe in the grips of a scoundrel?'

Jeannette gave a start.

'What do you mean?' she asked sharply.

Holst collected himself.

'You said yourself that you were married to an artist, didn't you? Are you unhappy? I adore you and I'll help you if you will trust me.'

He had got to his feet and bent over her; he wrapped his arms around her neck and kissed her eyes.

She was startled and looked up at him.

'No, I don't want to believe you. You're just like all the others – you're all the same – all of you.'

Holst felt that it was now or never. Maybe he could succeed with his onslaught, but if he didn't, she would probably slide out of his hands. She would hardly go as far with him as with Braun. But if he let on that he knew about her relationship, there was a danger that she would withdraw completely. It was a rather unusual situation, but the foray had to be carried through. Holst took both her hands in his and looked her in the eye with a firm, warm look.

'Dear Jeannette,' he said, 'I call you Jeannette, because that's what you call yourself. I don't know who you are, but I know how you live. I know the man who controls your destiny, who forces you to do the most degrading thing of all – to lie and deceive for his benefit, to mock that which is most beautiful and noble on Earth, to mock love itself, and to feign love for him and for others; all this to be repaid with evil words and scorn. I don't know you, Jeannette, but I know him, and if you wish it, I will save you from the hideous circumstances in which you live and deliver you from him and help you escape his clutches.'

Holst was still bent over her and had locked her in his arms.

The young girl looked up at him, frightened through her tears.

'Do you know Hugold?' she whispered, hardly audibly.

The name shot through Holst like a flame from head to toe. Like a steel spring snapping, he stood up straight, and with his blood pounding in his temples, he almost whispered the words between clenched teeth – Hugold and the girl's name, Gorin! The name from Elsinore. Now or never – if he was mistaken, the whole mission would be doomed. What did it matter to him who this woman was? But if it was how he sensed it could be, how it had to be, his luck had followed him, and he was now on the point of reaching his goal.

It only lasted a second, then he spoke.

'Yes, I know Hugold Sjöström, and no man in the world knows him better than I.'

His eyes rested upon her so searchingly and sharply that they were almost boring into her. She went deadly pale, threw her arms around his neck and burst into a sobbing that made her limbs tremble.

Holst became ice cold; it was like a fever pushing all the blood away from his head – he had to grasp the edge of the table to remain standing.

It was over in a flash.

He lifted the sobbing woman, laid her head against his shoulder and gently stroked her hair away from her forehead. It was as though Annie had instantaneously become alive, as if this sobbing girl was the Annie whose fate had filled his life for months, and without wanting it, without knowing how he formed the words, a phrase came whispering gently from his lips.

'Little Annie mustn't cry – little Annie mustn't cry.'

The name reached the girl's ears – she straightened up and looked at him with eyes that contained such astonishment that he immediately felt what was important and gathered himself to resist anything that could interfere with him and his duties.

The road had now opened up for him.

'Annie?' whispered the girl, 'Why do you say Annie – did you know Annie – which Annie?'

Holst bent his head towards her and kissed her forehead, but at that moment she wrapped her arms around his neck and pressed her lips against him in a kiss so hot that it scorched.

'Save me,' she whispered, 'if you love me, as you say, save me if you can.'

Running through Holst's head was the realisation that there was only one road – this girl can bring him into my hands, he has mistreated her, demeaned her. She has loved him, maybe still loves him. But there is only one road – only the one – I have to take action.

And Holst took action. He didn't talk to her about Sjöström and Annie or ask what her name was or who she was. He took her in his arms and whispered the most tender, warmest words in her ear, found the way to open her mouth and immediately closed it with his kisses. It was like an intoxication, but he didn't for a second lose sight of his goal while the soft Swedish language rang in his ears.

For the first time in his long service, Eigil Holst had broken out of the path he had faithfully followed. He was 26 years old, alone in a foreign country and stood on the road leading to his goal.

IV

HOLST AND JEANNETTE MET FOR LUNCH in the same restaurant where they had spent the evening before and plans for the breakaway were begun in earnest. Jeannette's ingenuity when it came to fooling men was almost unlimited.

It was certainly not going to be easy, but she was patient enough to move forward gradually, and Holst reinforced her in that, because for him it was precisely a matter of winning time. He first wanted to win Jeannette's wholehearted confidence and it made it so much easier that the young woman was clearly very much in love with him; he could thus be reassured that his role wasn't difficult at all, at least for the moment. He should just not estrange her, so that at a certain point, everything would work steadily and smoothly. Time would bring the rest.

Jeannette told him about herself. She was twenty years old, she said, which meant a little more, of course, although it wasn't far off. Her father had been a sergeant in a Scanian dragoon regiment, but later served as a stable keeper for a major Scanian landowner, a count from an old line. When the latter had moved to live in Paris, Ljunggren, as her father was called, went there with him and had spent eight years in France with his wife and children. It was then that Jeannette had learnt French, and she spoke it well enough. By the age of sixteen, she had become the young count's lover and when her father died and her mother returned to Sweden, her home was broken up and Jeannette came out into the world.

What else she said about her fate was hardly completely true and not of great interest either. She had met Sjöström in Paris; he was living there with Annie, whom he called his wife. But she was silent about these two. Holst would have liked to ask, but he had to tread carefully and at no point did he let on that he was interested in the couple.

During lunch, Jeannette reminded him that he had called her Annie the previous evening and asked him what he had meant.

Holst dodged the question.

Jeannette looked up at him and asked, 'So, what do you actually want with me?'

'To help you,' said Holst, 'if you are as unhappy as you said yesterday.'

Jeannette sighed.

'There isn't much for me to do here. I've had such a turbulent time the last few years that I can't imagine ever finding peace and quiet. But we don't want to think about that. We should just love each other, because you will love me, won't you?'

Holst would certainly do that – but practically speaking, it wasn't at all easy to arrange. Jeannette was probably quite pampered and Holst didn't have abundant funds. On the other hand, he was embarrassed to talk about that and he didn't really know how to handle the matter. He didn't want to tell her about

Braun. It went against the grain for him to hurt her; she was so pretty and chirping like a little bird in the sunshine. Besides, Sjöström was responsible for the situation and Holst had to be very careful with regard to everything concerning him.

'Tell me,' he said, 'do you want to go back to him, the one we talked about?'

'Are you bored with me already?' she asked with a quick look at him.

'Of course not, but we can't stay here – and aren't you living with him?'

Jeannette blushed.

'Yes, but if you want, I'll gladly leave him. I hate him – hate him,' she said, clenching her fists.

'Have you always hated him?' Holst asked her and gave her a serious look.

'I've never loved him, never. It was Annie I loved, but he was nasty to Annie, and I…I didn't have a thing in the world, so when Annie left, I had to go with him. That's what he wanted.'

'When was that?' Holst asked.

'Now, this winter,' she replied, 'I went with them to Copenhagen. Annie was good friends with a very rich young man who made a great fuss of her. Annie didn't care for him, but she wanted to marry him.'

She stopped herself.

'But here I am, talking about Annie – you don't know her at all.'

'Erm, yes,' said Holst, 'a little – Annie Cederlund – right?'

'Yes – so you know her – wasn't she lovely? And she was so good to me from the first day we met. God knows where she is now! I left them in Elsinore. Sjöström went off with her, but came back to Copenhagen alone. She's probably got married to her friend, but she's never written to me – and I don't think that's very nice of her, because she promised she would. She said she would think of me. I was waiting for a letter, and then Sjöström wanted us to travel to Nice. He lost a lot of money there gambling, money he'd got from Annie, and then he brought me to Venice, to this terrible life.'

'What terrible life?' asked Holst.

Jeannette got up and went over to him and put her arm around his neck.

'Won't you take me with you – please? I'm so terribly unhappy.'

She burst into tears.

Holst patted her cheek.

'Tell me everything – you can trust me with everything,' he said kindly.

'Not now – not now – but later,' she whispered. 'You'll get to know everything if you're good to me. You will be, Eigil, won't you? You're so good and honest. And I'm so terribly unhappy.'

'Do you want to leave him?' Holst asked.

Jeannette nodded.

'Right away, if I only could, but he'll do me harm.'

Holst smiled.

'You can trust me, Jeannette.'

Jeannette looked up in fright.

'No, you mustn't, you don't know how evil he can be – you mustn't go to him.'

Holst smiled.

'Don't be afraid. I have a message to him from his brother, who is a good, honourable man. The most sensible thing to do is for me to go to him quite calmly and deliver the message. Then when I've first talked to him, you'll see there could be something or other that I could tell him that would make a certain impression on him.'

Jeannette looked puzzled.

'Do you know him then?'

'Not personally, but I know a little about him. It will probably be best to take it quite calmly. Now we must part. I have some business to take care of.'

Jeannette grabbed his hand.

'But you won't leave me, will you? Eigil, you mustn't leave me. You're the only one who can rescue me. Listen to me – you must stay with me.'

She pressed herself against him and put her arm around his neck, while her eyes went misty with tears. Her plea cut Holst to the heart and he had to gently free himself. They were standing by the window on the first floor and life was beginning to get moving on the Riva – it was now late morning.

Suddenly Jeannette grabbed his arm with a faint cry and pointed down at the street.

'Look,' she said, 'Look, Annie's friend is walking down there – the three gentlemen there, he's the young one on the left. So Annie must be here too.'

Holst bent forward and looked in the direction in which she was pointing. In the middle of the street were three gentlemen in conversation. A slight shudder went through him and he stepped back instinctively. The three gentlemen were Captain Ankerkrone, Kurk and young Lieutenant Claes Ankerkrone. A few steps behind them walked the Danish district magistrate and by his side was Ulla, accompanied by a small lady with a slightly twisted back – Claes's wife, Holst guessed, for he hadn't seen her before. Blood rushed to Holst's head. So they were all in Venice. He clenched his teeth. Now he had to keep on his toes.

Jeannette noticed his step back.

'Do you know them?' she asked.

Holst nodded.

'Yes, I know them.'

Jeannette looked sharply at him.

'Who?'

'All of them,' said Holst, 'but I'll tell you more about this later. I have to go now. And you, Jeannette, must go home to where you live. I'm going to visit Sjöström today, but you mustn't tell him I'm coming.'

Jeannette went silent – doubt was eroding her trust of Holst; his manner had changed so much.

'Tell me where you live.'

Holst named his hotel.

'Alone?' Jeannette asked.

'I'm staying there with a young German called Dr Braun, a very nice young man I met on the trip down.'

Jeannette went crimson. Holst pretended as if nothing had happened but watched her intently. Jeannette was silent. They agreed to meet in her home that same afternoon and she left the hotel first. She was a little nervous, but Holst promised to keep his word and she said a very warm goodbye to him.

Holst smiled when the waiter presented him with the bill with many bows to 'His Excellency'. They were undoubtedly two of the most unusual bills he had ever put on his expenses during his activities as a policeman, but it was also probably the most remarkable experience he had ever had.

It was completely certain that if he had withdrawn discreetly that evening, his new friend would have been in her complete, unassailable right if she doubted his love. He knew who she was, a young girl who could count her lovers in the dozens; his power over her existed only in the love he had feigned for her at their meeting and later, when he had learnt her fate. If he stepped back now, she would instantly see through him, her wounded vanity would be woken, she would become his enemy, and the quarry he was pursuing would slip through his fingers.

He hadn't told her anything about Annie, but her name had been mentioned between them. Jeannette – she persisted in calling herself Jeannette, although she had been baptised Johanna – would hurry to her lover and warn him of the danger. One word from her about Annie would be enough. Holst still had no idea where Sjöström was to be found.

He had to admit to himself that what he had done was the only right thing – from a tactical standpoint.

But if he should be ashamed of himself or not – well, that was another matter. He had to honestly admit that he felt no shame – just a certain nervousness, although he fully realised that, in relation to such an experienced woman as Jeannette, his role wouldn't be as difficult as if he had been facing a more untainted woman.

He hurried back to the Hotel Bauer-Grünewald and met Dr Braun, who was very much in suspense about the outcome of the expedition.

Holst shrugged.

'Failed,' he said, 'the donna didn't turn up and I spent the evening with some countrymen I met yesterday in the Accademia.'

Braun was sceptical – but Holst gave him no further answer; he was too busy. It was necessary to make the necessary arrangements with regard to Sjöström.

V

Holst was happy to visit the Accademia; he was extremely interested in painting and was delighted with the rare collection of North Italian masterpieces, Titian, Paolo Veronese, Tintoretto etc., in connection with a large collection of genuine old pieces by Dutch painters who had come to study Italy's masters but left a series of motifs from their homeland. It was doubtful whether the future would give him an opportunity to see such things again, so he made good use of his time. When he had approached the central police station, the most senior officer was not in his office. He therefore decided to spend the waiting time on a visit to the Accademia. He might also have had an ulterior motive.

Unstoppable, like a surging current, the faces of strangers glided past him, faces he had seen at the hotel, in the square, on the Riva and on the excursions to the Lido, but constantly changing; there was only one of his countrymen, whom he knew from Copenhagen but whom he wasn't anxious to bump into – that was how comfortable he was here, far from everything familiar and customary. As he stood in front of Titian's famous Presentation of Maria at the Temple, and was delighting in the glorious detail at the foot of the staircase, he suddenly heard a strong voice in broad Danish.

'My goodness, here we have the famous Maria of Titian – so that's how she looks.'

Holst turned quickly and stood face to face with the district magistrate from North Zealand. There was no one else in the gallery other than the two of them and a young lady who had just turned her back and was looking at a small painting hanging on the opposite wall.

The magistrate cast a quick glance at Holst, and then continued in his usual tone without transition.

'...and also, my goodness, here is Lieutenant Holst of the capital's night-watchmen – so that's how he looks when abroad.'

The young lady turned quickly – it was Ulla Ankerkrone.

She blushed, and not at all just slightly, and Holst felt the blood shooting up to his cheeks too without him being able to stop it. It only lasted a few seconds. The young people exchanged friendly greetings and the conversation continued in a most conventional manner. The magistrate was an excellent travelling companion who had stripped away all of his rather odd bachelor manner. He told Holst about the sudden decision to travel and about the stay in the Tyrol and the pleasure he was finding in the journey and the excellent company.

He was particularly fond of Miss Ulla, who paid him such a wealth of attention in small ways, the sort that an old bachelor receives with a smile and gentle mockery, but not without great inner delight when it comes from a beautiful, young girl. Ulla had set herself to show the 'district chieftain' the world at its most beautiful and the district chieftain looked at the world and at Ulla and found them both beautiful.

His joy at bumping into Holst was sincere. Ulla's joy was less sincere, inasmuch as she sometimes tried to hide it without really succeeding. On the other hand, she was enormously pleased on her 'Pappa's' behalf, and she expressed this joy just as strongly as she felt obliged to withhold her own.

She was a lovely girl, Holst thought, and she had become even more beautiful since he last saw her. He felt something like a stab in the heart at the thought of yesterday's adventure – it preyed on his mind.

Captain Ankerkrone was staying at the Hotel Victoria on the Riva. He hadn't come out as he was not very well and an old friend of his accompanying him on the journey was keeping him company. They had all just arrived.

'Now the young lady is walking around with a poor old man like me, on steamers and gondolas, like a piece of luggage,' as the magistrate put it with a smile.

They didn't discuss the important business at all. The district magistrate was on leave and he was just as conscientious about his leave as about his duties.

Holst joined up with the magistrate and Ulla and they gave the Accademia a thorough viewing. Holst of course knew his way around and the young lady's eyes rested on him in wonder when he gave his account of the various artists and works of art. The magistrate invited him to dinner, but Holst had to apologise for not being able to accept the invitation. At the thought of the meeting he had agreed with Jeannette, he blushed slightly; it made it really difficult for him to proceed with his project now that he knew that a certain young lady whom he greatly appreciated was in the city and he could have spent the day in her company.

206

They walked together to the Riva. Holst took his leave of Ulla at the hotel, promising to visit the Ankerkrones; however, he asked the magistrate to grant him a brief conversation about important matters. The magistrate did so – but unwillingly.

Ulla was happy at meeting Holst; she spent more time thinking about him than she let on, and she felt quite bored in the company of the older men. The magistrate was a charming enough man and Captain Kurk – Uncle Holger – was an excellent uncle, but… In short, it was extremely pleasant that Holst was in Venice. She had no idea what he was doing there, but then she didn't think about it either.

The magistrate and Holst went into the hotel's reading room. Holst decided to tell the magistrate as much as he considered right and proper. He held back a lot about his venture, but disclosed that in the next few hours he would stand face to face with the murderer, and that the case would take a new direction that might necessitate the magistrate's return home. The magistrate could hardly believe his ears; he leapt to his feet and put his hands on Holst's shoulders.

'Is that true, my boy? It's like an adventure story.'

Holst bowed his head.

'Yes, it is an adventure and yet a quite natural one. The fellow is a scoundrel of the highest order – a gambler and waster who makes a living here in the vilest way. The money that his crime has brought him has been gambled away; he owns nothing any more, but he is probably a desperate type, so I won't be at peace until I've arrested him.'

'Have you secured the assistance of the local police?' asked the magistrate.

'No, not yet,' said Holst. 'As you are aware, I have relied entirely on my own resources in this case.'

'Yes, but now you're close to your goal. You really must be

careful. It's important to take action – after all, we have the arrest warrant. If I was in your place, I would take the man into custody as soon as possible. Yes, I know – I'm just an old man on holiday. But that's my advice. Get the man locked up first – we can discuss the rest later.'

Holst was silent for a couple of seconds. He wasn't quite sure whether he should tell the magistrate about the connection between the murdered woman and the Ankerkrone family. Perhaps it would be the right thing to do, but on the other hand he was unwilling to alert the old magistrate to the details of the case before it was absolutely necessary. He decided to hold his tongue.

'Sir, I think it will be best to tread very carefully,' he replied in a lighter tone. 'We're dealing here with an adventurer who can easily cause us a lot of bother and I think the safest step would be to arrest him for falsification and let the murder case wait. I'm afraid that if we play our trump cards right away, it will be harder to get a conviction and the attendant circumstances are still not at all clear. It may even turn out that he isn't the murderer.'

'Who should it then be?' asked the magistrate, a little puzzled.

'I think it's him, of course, but the falsification charge is obvious. It can hardly be denied, and if you have no objections, I would like to completely ignore the murder at this stage, also because of the newspapers. I've got this all arranged with the authorities back home, but I won't, of course, take any action without your approval. It shall be you who leads the investigation.'

'You're a kind young man, Holst, and I'll never forget you for this. I never expected that I would be managing my post in an important case – in a murder case, even – on the Riva degli Schiavoni in Venice. But no matter – do as you think best, but be careful and don't let yourself be outfoxed. Will you join us for lunch?'

Holst apologised and shortly afterwards took his leave, after changing his mind and promising to come to dinner at six o'clock in the hotel. He took care of the necessary matters in the Municipality and was given a couple of detectives for assistance that would be at the specified place at the agreed time. The arrest warrant was for falsification and fraud – he hadn't mentioned the murder.

VI

AT THREE O'CLOCK ON THE DOT, a gondola delivered Holst to the house where Sjöström lived. He was perfectly calm, though he had deemed it necessary to arm himself with a light pocket revolver, which he had never used before on duty, but which he knew how to use with great certainty, excellent shot that he was. He sent the gondolier away and went quickly up the stairs to the first floor where Jeannette had told him that the apartment was located. On the door was a nameplate: Montuori, Agenzia. He rang the bell and a wrinkled old woman appeared. She opened cautiously and asked for his name and business. Holst spoke poor Italian, but he could make himself understood and asked if he might speak with the Swedish gentleman. The old woman pretended not to understand, so he handed her the card on which the equerry had written a greeting. She closed the door and went away.

While Holst was waiting, he heard steps on the stairs

followed by a faint whistle, the signal that his Italian colleagues were in position. The agreement was that Holst should fire a shot at a window in the apartment if there was any need for help, but he wanted the whole operation to be peaceful so that as little attention as possible would be aroused. The old woman returned and invited him in. He followed her briskly through a narrow, dark entrance to a room facing the canal.

It was shoddily furnished, more like a kind of office; there were a couple of desks that gave the impression of a legal office or the like.

The room was quite bright and spacious. Holst heard voices in the neighbouring room. They were speaking Swedish; two male voices, one strong and rough, the other lighter. A lady's voice sounded like Jeannette's. So Sjöström wasn't alone.

The door opened and Sjöström entered.

Holst bowed and cast a quick glance at his opponent. Sjöström was about six foot tall and very strongly built. His face was reddish, his beard strong and blond; he looked like a soldier, except for his eyes being puffy and red, his hair thin at the temples and his face furrowed with many wrinkles. He had been a magnificent soldier, that was obvious, but there was an uneasiness in his eyes and a pervasive nervousness about his bearing that marked him out as an adventurer, an insecure man.

He bowed a little stiffly to Holst and asked him to sit down.

Holst took a chair and made himself comfortable as he put his hat on a table.

'To what do I owe the honour of your visit, Lieutenant?' asked Sjöström with a slight bow.

'Your brother, the equerry, Bror Sjöström, as you will see from the card I gave your servant, has asked me to visit you to bring you his regards,' Holst said in a friendly tone. 'I have

211

the honour of knowing your brother rather well and I couldn't neglect the fulfilment of his wish.'

'Oh, really...' replied Sjöström.

Holst shuffled comfortably in his chair, like someone who had plenty of time.

'Your brother was very concerned because he hadn't heard anything from you, apart from occasional messages from countrymen who had met you in Nice. He was frankly afraid that something unpleasant may have happened to you. As you know, rumours spread very fast. So I promised to look you up and find out at first hand.'

'Oh, really...'

Sjöström didn't seem very communicative. It was apparent that his thoughts were in the other room, where the conversation appeared to have stopped. Holst didn't get put off by Sjöström's attitude, but continued in the same friendly tone.

'In particular, it caused your brother some concern that you didn't visit him in March this year when you were in Helsingborg.'

'How do you know I was in Helsingborg?' Sjöström blurted out.

'Oh, Sweden isn't that big a place – Scania, I mean. Then there is a certain Mr Karlkvist from Kristianstad, who, to put it bluntly, has been bothering your brother a great deal.'

'Karlkvist...'

Sjöström's eyes blinked then he directed them sharply at Holst.

'I beg you to speak more clearly, Lieutenant. What do you want of me?'

'But I have told you my errand,' said Holst in the same mild tone. 'Your brother has instructed me to seek you out. He imagined you were in some difficulty and that you might be in need of some money – yes, I'm sorry to speak so indiscreetly, but your brother is my friend. So to put it plainly: if you would be so kind as to come with me to the Austrian Bank, I will be able to pay you an amount according to your brother's wishes.'

'I don't need any money,' said Sjöström curtly, before seeming to think better of it. 'Besides, I don't need to come with you. A cheque would do just as well.'

Holst smiled amiably.

'In order to insure himself against all eventualities, your brother wanted the money paid out in my presence.' He looked very sharply at Sjöström. 'Because of all eventualities.'

Sjöström became uneasy. He made his choice and got up quickly.

'You must excuse me, Lieutenant, but I have guests. I don't know you but I thank you for the greetings from my brother. I don't need any money – not at all. Yes, I don't wish to be rude to a stranger – a friend of my brother, no less – but, as I said, I don't have a lot of time. Perhaps I could visit you where you're staying. At present, it's impossible for me to talk to you any further.'

Holst remained quietly seated.

Sjöström stood in front of him, looking at him with suppressed ill-temper. His gaze wandered uneasily and he glanced now and then at the door.

'Well now, so Mr Sjöström doesn't need any money,' continued Holst in a slightly teasing tone; he had made his decision when he failed to lure Sjöström out of the house. The friend in there was apparently a golden goose who promised Sjöström some good profits. There was therefore nothing else to do than get on with arresting him. But on the other hand, Holst was reluctant to raise the alarm while a stranger was in the house. He had to take action and make sure everything happened peacefully.

'Mr Sjöström's lack of need surprises me,' he continued. 'I was under the impression that the ninety thousand kroner Mr Sjöström picked up in Helsingborg in March found a big hole in his pocket in Nice.'

Sjöström went pale and gripped the back of the chair.

'But perhaps the money is still in your possession?' continued Holst.

'Who are you?' asked Sjöström. 'How dare you force your way into my house and poke your nose into my business? Will you leave, please?'

'No, I will not,' said Holst, 'that is, not unless you will come with me, Mr Sjöström.'

'With you…?'

'Yes, with me. I have an errand in addition to the greeting you didn't seem to appreciate and the offer you didn't want to accept. It's in connection with your settlement with Mr Karlkvist and Enskilda Banken in Scania. It appears that you have drawn too much, Mr Sjöström. At least, that's the bank's opinion and it has delegated me to settle this balance with you.'

Sjöström had gone pale, but he mastered his emotions perfectly.

'Lieutenant, I don't understand you and I am terminating this conversation. You may go.'

He drew back to the door. Holst stood up calmly and fixed him with a firm look.

'My apologies, Mr Sjöström, at having to be so disagreeable towards you, but it is my duty to inform you that at the moment you take one step closer to that door, a shot will sound that will in consequence bring a little commotion into the building that can be avoided if you will come with me willingly.'

Sjöström stood for a moment like a tiger about to leap, before collecting himself and running at Holst with lightning

214

speed, but Holst had been carefully watching every one of his movements and he quickly grabbed his chair, flung it at him, stopping him in mid-leap and causing him to fall on the floor with a mighty crash a few steps from Holst.

The door of the neighbouring room opened and Jeannette appeared in the doorway – white as a sheet. Behind her a young man stepped forward and rushed at Holst to assist the master of the house. Jeannette tried to hold him back. Sjöström was rolling around trying to get free of the chair. Holst stood calmly in front of the door to the entrance hall, the revolver gleaming in his hand. When he caught sight of the young man, he looked down instinctively. It was Claes Ankerkrone.

The young Swede remained where he was in deep surprise.

'The detective – Papa's detective – what the devil are you up to with Hugold Sjöström?'

Jeannette's gaze rested on Holst. At the word 'detective', she gave a start and stood stock still. Sjöström had got to his feet; he was bending over, supported by the chair, the seat of which had broken off.

'Mr Sjöström,' said Holst, recovering himself, 'I would have preferred to avoid any scene in the presence of this lady and the young gentleman. It is your fault that it hasn't been avoided. Mr Ankerkrone knows me and my position. I have been ordered to arrest you and I therefore declare you arrested. You will kindly come with me.'

Sjöström raised the chair as a weapon, but Claes Ankerkrone intervened.

'No stupidity, Hugold – allow me, I know the gentleman.'

Sjöström lowered the chair. Claes turned to Holst.

'Lieutenant Sjöström is my friend,' he began in a cold, slightly supercilious tone. 'Perhaps I might ask what right a Danish detective has to arrest a Swedish subject on international soil?'

'Mr Ankerkrone,' Holst answered calmly. 'It would be best for you to keep out of this case for the time being. I am acting on my responsibility and under orders.'

'It's an injustice and we won't stand for it,' Ankerkrone exclaimed vehemently. 'I'm speaking for Hugold.'

Holst smiled.

'This could become harder than you think, Lieutenant.'

'A man is at least entitled to know why he is being arrested.'

'Falsification and fraud is all I am allowed to say.'

'For how much?' asked Ankerkrone.

'A trifle,' said Holst with a smile, 'just a few thousand kroner.'

'I'll raise it,' Claes cut in.

'Eighty-nine thousand kroner – it's quite a lot of money.'

'Means nothing – give me time and I'll settle the matter. It can be done with less, I suppose?'

Sjöström stood motionless. He felt that Holst's eyes were fixed on him.

'Will the lady be so kind as to open up?' Holst said with a firm look at Jeannette. 'There are two gentlemen outside the door who want to come in.'

Jeannette hesitated.

'Everything will depend on whether or not the lady will – if she won't, she will have to take the consequences.'

Jeannette looked closely at Holst with an enquiring look in her eyes – he bowed his head and she was out of the door like lightning.

Before Sjöström had pulled himself together, the door to the hall was flung open and the two Italian police officers stepped into the living room. Ankerkrone protested, but Holst intervened and put his hand on his arm.

'Out of regard for your father, you should think seriously about what you're doing, Lieutenant Ankerkrone,' he said.

Sjöström tried to free himself from the two Italians standing by his side, but a brief steely click betrayed that the handcuffs had been fastened around his wrists. The veins in his forehead swelled and he made a cramped move to free himself, but sank exhausted on a chair. Ankerkrone stood silently, his cheeks coloured with indignation.

'This is a dirty trick,' he said in Swedish. 'I'm going to the consulate.'

Holst turned calmly to him.

'If you'll take my advice, Lieutenant, you'll go to your father first; I give you my word of honour that this business is more serious than you might think.' He leant towards him and whispered, 'Annie...'

Claes Ankerkrone went pale.

Sjöström stood up and addressed his friend in a subdued tone. 'Do what you can for me, Claes, and for her over there.'

One of the officers threw a cloak around him and led him away. Ankerkrone was left standing undecided on the threshold of the living room. Jeannette was leaning against a desk, her face frozen, and the old woman appeared in the door with great consternation.

Holst turned to Ankerkrone.

'The lieutenant can calmly leave me to take care of everything. You should go. I'll make the necessary explanations later.'

Ankerkrone lifted his head defiantly.

'I promised Sjöström that I would look after the young lady.'

'That's not necessary, Lieutenant. I'll take that responsibility – isn't that so, Madame?'

Jeannette bowed her head weakly. Ankerkrone wanted to protest, but Holst turned to face him.

'What has taken place here will show you that I have the authority,' he said firmly. 'I intend to use it and beg you for the last time, seriously: Go!'

The lieutenant took a step back; on a sign from Jeannette, the old woman brought his hat and stick and, with a slight bow to Jeannette, he left the room, giving Holst an almost imperceptible nod. When the door closed behind him, Holst turned smiling to Jeannette.

'Well now, my little friend, now you can see who was the strongest.'

With a leap, Jeannette threw herself into his arms, while the old woman stood in the doorway, gazing at them open-mouthed. Holst gave Jeanette a light kiss on her forehead.

'You won't be seeing him again soon, Jeannette. Let us two now consider what is wisest for us and, first of all, put this elderly lady in the picture. I need to take a little break after all this excitement.'

VII

THE RESPECTABLE OLD SIGNORA MONTUORI was born in Vienna and had emigrated to Venice during the time of the Austrian Empire. Her husband, a southern Italian, had an indeterminate business, which could very well be described as an Agenzia, a mixture of pettifogger and usurer, which is what he was. For the time being, more for the sake of his health than for his sins, he was away for a longish term on what the Italians call by the melodious name of *ergastolo*; we would call it a life sentence. Holst entertained himself animatedly with Signora Montuori, who, after what had just happened, regarded him with superstitious horror. He spoke kindly to her, he was in excellent spirits and in the mood for all kinds of gentle jokes.

'Honourable lady,' he said, 'I have the pleasure of bringing you a greeting from one of my friends who was so happy to visit you in your home a few days ago. He was so gullible as to entrust you with storing some effects that had some value for him: a ring of cut diamonds, a gold watch and a hundred and fifty lire in banknotes and gold coin. Unfortunately, he's unable to come personally and pick up his effects and he was therefore thinking about sending the two gentlemen who took such tender care of Lieutenant Sjöström. I told him that I could carry out his errand and I am quite certain that you, most honourable Mrs Montuori, will entrust me with the named items.'

The old woman shook like a leaf and her toothless gums twitched with terror. But she said she didn't understand a thing. Jeannette came over to him. Holst put an arm around her waist and pulled her down on his lap.

'Little Jeannette,' he said, 'Signora Montuori and I are unable to reach an agreement. She won't believe my friend Dr Braun has delegated me to pick up some effects he has entrusted to the custody of this house. It's quite likely that the 'rozzers' will find it necessary to institute an inspection of this house and my friend therefore thinks it's better that these items are entrusted to me. Don't you think so too, Jeannette?'

Jeannette had gone deathly pale. She wanted to get up, but with Holst's arm firmly around her waist, she couldn't free herself. She leant her head down on his shoulder and burst into intense weeping.

'So that's what you wanted of me,' she whispered through her tears.

The old woman stood trembling. Holst stroked the weeping girl's hair back over her forehead and kissed her.

'You little fool,' he said, 'do you think I would harm you?'

She looked enquiringly at him through her tears. Holst smiled so kindly that she believed him and put an arm around his neck, pressing up against him.

'You will take me with you, won't you?'

Holst nodded silently and looked up at the lady of the house.

'Well, most honourable lady, have you reconsidered?'

Signora Montuori hesitated. Holst pushed Jeannette softly off his lap.

'The young lady is under my protection, but you will immediately be handed over to the authorities. Do you understand?'

Jeannette went over to the old woman.

'It would be best if you hand over the items.'

Holst rolled a cigarette, before standing up and going over to the Signora and putting his hand on her shoulder.

'Do as I say, little lady – it's in your best interests. In addition, that's all I will demand of you – and that you put one of your excellent rooms at my disposal. I like the apartment and I intend to stay here with you if you will have me. You might well be in need of me, and as far as payment is concerned, you can ask for what you want, but I will have those stolen goods.'

Jeannette clapped her hands and found the idea adorable. Signora Montuori didn't share her enthusiasm, but she realised she was in the weaker position and left the room shaking her head.

It would be unfair, and at the same time untrue, to assert that Holst at this moment felt like a working policeman – it would be unreasonable to expect it too.

Jeannette looked at him with big, pleading eyes.

'Not another word about Dr Braun…'

She warded off the answer with a kiss that couldn't mean anything else but consent, because it was honestly answered. Holst promised himself that he would do something for this girl. To put her in a home for fallen women was not, despite the seriousness of his moral code and, for that matter, the purity of his character, the first thing to enter his mind. Signora Montuori handed over the booty, which out of prudence hadn't yet been sold, and Holst was so generous as to give her twenty-five lire as a kind of reward for her good deed.

The whole scenario amused him immensely, but he had grown enormously in the old lady's respect and very soon she and Jeannette were eagerly in the process of smartening up the apartment for the new tenant. It was now five o'clock and Holst had to go back to the hotel to dress for dinner. At the same time, he took steps to transfer his light luggage to his new neighbourhood.

VIII

Holst met Dr Braun in the hotel's dining room, where he was eating dinner alone. Holst sat opposite him and told him with a little smile on his face that his expedition had been successful.

'I thus have the pleasure of placing the *corpora delicti* in front of you and hereby hand over your watch, your ring and 125 lire – the other twenty-five went to expenses.'

Braun went bright red.

'And the lady?' he asked.

Holst smiled.

'The lady, the old witch and the terrifying husband are all under police supervision.'

Braun shook his head.

'Poor young woman, she was so enchantingly sweet.'

'You needn't be concerned,' said Holst. 'I've taken care that everything is being done without awaking attention, and the police officer whose special supervision she is under will be good to her.'

'Oh yes, I'm sure,' interrupted Braun. 'The police are presumably just as utterly depraved and immoral here as they are everywhere else.'

'That's possible,' said Holst, getting to his feet.

Braun didn't want to let him go; he wanted the opportunity to show his gratitude, which was amplified further by the fact that he didn't have to have anything to do with the police and that everything had been settled with the twenty-five lire's outlay. But Holst was evasive.

'In this case, you have done me a greater service than I have for you and I have no claim on your gratitude.'

Braun didn't understand that at all; hadn't Holst himself gone into the lion's den? Ah well, he wouldn't speak about it, so it would be importunate to ask. He had his belongings back and he was happy.

Holst dressed for dinner and at six o'clock he was standing in the entrance hall of the Hotel Victoria. His heart was pounding a little at the thought of meeting Captain Ankerkrone again. The district magistrate was the first man to appear. Holst told him briefly about what had happened. The murderer was now arrested, charged with falsification and fraud, and the necessary formalities for organising his extradition would be initiated the next day. Holst would personally inform the consulate about the case, but since the detainee was a Swedish subject, the negotiations would no doubt be quite complicated and take time. The district magistrate found this rather fortunate, since it meant that he wouldn't have to interrupt his overseas trip.

Holst asked the magistrate not to say anything about the case.

While they were talking about this, Captain Ankerkrone, Ulla and Captain Kurk came down. Ankerkrone greeted Holst with great warmth. Holst was struck by how tired and infirm he looked and he made a remark about it.

'No, I'm not at all well, my friend – the machinery isn't working any more,' replied Ankerkrone with a weak smile.

Captain Kurk was very formal; Holst thought him almost unfriendly and found this totally unjustified, but he recalled that the man needed time to thaw out. He hadn't been particularly forthcoming in Kristianstad either. Ulla was enchanting in a light silk dress with dark red roses that matched her pale complexion and dark hair. Holst looked admiringly at her and caught himself thinking that one woman at least would have fretted in silence if she had seen them together.

The experiences of the last few days and the spontaneous eroticism that exudes over the Queen of the Adriatic were having an irresistible effect on Holst, making him feel quite differently available and self-controlled towards the beautiful young women. He had to admit to himself that he was flirting outrageously with Ulla and the three elderly gentlemen were eyeing him with great attention. The district magistrate teased him slightly. Claes Ankerkrone had sent his apologies; he couldn't come until after dinner.

It was apparent that Captain Ankerkrone didn't know anything about the arrest, but Holst understood from a few words that Kurk let slip that Lieutenant Claes had acquainted him with the story. But it was only a couple of words. Otherwise there was no mention of this event and the atmosphere lightened significantly during the meal. Only Captain Kurk seemed dispirited and taciturn.

They took coffee on the hotel terrace. The evening was quiet and warm, though a light sea breeze was blowing over the lagoon. Holst and Ulla sat together and talked about summer in the Nordic countries and the green beech forests.

'Don't you long for it?' Ulla asked.

'Well now,' he replied, 'long for it – I wouldn't call it that exactly. There are mysterious powers in the nature down here. Yes, I know that sounds strange, but it's true. They talk about the great Goethe, about him coming to Venice and being seized by a strange mood, actually a spirit that cavorted in him, far different from the spirit of German speculative romantic poetry.'

Holst blushed.

'I'm no poet, not in the slightest, but I have the same feeling.'

Ulla smiled.

'You mean that when you, like young Werther, sat on the bench by the little lake up there, you wanted to escape when you saw me coming and now...'

Holst looked at her.

'How strange that your thoughts follow precisely the same track as mine – that's exactly what I was thinking.'

Ulla blushed.

'...And now...?'

'Now I would like...'

Holst went silent. She looked at him with a strange, questioning look, and he felt a kind of trickling spring, deep inside, that spread through him.

Two people can meet in love with a glance for a short second, and it happened here. There was no way back from such a meeting. It was as if little Jeannette had opened the gate for Holst to areas where he had never walked before, as if she had directed his path over flower-sprinkled fields towards the greater goal, and while his gaze rested on the beautiful young woman in front of him, with her blushing cheeks and her large, enquiring eyes, his lips whispered a thank you to little Jeanette, who had taught him more in one day than life had taught him in many years.

There was no sadness in the memory, only a swelling hope for the future; it was a life purpose, the first real one he had experienced.

Captain Kurk interrupted the young couple; he wanted to exchange a few words with Holst. The obvious disappointment which marked Ulla's face at the interruption reconciled Holst to the separation. The gentlemen retired to the captain's room to be undisturbed.

It was obvious that Captain Kurk wanted to know the whole story, but the moment Holst realised that Kurk was on another person's errand, he abandoned his gentle mood and gathered himself to receive the attack coldly, clearly and sensibly. He realised that the moment had arrived when he had to take a position on the question of Captain Ankerkrone's relationship to the unfolding drama. He was in a foreign country; the case was solely dependent on him; he had it in his power to lead it, and they all understood that. But he was a soldier and no atmosphere in the world would take him away from the path of duty that lay before him, sharply outlined by what he already knew and what they would have to tell him if he wanted to know about it.

IX

Captain Kurk asked Holst to take a seat and offered him one of those excellent cigars which mean so much in Italy, where the desire for tobacco has to be satisfied, along with Minghetti, Cavour and other deceased statesmen, by damp, unpleasant tobacco or by Virginia and Trabuco, which lasts for weeks and costs a fortune in matches.

Holst lit it and sat down, on his guard.

'Lieutenant,' began the Captain, 'I understand that Sjöström has been arrested.'

Holst nodded.

'Lieutenant Ankerkrone came to me extremely agitated and told me that you had carried out the arrest in Lieutenant Sjöström's home where he lives with his mistress. The lieutenant said that the charge is falsification and fraud. Is that correct?'

Holst nodded.

'Will the charge be limited to this?' asked Kurk with an

inquisitive look.

'Provisionally, yes,' replied Holst.

'Provisionally – but what about later? Claes disclosed that you had mentioned a name that you know because of me, as I'm sure you will recall. Do you consider Sjöström guilty of the murder of Annie, and is that why you have arrested him?'

Holst looked up calmly at Kurk.

'It's against my principles to comment on my suspicions at such an early stage of a case. I believe I can prove that Lieutenant Hugold Sjöström has falsified a cheque issued by Annie Cederlund and appropriated a considerable amount of money hereby – or rather, I am in possession of the document and there is a strong probability that the falsification can be proved. With regard to the murder, I have no presumptions at all – I only know that in this case I will have to negotiate personally with people, not with their representatives.'

The captain bit his lip.

'You seem to be forgetting, Lieutenant, that when you presented yourself to me some time ago, you invoked a bond that ties us together and that I respected your approach to engage me in dialogue. I told you what I knew. It seems to me simple gratitude to return the favour.'

Holst looked firmly at him.

'My dear Captain,' he said, 'what you told me was what you felt fully disposed to tell, no more. I can't tell you about the deliberations of my superiors. I'm merely a subordinate and my duty, as you know, goes above everything else.'

Captain Kurk switched to a more familiar tone.

'Of course, it's up to you. It might seem more satisfactory that Arvid Ankerkrone spoke to you personally, but he is ill. His health has suddenly been undermined in recent days and he can't take a lot of mental exertion.'

'I have plenty of time,' said Holst kindly. 'My friendship with Captain Ankerkrone and his family is so warm that you must trust, dear Captain, that I won't take any action against anyone of that name without due warning.'

'Will you give me your word on this?' asked the Captain. 'And that you won't use your acquaintanceship and the confidentiality which you enjoy with the family in the conduct of your office?'

Holst stood up and gave the captain his hand.

'Sir,' he said, 'on the day when my civil duties require me to take any step against Captain Ankerkrone or any of his family that is against their desire and will, on that day I will step back and ask someone else to do it. I won't seek any information that isn't voluntarily given to me, and before I disclose the name which hasn't yet been mentioned in any official document, and not even to the district magistrate, I will present myself to the head of the family and tell him why I am disclosing it and give him every chance for it to remain unmentioned.'

Kurk was a little uncertain for a moment.

'Do you think it will be necessary to disclose it?'

Holst shook his head.

'I can't say. Tomorrow I'll be talking to the man I've had arrested and much will depend on what he tells me. With the best will in the world, I can't tell you more than that today.'

The conversation was closed and the two gentlemen returned to the others. Claes and his wife had arrived in the meantime. The young Englishwoman paid special attention to Holst; she wasn't very pretty – indeed, not particularly charming either – but her eyes sparkled with intelligence and her ability to look at people and relationships and judge them coldly and clearly was uncommon. She appeared to be very much in love with her husband, but seemed cooler towards her father-in-law and sister-in-law. She treated Captain Kurk with a striking lack of affinity.

Claes Ankerkrone pretended to have completely forgotten the scene at Sjöström's apartment; he was overwhelmingly gracious towards Holst, extremely charming, but hardly totally honest. Holst didn't take to him. He dedicated his evening to Ulla, and in her company forgot about other people and other matters. When he left them, she gave his hand a long, firm squeeze and asked him to come by and accompany her on a trip through the wonderful city. He promised to do that.

Upon his return home, he pushed the waiting Jeannette gently aside and went to his room to be alone with his thoughts and his young hope.

X

CAPTAIN HOLGER KURK SLEPT VERY LITTLE the night after his conversation with Holst. He was nervous after Sjöström's arrest, which only he, the district magistrate and Claes knew about. He knew more than the young lieutenant; he knew that the true reason for the arrest was the suspicion that Sjöström was Annie's murderer. He shared that suspicion, but at the same time, he realised that this case could well expose his old friend's name in a court case, the scope of which could not be ignored.

Ankerkrone was ill; admittedly his health had improved recently, but he couldn't take too much mental stress. There was a brief mention in the morning newspapers of the arrest, which would, of course, immediately be communicated to Sweden telegraphically. Ankerkrone would thus get wind of it and what would happen then was impossible for anyone to calculate.

When Kurk had informed Holst of what he knew about Annie, he had intentionally withheld the name of Arvid Ankerkrone, but he realised that Holst, who already at that point had been on the trail, now knew a lot more – indeed, it could be that Holst knew even more than he did, because he had certainly found out about most of what had happened between Ankerkrone and the murdered girl before the last fateful events. He only had his suspicions about these, nothing definite. Ankerkrone had involved him in order to try and restrain his son, but this hadn't succeeded, and Ankerkrone had had to take action himself. He had informed Kurk that it had been successful, but that the price had been higher than he would ever have thought possible. At first, he had thought it was about money. After Holst's visit to Kristianstad, he had been nagged by the most painful doubts and the heaviest suspicions and immediately sought out his friend. He had arrived just as Ankerkrone had received Holst's messages, which had caused Ankerkrone great anxiety. Kurk hadn't been told anything and the Captain had rejected all his attempts to find out more. But he had been very ill, that much was clear.

Kurk didn't want to believe that there could have been anything really important between Arvid Ankerkrone and Hugold Sjöström. He knew better than anyone else what had happened earlier, but this – no; and Arvid Ankerkrone neither would nor could. Annie was dead, murdered, and Sjöström was her murderer, but Arvid Ankerkrone had been in the vicinity and might have negotiated with her shortly before. He had to know more than he had said and therein lay the foundation for his silence and illness.

Holst was a dangerous man, for he would do his duty; his friendship with Captain Ankerkrone would have to take second place. There was only a flimsy foundation of hope to build upon – he was captivated by Ulla. But sacrifice her to save the family's honour? Not even Ankerkrone himself would do that.

And the district magistrate was a good-natured, helpful person whose indecision concerning his responsibilities would only make the case even more complicated. Even though it might be possible to win Holst over, what position would the old civil servant take when suddenly faced with his old friend who had to be dragged into a case where the whole of the Nordic region would be a curious spectator? The Danish judiciary was a race that was well-known in Scania as well, and the profession wasn't exactly bathed in glory, thanks to the treatment that the country's old and new literature and the press had rightly or wrongly given it. Would the friendship hold?

Claes was a stupid boy who would only worsen the case; he had to be kept at one remove. And Ulla – never. No, there was nothing else to do but to force Arvid Ankerkrone to speak up if Holst wouldn't lend him a helping hand. Captain Kurk still didn't trust Holst.

Early the next morning, he went to Ankerkrone to speak honestly to him.

Arvid Ankerkrone received him in the living room on the first floor of the hotel; he was quite well and greeted him cheerfully. It was very painful for Kurk, but there was no way around it. He began to talk about Holst and his well-mannered bearing.

The Captain nodded.

'He's extremely captivated by Ulla,' said Kurk, 'and do you know what I think? Ulla is extremely captivated by him too.'

The Captain smiled.

'They would be a handsome couple. Holst is a complete gentleman and he will surely be able to reach a position of high standing – he's an unusual talent.'

'Do you think so?' mumbled Kurk. 'It's an ignoble occupation – he should give it up.'

'He could no doubt be persuaded to do that,' said Ankerkrone seriously, 'if some incentive was used. But, as you know, I'm not all that well-off and Ulla has nothing except her inheritance from her mother's side, which won't stretch very far. It could be difficult to get him another position.'

'So you've already been thinking really seriously about it?' said Kurk.

'Often,' said Ankerkrone, before adding in a strange, hollow voice, 'it's also the only way.'

'What do you mean?' asked Kurk.

'Nothing,' said the Captain with a weak smile.

'Do you know that Holst has made a catch here in Venice?' asked Kurk, with a searching look at his friend.

'No. What catch?'

'Yesterday he arrested Hugold Sjöström for falsification and fraud.'

'Well I never,' said Ankerkrone, 'and you don't tell me this until today – or didn't you know yesterday?'

'Yes, I did,' replied Kurk hesitantly.

'Then you should have told me so that I could have wished Holst good luck with his catch. That Sjöström fellow has a great deal on his conscience.'

Kurk looked surprised, while Ankerkrone sat quite calmly, although Kurk thought that his mouth was set in a strangely fixed manner, as if on a man who had made a decision and was determined to carry it through.

'Arvid,' said Captain Kurk, 'you're not being honest with me.'

'I don't know what you mean. Why should I take a keen interest in Hugold Sjöström's fate? After all, he's closer to you than to me. He was a bright soldier in the old days, but now he's become a criminal capable of the lowest of the low.'

'Murder too?' asked Kurk.

'Everything,' answered Ankerkrone.

'Don't you know what the true reason for his arrest is?'

'I don't know anything except what you've told me. I didn't even know that Sjöström was here – he hasn't sought me out.'

'So you aren't interested in the case in the slightest?'

Arvid Ankerkrone stood up and went over to the captain, put both hands on his shoulders and looked him firmly in the eye.

'Brother Holger, I've been weak three times in my life, and all three times it was because of the same woman. She's now dead. I've stood beside her body. On that occasion, I was calm and now I'll never be weak again. Dear brother, I know that I can count on you and therefore I entrust you with the task that I can't do myself. You know that Sjöström has only been in contact with us on the one occasion. That time it was a matter that must remain a family secret, which mustn't be spread to thousands of curious, scandal-seeking strangers. We're now facing a court case in which Sjöström's arrest is the first vague beginning. If that case is going to be extended depends on you.'

Kurk looked questioningly him – he didn't understand a word.

Ankerkrone smiled weakly.

'Brother, it's too early in the case, too early in the day too. Now the threads are resting in my hand and it isn't shaking any more. But you must be patient. You will remember that, in the old days, there were three of us. I was always the head, you were the heart, and Cedersköld was the hand. The hand became unfaithful to us, and that's why it withered. Now you must be the hand, Holger – the heart must stay cold. We don't only hold sway over our own destiny. Don't lose courage, brother, because you don't understand me, but you should know that I can and will act so firmly now that nothing will divert me from my path.'

Kurk shook his head, but he felt that Arvid Ankerkrone himself was the one in charge. And he became calm because he knew that Arvid was stronger than he was. Then Ulla arrived and her bright smile brought the sunshine into the living room where the three were soon seated around an enjoyable lunch table.

Ankerkrone wrote a few words to Holst and asked him to be his guest on an excursion to the Lido.

XI

Holst presented himself at the hotel at the stipulated time. The whole group was assembled and Ulla greeted him with a radiant smile. Captain Ankerkrone was apparently much better; he looked more recovered and it struck Holst that his whole demeanour bore traces of considerable determination and dignity.

Kurk was slumped and said little, keeping his distance from Holst, and devoted himself mostly to the district magistrate, whose happy old man's chatter sounded strangely alien here, where an intensely uneasy energy pulsed under a smiling surface.

They all took the steamer to the Lido; the sun was shining warmly, while a fresh breeze made the flag on the steamer's mast flap and ruffled the tops of the yellow waves. It was as if all the nations of the world had gathered together on the deck of the little steamer, and the plethora of languages sounded like a Babylonian tumult, with the women's laughter chirping animatedly and a group of German students who had gathered in the ship's prow singing their soulful German songs.

Captain Ankerkrone was leaning against the gunwale and observing the people on the deck. Holst went over to him.

'How many sorrows do you think are hiding behind this noisy bustle? How much adversity do you think these people are trying to escape from? There lies the City of Neptune, as Goethe calls it in his immortal epigrams, as you know.' Ankerkrone smiled weakly. 'I brought them with me to Venice twenty-five years ago when, as a young man, I saw this city for the first time. And they've been with me ever since. Look at all of these pilgrims to Venice who are searching for the place where the great spirits lived and loved; look at how they stare and listen to their chatter. They're all looking for the same thing – everyone believes they have found in Venice what they were looking for: to stand at the door of happiness. Poor pilgrims, listen to what the master says: *Seh'ich den Pilgrim, so kann ich mich nie Thränen enthalten. O, wie beseliget uns Menschen ein falscher Begriff!* 'If I see a pilgrim, I can never hold back my tears; Oh, how enraptured we humans are by false notions.' As you see, I'm still quoting Goethe.'

Holst didn't answer; the Captain's gaze rested on him with friendly seriousness.

'You, too, Eigil Holst, have believed you would find what you were looking for in Venice, in more ways than one, haven't you? And you stopped on the threshold because you didn't dare to seize the opportunity.'

He paused.

'Just seize it.'

Holst looked up at him seriously.

'I don't understand.'

The Captain smiled with a strange wistful smile.

'I'm just saying, seize it, my friend, and so that you understand me better, I say, seize both the father and the daughter.'

Holst went bright red.

'Isn't that right? You understand me? Pilgrim, you believe you're standing at the end of the road and your false notion makes you happy, it's just that your happiness is of a kind of its own. You should know that I've been following your journey and that a plan and not chance have brought us together today. When I saw you for the first time, I received you with friendship and it turned out that you became the one who held my destiny in your hand because I put it in your hand myself, and encouraged that old man over there in his choice of you. Now you're at your goal and you're hesitant to seize the opportunity. How strange we humans are.'

Holst stayed silent; he didn't want to talk now, even though Captain Ankerkrone had touched upon the letter and the diary – in fact upon even more than he had written and more than he had promised to talk about.

The Captain put a hand on his shoulder.

'Now we two are on this journey together and your thoughts take only the path you most prefer. When you return, if your thoughts are still following the same path, we will read my diary together and we will talk. When we parted after our time together up there, where you were working so eagerly, I told you that your path would lead you to me and that you would need my help. You can see for yourself that that's exactly what has happened and you will receive my help. My life has only one goal now and that single goal is also yours, my dear friend. That's why we two are so ideally suited to work together.'

Ankerkrone's gaze glided along the gunwale to where Ulla was standing propped up against a staircase in cheerful

240

conversation with the district magistrate. Holst's gaze followed the Captain's and he blushed.

The steamer docked at the jetty by the Lido. Holst and Ulla walked together along the beach where the bathing was in full swing and hundreds of happy people were rolling around in the sand, laughing and joking, as the sun reflected off the windows of the casino and cast its rays over balconies and galleries.

Ulla stopped.

'This isn't the real Venice for me. For me, Venice is the silent, sighing streets, the dark churches with their treasures and the magnificent paintings in the Doge's Palace and the Accademia, but most of all, St Mark's Square. Father loves Venice, where he first met mother, who died when I was quite small. Pictures from Venice have always adorned our walls, and father is always quoting from Goethe's Venetian Epigrams; he knows them by heart, but he will never really explain them to me and I don't understand them at all.'

Holst smiled.

'Understanding them isn't always easy either.'

'But you understand them,' Ulla interrupted eagerly. 'You must be able to explain a lot of it to me...' She blushed, 'Of course not everything – but something of what you understand, which you could...'

Ulla had once again entered one of those blind alleys out of which she never seemed able to escape.

'Like this one,' she blurted out quickly. '"*Sanct Johannes im Koth heißt eine Kirche; Venedig –nenn' ich mit doppeltem Recht heute Sanct Marcus im Koth.*"'[10]

Holst smiled.

'It probably means that Venice is built on marshy, clayey ground.'

Ulla looked up at him.

'– clayey ground – yes, but…'

Holst looked her right in the eye.

'Miss Ulla. If you want, we can meet up in the afternoon in St Mark's – then we can perhaps see on what ground St Mark stands.'

Ulla blushed. 'Five o'clock?'

'Five o'clock.'

The district magistrate waved to them that their meal was ready. They returned to Venice just after midday.

XII

THE PATRIARCH IN VENICE was saying mass in St Mark's. He stood in front of the high altar dressed in his gold-braided vestments with the bishop's mitre on his head and surrounded by a boys' choir and prelates with crosses and censers. The music swirled down from the organ over the congregation, while the heavy incense spread its scent through the vaulted space. The sunlight shone strongly through the stained-glass windows; the mosaic on the ceiling glimmered with gold and rich colours, while the smoke in the light, pulsating air was yellowish in the light from the candles.

Devout believers were kneeling on the floor while curious strangers stood and watched. The occasional Catholic bowed in reverence, but the majority – indifferent Englishmen – chatted undisturbed, as if it was a popular theatre piece they were watching.

The hymns and the sound of the organ swelled more strongly

and then a single lovely voice echoed alone through the vault. The boys' choir joined in, merging with the voice and dying in a wealth of different tones. The music went silent and a dry, old man's voice read from the book by the high altar, two voices responded, and once again the organ and trombones sounded while the choir weaved the Latin psalms into readings given by alternating voices and interrupted by the strong, full-toned solo.

The clergy in front of the high altar began moving; they removed the mitre from the bishop's head and replaced it with one glittering with gold; the boys fastened a shining, golden robe around his shoulders, and constantly switched places around him, handing him a vessel and cloth, gathering around before breaking away once more, while the liturgy resonated incessantly and the incense rose towards the mosaics on the ceiling in the flickering candlelight. Sometimes the psalms were more subdued, sometimes only murmuring faintly, while the believers knelt on the sharp stones, which, with their strange, colourful images, formed the floor of the eternal church of St Mark.

In a corner close to the entrance to the sacristy, from which the priesthood had emerged, stood a young man and a young woman, arm in arm. They weren't talking to each other, but she was leaning against him, and her head was resting on his shoulder. It was as if their thoughts were being borne by the lovely music to distant realms and the mighty power that lies in the centuries' old church's strange traditions was forcing them under its dominion. They didn't understand the words, but they understood that behind the psalms and hymns, behind the music, was a kingdom that no human eye will ever see but which is there because the human race, in the hundreds of years that have passed, has built this kingdom into its hopes.

When mankind's path goes past the threshold of this kingdom – and it happens when serious decisions are made, when sorrow and happiness grasp our souls deepest – the mind bows under this mighty power, and even someone who doubts or denies feels in such a moment the stronger power which he doesn't understand. But this is felt most deeply if two people stand at each other's side at the very moment they have linked their hearts to each other so that they swell in the rich hope of love.

Then it isn't a theatre piece, even though it seems strange and foreign, even though the devotion of the believers seems simple-minded and the activity of the priests incomprehensible and unfounded. The singing, the smell of incense and the light merge in the space, combining with the vaults in the lovely basilica into a dream that carries the thoughts far away to where happiness must be eternal, as long as happiness exists, and eternity at such a moment is happiness.

And for these two standing there in their dream, everything was forgotten at this moment, everything else but this one thing: that they were two and happy in a dream that would last forever.

The mass ended and the prelates left to the blare of the organ on their way to the sacristy. In front of them, the choir boys carried the cross and the censers; the venerable patriarch went past, and when he cast his eyes on the two standing in the nook, he saw two people bending towards each other in a kiss of warm love.

The patriarch smiled under his mitre, he who would later bear the tiara that adorns pontifex maximus.

XIII

WHEN HOLST CAME HOME THAT EVENING, Jeannette received him with melancholic seriousness.

Jeannette's infatuation was of a strangely humble nature; she bent herself to her chosen master's wishes like an Eastern slave woman, fearing his great power and authority. But she was seriously in love and her feeling was genuine enough. She was young, but she had been through a lot and she had gradually become accustomed to humiliation, but also to humility. She hated Sjöström and the fate that had struck him hadn't taken the edge off her hatred. Holst was not especially well acquainted with women and their feelings, but he understood that Jeannette had become attached to him and that she would follow him like an obedient dog. After what had just happened, it was impossible for him to continue with the little adventure that had taken him unawares.

It troubled him that he couldn't offer her even the insignificant crumbs she would be happy with, but she was young and healthy, and, particularly in the mood that had now captured him, he was happy for youth and health and for the thousands of little things that a woman in love creates around her loved one. He had deliberately chosen Signora Montuori's house as his residence in order to be able to find out everything Jeannette knew about Annie, but that was the only reason.

Jeannette was curious about the people whose guest Holst had been, and he told her who they were and how the trip had gone. He only mentioned Ulla in passing, but Jeannette guessed at a lot from his few words and doubled her tenderness so that he would forget her. It had gone quiet now that night had fallen and it was very warm in the narrow canal streets. Holst couldn't sleep, so they sat together in a large room facing the canal with the water lapping against the foot of the house and talked for a long time; and strangely enough, what Holst learnt from the young woman in the quiet of the night cast the first really sharp light on the case that was filling his thoughts. Jeannette told him about herself and gradually there grew out of her narrative exactly what Holst had a foreboding of but didn't dare believe until it lay before him in all its sharp clarity, like cold, hard-headed reality that threatened that to which he was tying the warmest aspirations of his life. Jeannette told him about herself and her childhood:

'Daddy was an officer of the watch in the Scanian Dragoons based in Ystad. I still remember so clearly the farm at home, where we siblings played, and where Glimmingehus Manor, with its big stone trolls and bare boulder walls not a hundred yards from our playground, reared up out of the green fields. And when the soldiers met up for manoeuvres and exercises, when Daddy's squadron came riding down the road with the big, shiny brown horses and the trumpets on the massive roans, they often stopped in front of the farm and Mummy came out with us children, and Daddy's Captain on his grand, black and brown horse rode up in front of the door and was given a soft drink and asked about us and pinched our cheeks. Do you know who that Captain was? It was the father of the young man you saw here yesterday when you arrested Hugold, Captain Ankerkrone. He had a magnificent manor house up near Kristianstad, but his wife was dead. They said her story was a sad one, but I didn't hear it until later. Daddy told me a lot about it later, after we had come to Paris with the Falkenbergs. Because the year I had my eighth birthday, there was such a huge exhibition in Copenhagen that Daddy and Mummy and my brother, who was twelve, and I went first to Copenhagen and afterwards to Paris with the grand Count of Riddartofte. He was a delightful man, one of the finest old men I've ever seen, and he was very charitable too. Hugold's brother came to serve there as an equerry. The old Count is dead now, but the son is said to be like his father – Tage, that is – because the younger one, Otto, I won't say anything good about him, not after how badly he treated me later.'

Jeannette sighed and became lost in thought, but Holst, sitting quietly and listening to her chatter, asked her to tell him more.

'I remember it so clearly,' she continued, 'I must have been twelve to fourteen years old – she came, the one you mentioned, Annie Cederlund, to Daddy for the first time. She was so unhappy, she said. She'd been rich and had important friends, but the last one, an Austrian Count, had suffered a big bankruptcy that everyone was talking about in Paris, and now Annie was ill and she thought she was going to die. She had once had quite a lot of money, but it had all gone on her lavish lifestyle, and she'd been thinking of drowning herself in the Seine – just like me before I met you. I've often thought about jumping into the canal here and sinking to the bottom away from all my sorrows. But she had a little child at home in Kristianstad where she had been and wasn't it strange? It was precisely with Daddy's old Captain, Ankerkrone, that she had had the child. She loved him so terribly, but he had rejected her, and Daddy often said later that Annie had been responsible for the death of the Captain's wife.'

Holst, who had been sitting half in his own thoughts, immediately began to pay attention.

'If you know anything about that matter, you must tell me everything you know,' he said, giving Jeanette a sharp look.

Jeannette shook her head.

'No, I only know what Daddy said, that Ankerkrone had been in love with Annie when she was a young girl up in Småland many years ago, and his wife had been so weak after her last child, a girl, and then it hadn't gone well for them living together, the Captain and his wife. But she had recovered and it had been better between them until one day she died suddenly. And Annie had caused ill-feeling between her and the Captain, because she could be vengeful, even though she could be so good too. She wasn't like me. I could never hurt a man I really loved, and Annie loved Arvid Ankerkrone much more than they could write about in any novel.'

'How do you know that?' asked Holst with a little smile.

'Because she told me hundreds of times – you should know that Annie was like a mother to me, but that was later, after everything had gone wrong for me. And that's why I can't understand that I've never heard a word from her since she left me in the spring in Elsinore. I asked Claes Ankerkrone about her yesterday, but he didn't want to say anything; he went very quiet, and he loved her more than anyone would believe, but she didn't like him. He wanted to divorce his wife and marry Annie, even though she was much older than him, but she looked young – then suddenly it was all over and it was his father who caused it. I know because I personally had a visit from him that day.'

Jeannette's story was jumping around a lot; Holst tried to force it back on an even keel because every word she could tell about this was of paramount importance to him. It was clear to him that this young woman knew better than anyone else what had happened just before the crime was committed in the forest north of Esrum on 27th March, and he wanted to know everything.

'So you met Annie for the first time in 1894?'

Jeannette thought about it.

'It was the summer they assassinated the French President, I remember that clearly – yes, it was in 1894. She lived with us for a whole year and recovered completely. Then she went back home to look after her child, who I suppose was about ten. A couple of years later, Otto Falkenberg came down to his father; he was a kind of attaché, they called him, but there was no goodness in him. I was so proud that he made so much fuss of me. I was good at riding, and we rode together, and he told me so much about everything he was going to do for me, and that's how it all went wrong. He was the first gentleman I got mixed up with, and he seduced me without me realising how wrong it was. Then Daddy fell ill and died, and on the same day the old Count died. It was a dreadful time because I was going to have a baby and I was very ill and the child died too. But Mummy was grieving so much and my brother, a soldier stationed in Ystad, came down to fetch her. But I didn't want to go with them so I left with Otto to Germany. Then they wrote to him so much and he met someone else, so he left me, and I was alone in a foreign country with only a little money. I didn't want to go home because I felt ashamed towards my brother and my mother, and I accepted a job in a circus where I rode a little and also danced in the ballet. It was a difficult time, but then we arrived in Berlin. Yes, that was some time after, it must have been in '98, and I met Hugold there; he spoke to me in the ring – he'd probably found out that I was Swedish, and then I saw that Annie was with him.

They were in Berlin, and incidentally were almost penniless, but she was very good to me, and I came to live with them too, and we travelled together because I left the circus. I'll never forget Annie for that year, she was so very good to me, but they didn't have any money, and I wanted to have some fun and I knew many gentlemen, but nobody I cared about, because you should know that you're the first one I've really loved, and I did that the moment I saw you. So you must also love me.'

Jeannette looked up at her protector with questioning, trusting eyes.

He bent towards her.

'Of course I'll be good to you, you poor little thing.'

Holst looked at her for a long time, then took hold of both her hands.

'Jeannette, you're a good, honest girl, and I trust you. You don't know how important you can be for me and it's no coincidence that we two have met each other. You also need to know why I'm here and you're going to help me with a job which is so difficult that you'll hardly believe you can manage it, but you'll see that I trust you. But first I want to tell you that I won't try to pull the wool over your eyes.'

Jeannette looked up anxiously.

'Are you married?'

'No,' said Holst with a smile.

'But you have a girlfriend?' she whispered almost silently.

'Maybe,' replied Holst and Jeannette put both arms around his neck. Holst pushed her gently away.

'Jeannette,' he said, 'I can't give you my love, because there is someone else I care about.'

Jeannette gave a start.

'Someone else – so why did you tell me you loved me?'

Holst took her hand.

'Jeannette, you know what I am, don't you? It was because of Dr Braun that we two got together – at the time I didn't know everything I know now. Tell me honestly, Jeannette, when you now know that I love someone else, someone whom I have told today that I love her, will you keep being honest with me like you are now?'

'Is she a fine lady?' asked Jeannette. 'One you want to marry?'

Holst didn't answer.

'If that's the case – if it's a fine lady you're in love with and who you want to marry, you can still stay here with me a little while yet, can't you? You mustn't leave me. If you do, I'll drown myself and it'll be your fault.'

Jeannette clung to him and tears came to her eyes.

Holst looked at her in silence, then he took her hand once more. He was sure of her and he decided to tell her everything.

'You should know,' he said, 'that my presence here has a bigger goal than what you already know. It's about Annie – the same Annie you were talking about. When she left you in Elsinore that day which you talked about, she was murdered. A couple of months later, I found her body in a quarry in North Zealand, and the man I had arrested here in this house yesterday is her murderer.'

Jeannette went deathly pale.

'Murdered! Annie murdered by Hugold! No, no, that can't be

true. Hugold hasn't murdered Annie…he hasn't…it must have been…'

Her eyes became glassy and she gasped for air.

Holst kept a firm grip on her hand.

'Who?'

Her voice sank to a whisper.

'It's him…the other one…'

'Claes Ankerkrone?'

'No, no…the other one…his father, the Captain, Arvid Ankerkrone…'

Holst's blood froze to ice in his veins.

They sat totally silent for a couple of minutes while the water lapped against the wall of the house, and the wind, which had now started blowing round the corner of the canal, rattled the shutters outside the open windows.

Holst broke the silence.

'Arvid Ankerkrone!'

Jeannette froze, her shoulders shook and she rubbed her hands together.

'Annie murdered! So he's done what she feared, just as she thought everything would turn out well.'

'Who do you mean?' Holst asked.

'It was Claes Ankerkrone's father, the Captain, whom Annie was going to marry on the day she said goodbye to me.'

'But you told me it was the son,' said Holst, subdued.

'Yes, because no one was supposed to know about the other arrangement and I promised Annie to keep quiet and not tell anyone.'

Jeannette bent down over Holst and cried convulsively with her head pressed down against his knee. Holst sat totally still; it was as if everything had stopped, as if his thoughts were suddenly silenced. He couldn't think and if he tried to it was as if all his diffuse suspicions, all the forebodings he had held back, gathered together, towering up over him in one voice: 'But you knew it was him all along, you must have been able to see that it was him. Each step you've taken pointed to this one person. You haven't wanted to see it. You've betrayed your duty. Now you know how it is, you must act like a man.'

For the first time in his life, Holst broke down. He sat bowed over the sobbing woman while his heart constricted. He couldn't fight his way out. He felt that if this had happened just one day, just half a day earlier, he would have been capable of bearing it like a man, and he would have been able to do his duty without looking to right or left, without hesitation.

Now it was impossible. He couldn't raise his hand against her father.

He lifted up the weeping Jeannette, led her to her bed and gently covered her. She wanted to speak, but he asked her to be silent. She looked up, and with that intuition that every woman owns, she guessed his thoughts.

'Is it his daughter?' she asked very gently.

Holst didn't answer. He sat silently on the edge of the bed, until Jeannette's breathing showed that she was asleep.

XIV

IT WAS MIDNIGHT. HOLST GOT UP and left the house. He walked through the narrow alleys down to the Riva, from where he saw the moon shining like a narrow disc and the countless stars reflecting in the lagoon. The wind was now blowing quite briskly. Holst stopped in front of the hotel. He looked up at a certain window behind which a flickering light burned. Was Ulla asleep, he wondered. After what had happened, she couldn't sleep. His gaze switched to the window next to hers, where a clear, calmly burning lamplight testified that Captain Ankerkrone hadn't yet gone to bed.

A door opened out to the balcony in front of the Captain's room and Holst saw how Ulla stepped out supported by her father's arm. There they stood for a long time while she leant her head on his shoulder. Holst saw that he put his arm around her shoulders and kissed her forehead.

Holst took a firm grip on an iron railing beside a stairway

which led down to the water from where he was standing.

No – that surely couldn't be the meaning of life; that, in order to follow one's duty, a random job laid on our shoulders, we humans should have to spurn the richest happiness of our lives. If it were true that the man who stood there on the balcony had taken another person's life, taken it in order to revenge himself or protect someone else, then the higher powers that watched over what men call eternal justice could bring their will to pass without him.

His place was with these people, to support them with advice and deeds. Anything else would be treason against the greatest of all things, against his young, burning love, against happiness, that was smiling on him for the first time after an arduous life of hard work.

And at this moment, Holst decided to betray what he had called his duty to follow the voice that spoke to him in the beating of his heart.

He stretched out his arms towards the two and spoke her name in a loud voice.

'Ulla!'

It echoed across the silent Riva, across the lapping waters of the lagoon.

Ulla reached out towards him too and he quickly headed over to the high portal to the hotel and, after a few minutes, was standing up there, where the light had been blinking at him, with the two people to whose fate he would be inextricably bound in the future.

Ulla left them after a while to go to bed and Holst found himself alone with Captain Ankerkrone, who looked at him sadly and laid a hand on his shoulder.

'Eigil,' he said, 'we two have yet more words to exchange with each other.'

'About Ulla, yes,' replied Holst, 'but not about anything else.'

'And Annie?' asked Ankerkrone.

'No,' said Holst, 'from today, I'm stepping back from everything to do with Annie. It was a case I volunteered for and no one will force me to take any more steps along the paths which lead to solving it.'

'You will betray your duty?' asked Ankerkrone.

'Yes.'

'And the murderer?'

'He must stand to account to God for his actions. If earthly justice is to reach him, it won't be at my hand.'

The Captain looked acutely at Holst.

'So you now know who the murderer is?'

'Yes, I do,' replied Holst.

'And despite this knowledge, you want to marry his daughter?'

Holst grabbed the Captain's hand and squeezed it firmly, while bowing his head in a silent answer.

A glimmer of victory flickered in Ankerkrone's eyes, while he held the young man's hand in his and drew himself up proudly, as if all his bodily weakness slipped away in this moment because of the silent response and the warm handshake.

'Thank you, Eigil, for your answer; now I dare to speak and tell you everything.'

'You've guessed right. I'm Annie's murderer, me and no one else. Even if it may be Sjöström who'll be held responsible in a human court, in the court of God, it is me and me alone.'

'What are you saying?' Holst cut in. 'Sjöström – but then it's…'

Ankerkrone smiled wistfully.

'Take a seat, my dear friend, and I'll tell you what I'm now free to reveal to you, because you've made your choice and bound your destiny to me and my daughter. From the diary and letters I sent you, you know all that happened between Annie and me up until the day when I decided to save my son from the disgrace that awaited him if he followed his foolish love for that woman and betrayed his duty to his wife and children. I could have prevented the fate that befell her. I didn't. I have demanded a 'divine judgement' before, when I forced Cedersköld to dare to attempt the leap at the cliffs in Stilfserjoch. I once again demanded a divine judgement when I sent Annie away to meet the fate which Sjöström, in his insatiable lust for her money, had prepared for her. In both cases, the judgement was death and the responsibility mine – I don't deny it. They were both instrumental in Giulia's death.'

Holst sat silently. During Ankerkrone's speech, his thoughts had reverted to their customary path. So it was definitely Sjöström and not the Captain who had carried out the murder. By going on what Jeannette had said and the Captain's communications, he had allowed himself to be led to the suspicion that had now proved unfounded. He looked up at Ankerkrone who was standing in front of him with a strange, dreamy facial expression.

'Have you assigned Sjöström to kill Annie and paid him for it?' asked Holst.

'No,' replied the Captain, 'but I don't claim any credit for that either. It was unnecessary and I dare say I wouldn't have done it even if it had been necessary.'

Holst smiled; he had recovered his balance.

'Captain Ankerkrone,' he said, 'this strange case has really driven me, level-headed and pragmatic Copenhagener that I am, out into realms that so far have been way beyond my experience. It's your fault; in your diary and your letters as well as in your speech tonight, you've travelled so far away from everyday life that you seem to be moving in the foggy world of

258

the novel, where your son-in-law, Eigil, delights in taking walks with your lovely daughter Ulla, but where Sergeant Holst, for purely official reasons, doesn't dare to venture. You will perhaps allow me for the first, and hopefully the last, time to ask you to tell me, in an earthly language, what you were doing in the days from 22nd to 27th March 1902.'

'Are you interrogating me?' asked Ankerkrone.

'With your permission, yes,' Holst replied, 'but only the actual facts. The novel is Ulla's and mine, the everyday story is yours.'

Ankerkrone sat down in an armchair opposite Holst. He collected his thoughts for a few minutes, before briefly and clearly explaining what had happened.

'As you know, I had decided to prevent Claes from the folly he was in the process of committing in marrying Annie and abandoning his marriage. On 23rd March, Emily and I arrived in Copenhagen and went to the Hotel d'Angleterre. I had discovered that Claes and Annie, along with a kind of lady's companion, a daughter of my former Captain of the Guard, Ljunggren, had arrived in Copenhagen a few days before. They had taken residence at the Hotel Kongen af Danmark. I had previously used Ljunggren's daughter as a kind of spy. She told me that Annie and Claes had gone to Helsingborg. I decided to go after them, but on the same day Sjöström arrived, a man I knew quite well from the time he served in the army as a young man. He sought me out and I learnt very quickly that this man, who up to then had taken every advantage of Annie's relationship with Claes, had become afraid. From the turn events had taken, he was frightened of losing the benefits his relationship with Annie offered. I therefore decided to try to bring about that Annie married him, and in so doing ward off the danger.

'We only travelled together as far as Elsinore, as I didn't want to attract attention by appearing with these people in Scania. Sjöström went on to Helsingborg and returned to Elsinore on 25th March with Claes and Annie. It proved impossible to dissuade Claes, and Annie wanted nothing to do with Sjöström. She said she had come to terms with him for a generous sum, and now it was enough.

'On the evening of the 25th, I had a long conversation with Annie. In the beginning, she was contrary and spiteful, but bit by bit I gained my old dominion over her, and she became moved and compliant. I had told Claes what had occurred between us, but he was completely out of reach, so I came up with a plan that I immediately carried into effect.

'I promised Annie I would marry her, and through this I got her to tell Claes that she didn't care about him and never had. That helped. A fierce argument arose between Claes and myself, but when Claes, who stomped off in anger, had met Emily in Copenhagen, she managed to regain some power over him, and the danger thus seemed to have been eliminated at a stroke. Annie was happy; she had now achieved the goal of all her life's wishes, she said, and as for me – well to be quite honest, it was only consideration for Ulla that held me back. I didn't love Annie, but I had committed great injustices against her. I'm now an old man and, in many ways, look at things differently than I did in my younger days.

'Annie was afraid of Sjöström. She told me that he had twice threatened her life in order to get hold of her money and that, as Sjöström had now learnt how rich she was from her lawyer, a man named Karlkvist in Kristianstad, she was in great danger if I didn't protect her. She didn't want to sacrifice her fortune, which amounted to about one hundred and fifty thousand kroner, even though I informed her I didn't want anything to do with this money.

'I hesitated in my decision; as I said, entirely out of consideration for Ulla. Then Sjöström sought me out and tried to squeeze money out of me by declaring that he would disgrace both of us if we didn't agree terms with him. He seemed close to desperation. It was clear that nothing would stop him. I managed to put him off.

'I spent the 26th together with Annie, who seemed happy and well-satisfied and it broke my heart to see her like that. I couldn't decide, but on that day, I learnt what you now know from the letter Annie had once written to me during an illness and which her mother had received for safekeeping. You will understand that this letter sealed Annie's fate. I held my peace – I couldn't have talked that evening and I can hardly recall exactly what I was doing. I was acting as if in my sleep. I only recall that Annie and I agreed that I should arrange everything so that our wedding could take place in the little church near the town where we had lived together before her child was born. I was to travel there in advance and Sjöström and Annie were to follow me there the next day. He and the farmer whom I had met in town the day before, and who knew us both, were going to be witnesses.

'When I left Annie, I visited Sjöström and told him that we were going to meet at the little lake in the forest which Annie knew. I didn't want anyone to know anything about that. Sjöström asked me how I was going to proceed with regard to the money and I replied that he could act as he wanted, but I added – and it's here my responsibility lies heaviest – 'If I don't turn up tomorrow, I will never ask any questions about you or Annie or anything that concerns either of you. So Annie's fate is in your hands.' He didn't reply – after a few minutes of silence, he simply asked me if I loved Annie, to which I just replied, 'Annie has killed my wife, whom I loved.' Then I left.

I returned to Copenhagen the same evening. I was convinced that Sjöström would make every effort to go through with his plan. Yes, I don't deny it – I felt convinced that Annie's death sentence had fallen. She hated Sjöström and wouldn't bend for him, and for him the only thing that mattered was to get hold of her money.

'I lay low for a month in my house in Malmö with Ulla, until anxiety drove me to the place where my thoughts went all the time. I rented rooms for myself at the farm where we met each other and my path took me daily to the lake where we two met each other that day in May.

'When they emptied the quarry and Annie's body appeared, I got peace of mind. Now I knew what had happened to her, but you will understand why I was so deeply interested in everything that was happening in those days. It was me who encouraged the district magistrate to summon you, and from the outset, I had the feeling that this day would come. Now you know my responsibility and you know I've put everything in your hands so far. I think you should continue your work. I'm prepared to bear my responsibility.'

Holst got up and went over to Captain Ankerkrone.

'For Ulla's sake, you should consider what you're doing,' he said in a gentle, subdued voice.

'Ulla should know everything,' said Ankerkrone seriously.

'Yes, she should,' replied Holst, 'but she shouldn't learn it from your mouth, but from mine when she becomes my wife and life has taught her to understand what her pure young woman's mind isn't capable of taking in now.'

The Captain pressed his hand warmly.

'You're right, Eigil – you're quite right. It shall be as you wish.'

They sat in silence for a while. Ankerkrone was the first to break it.

'There's still another way out – one I want to try.'

'And that is?' asked Holst.

Captain Ankerkrone smiled sadly.

'No, my friend, this is a matter for me, me alone – and Kurk, if he will.'

Holst didn't ask anything more. The morning was already becoming light and he needed rest. Early that morning, Ankerkrone sent a message to Kurk to come to him and the two old friends sat talking together for a long time. When Kurk left the Captain, his face was serious, but his firmly set mouth testified that the two men's conversation had led them both to a solemn decision, the responsibility for which they were willing to bear.

In the hotel's vestibule, Kurk met a man whose presence in this place at this moment didn't surprise him in the least. He stopped and uttered his name. The stranger opened his arms, as if to embrace him. They went off together and talked for a long time, and when Kurk left him, his face, while still solemn, was much calmer than when he had left Captain Ankerkrone.

The newcomer was the happy equerry from Riddartofte, Bror Sjöström, who had been summoned to Venice by reports in the Swedish press. He obtained permission through the consulate to visit the prisoner along with Kurk.

XV

JEANNETTE HAD NOT SLEPT WELL THAT NIGHT. She had attached a faint hope to the effect of what she had told Holst, but she soon realised that for her there was nothing for it but to give up any hope of binding her destiny to Holst in even the loosest way. While he was gone, she got up and started gathering her jewellery and belongings together to think about how she could meet the demands that life would present her with in the near future. She didn't want to accept anything from Holst. She didn't own very much, but she had gradually collected some jewellery. She recalled that Sjöström had shown her a secret space in a writing desk, where he had hidden some items of value and she decided to check this hideaway. Initially, she didn't find very much in there, but among the items was a small box, wrapped in thick paper and sealed. She broke the seal and, in the box, she found to her astonishment a little diamond-studded lady's watch, a couple of lockets and some rings she recognised, as well as the jewellery Annie had always worn.

She didn't understand how they had come here. So, Sjöström must have… She shivered and thought about Annie's fate and Sjöström's hardness and brutality towards her.

The next morning, she told Holst about her discovery and it surprised her that he didn't have a stronger reaction to it. But he didn't say a word about Annie. She thought he was so strangely silent and withdrawn.

Later in the day, Holst received a visit from Lieutenant Claes.

Jeannette had lain down again, while Holst was working on the official report and the letters to the consulates. Signora Montuori, who tended to glide around him with feline stealth, approached him and announced that a young gentleman wanted to talk to him. She handed him a card, which he took and read: 'Claes Ankerkrone, Lieutenant in the Crown Prince's Hussars, Proprietor of Gammalstorp'.

'Have him come in,' he said abruptly, and Claes entered the room wearing a weak smile.

He bowed minimally. Holst offered him a chair and the lieutenant sat down without showing any embarrassment.

'I really came to see Donna Jeannette. I hadn't expected that Lieutenant Holst would have construed poor Hugold's request to protect the lady so literally, but she isn't wanting for anything, I can see.'

Holst blushed but forced himself into a polite question.

'Was there anything else, Lieutenant?'

Claes became serious.

'Yes, Hugold Sjöström and I were friends once upon a time. I don't usually desert a friend in need. You are in the strongest position, so I will use the opportunity to ask you how much would be required to get Hugold out of this embarrassing situation.'

Holst shook his head.

'I'm afraid that's hardly possible. As I told you yesterday, it's a very significant amount.'

Claes smiled a little haughtily.

'There's a difference in what one considers to be significant, Lieutenant Holst. I don't usually take money so seriously.'

'Your wife, you mean,' Holst chipped in, irritated by the young man's demeanour.

Claes bit his lip.

'I haven't come to pick a quarrel.'

'Good Lord no,' said Holst with a slight bow, 'but you are mistaken about the situation. I have had the task of having Sjöström arrested. I lack the authority to negotiate his release. I can only advise you to find a lawyer who can get access to him, but I would advise you against it.'

'Why?' asked Claes – he would have added a few snide words about Jeannette, but thought better of it.

Holst got up and went over to the young man.

'Lieutenant Ankerkrone,' he said, 'your father is my friend. I feel more friendship for your family than you suspect. I could also be of some service to you if you would trust me. Among gentlemen, it is customary to trust someone's word. If you wish to be my friend, you won't regret it.'

Claes shifted slightly.

'You must forgive me, Mr Holst, but I am an officer, you are a detective – it's a very honourable profession, I understand, but…well…that's impossible.'

'I didn't think you were stupid, Lieutenant Ankerkrone,' said Holst sharply.

Claes was startled.

'I have serious matters to deal with and I have no intention of allowing my plans to be thwarted by stupidity. You can thank your name and my friendship with your father for my not acting differently in this case from how I am proceeding. You probably remember what you were doing around 27th March this year and you probably know that if your father hadn't acted like he did on that occasion, you would now have found yourself in a very similar position to your friend, Hugold Sjöström. You forget rather too quickly, Lieutenant, but you ought to know that you're talking to a man who knows you and your circumstances more intimately than you may suspect. I have hardly any use for you, but I would advise you not to get in my way. It could turn out to be more expensive than you could manage, no matter how little importance you think you attach to the value of money.'

Claes had gone pale and he clenched his teeth.

'What do you mean?'

'Lieutenant Ankerkrone, I don't know how eager you are to appear as a witness in a court case pursued against Hugold Sjöström for falsification and fraud against your former mistress, Annie Cederlund, or if you want a Swedish jury to enter the bar along with Mr Karlkvist from Kristianstad. It's possible, though, that your wife would know how to judge that scandal for its worth – and that your neighbours and friends in Scania would feel terribly concerned at reading in their morning newspapers a testimony that could be just as interesting as any recent scandals.'

Claes held his tongue.

'You might prefer, Lieutenant Ankerkrone, to continue negotiations in a somewhat more courteous tone – I'm perfectly agreeable. I don't usually offer my friendship twice, but I make an exception with you for the reasons already mentioned.'

Holst stretched out his hand.

Claes took it reluctantly.

Holst smiled.

'As you will see, we two can easily become friends, even though I'm a "detective", as you call it. I'm quite used to mixing with people and quite cooperative. In addition, we two have common interests. It's a question of avoiding the process I talked about, and that will be simplest if you conduct yourself in a rather passive manner in the meantime. It's not certain that there won't be any need for the funds you seem to have so extravagantly at your disposal and there will no doubt be ample opportunity for you to become of primary importance. But for the time being, it will be best for the case if you keep yourself on a secondary level.'

It was apparent that Holst had made a deep impression on the young man and they parted on tolerably good terms. Holst had to admit that from the very beginning he had found a footing with his distinguished and wealthy brother-in-law, which would certainly be beneficial to both when the brother-in-law relationship became known to Lieutenant Claes.

On the same day, Holst informed Captain Ankerkrone of the discovery of Annie's jewellery, the pivotal damning evidence against Sjöström.

XVI

THE BRIDGE OF SIGHS LEADS THE WANDERER from the Doge's Palace over the canal to the institutions of justice. Hugold Sjöström was incarcerated here in a narrow cell, sitting on a wooden bed at a small table fixed to the wall. The days passed slowly for him and, in deep uncertainty, he sat bowed and staring straight ahead. He hardly dared to think. It was true that no-one had told him anything else except that the reason for his imprisonment was the falsification, but he sensed that there was more to it than that. Just the fact that it was a Danish police officer who had effected his imprisonment made him unsure. What business was the falsification in Helsingborg of the Danish police? And who could have reported it, now when Annie was sleeping for eternity on the bottom of the quarry? He hadn't seen anything about the finding of the body, because he didn't read Danish or Swedish newspapers, but he suspected that Annie's disappearance must have attracted attention and that and that alone was the reason for his imprisonment.

Jeannette must have betrayed him; she was in collusion with the police officer, that much was clear, and Claes Ankerkrone – he whom he had met once again and tried to inveigle into his plans with Jeannette's help – what about him? No, that was unthinkable. But it was possible that Captain Ankerkrone had discovered his new plot and had broken his word in order to protect his son from new dangers.

That was how it must be, but it would cost him dearly if he tried to cast him into misfortune.

He laid his plans. He would deny everything and blame the Captain, who had told him that Annie had killed his wife. No person in the world could know what had actually happened that morning, when he had tried to persuade Annie to voluntarily assign him everything through marriage. And while he was thinking about this, the scene that morning in the forest appeared so clearly to him. He saw Annie in her tight travel suit and black hat, happily smiling in the anticipation and certainty of standing at her goal. He was reminded of her anxiety when the waiting time stretched out and the Captain hadn't turned up. He remembered so clearly how he had spoken to her and told her that the Captain had told him that she was his wife's murderer and that there was no hope for her; how he had tried to force her and how, when her anger rose and she mocked him using the coarsest words she could find, he had decided to execute the plan he had put together when he heard at the hotel that Ankerkrone had departed for the south on the previous evening.

He had talked to her once again, and when she had wanted to leave him and rush away, he had spoken kindly to her and tried to help her pull herself together and enjoy a bracing glass of cognac. She had screamed and said, 'Are you trying to kill me with poison!' He had laughed and handed her the glass and she had given him a strange look and drunk it, almost as if she knew it was poison, almost as if she wanted to die because she couldn't survive the bitter sorrow that had struck her.

The poison had worked straight away and she had collapsed almost instantly. He still remembered how he had undressed her body and lowered it into the lake, bound to large stones; how feverishly he had worked in the thickets; how he had fled with the basket where he had hidden the clothes, after pocketing the watch and the rings to make sure they didn't lead to recognition. How he had met Karlkvist in Helsingborg and bribed him to be helpful before quickly leaving the country with Jeannette to lose all the rich spoils at the damned green table in Monte Carlo. Now it was over. They must know everything, and now they would take him back to Sweden or Denmark and try to force him to talk.

But he wouldn't talk, and woe to anyone who had betrayed him. There was no evidence against him.

The key rattled in the heavy door; he got to his feet and, standing in front of him, he was startled to see the only two men who had ever cared for him, the two who had always been ready to help no matter how desperate a state he had been in: Captain Holger Kurk and Bror, his brother.

He remained standing, unable to speak. What should he say?

Kurk approached him; the turnkey was still standing in the door but, on a sign from the Captain, he withdrew.

The three were left alone.

Captain Kurk's face was serious, indicating that a firm decision had been made.

Bror Sjöström stood with his eyes lowered and was deeply moved.

Hugold offered to shake Kurk's hand, but he didn't take it.

Bror turned away when Hugold approached him.

'What do you want of me?' asked Hugold impassively.

Kurk looked at him firmly.

'To help you, Hugold, for the last time in your life,' he said with full seriousness.

Hope brightened in the face of the prisoner, but Kurk quickly continued.

'Not how you may think, Hugold. We can't open this prison door for you. We've helped you previously, even though you've rewarded us poorly and dragged your brother's honourable name in the mud throughout Europe. But we can't help a murderer, an assassin, Hugold, because that's what you are, and you are condemned to judgement.'

'You're lying, Captain – it's not true.'

'And Annie's watch, locket and rings which Holst has found in your possession?' replied Kurk softly and calmly.

Hugold went pale and supported himself against the bed.

'There's no way around it, Hugold,' continued Kurk. 'The body of the woman you murdered has been found, and in a short time you will stand face-to-face with your victim. Denying it won't help, because your steps have been followed one by one, and evidence will be presented which you won't be able to contradict.'

Hugold pulled himself together.

'You're lying, Captain – the murderer is Arvid Ankerkrone…'

'Do you think that lies can save you now?' Kurk had taken a step towards him. 'Don't even try to imagine that you can avoid your fate. Or perhaps you believe you can? There is plenty of evidence as to where Arvid Ankerkrone was on 27th March this year, but where were you and what was in the basket that you bought in Elsinore and that you left on the train when you went back to Karlkvist in Helsingborg via Copenhagen? Or do you think anyone will accuse Arvid Ankerkrone of mixing poison into the cognac bottle you left in the basket with Annie's clothes?'

Kurk spoke calmly, but with a strong emphasis on each word.

Hugold shuddered – he could feel he was lost. Just the fact that Kurk could tell him word for word how everything had happened, and that Ankerkrone would be cleared by the evidence that could be obtained of his presence elsewhere, while he himself would be convicted by the large number of testimonies from all who had seen him. He collapsed and put his head in his hands. When he looked up, Kurk was standing bent over him.

'Hugold,' he said, 'there was once a time when you were a bright lad and when I loved you like my own son. Much has happened since then, but I still have enough left for you that I will save you from the shame of standing before the court as a murderer and from having to lay your head under the executioner's axe. This will be your lot. You were a soldier, a brave one at that. There's still one path open for you. I can't see any other, Hugold. Make your atonement to He who is above us all, and then take that path, the only one left.'

Hugold rose and stretched out his hand towards his brother. The equerry shook his head.

'I can't help you,' said Bror in a subdued, quivering voice. 'Nor can I call you brother any more – what you've done is too hideous. You must listen to what Holger says, because I can't, Hugold, I just can't.'

The equerry turned away.

Kurk was standing with folded arms and looked firmly at the prisoner. Hugold was fighting a fierce inner battle, but he couldn't speak.

The turnkey appeared in the doorway – the rules decreed

that the visit must end.

Bror took Hugold's hand, but released it quickly – it was cold; he turned and walked out quickly.

Kurk remained for a moment. It was as if a gleam had been lit in the eye of the prisoner that was promising.

'Courage, my boy, courage,' whispered the Captain and pressed his hand while looking him stiffly in the eye. Then the door closed behind them.

Hugold collapsed in icy despair – and as his head bent over the table, he saw a small white package lying close to the wall.

Two days later, Holst received a message from the prison that the Swedish lieutenant being held under arrest had died suddenly. The cause was unknown.

Bror Sjöström sat in Holst's apartments the day after the news of his brother's death. He was saddened, but he had to admit that what had happened was the best for all concerned. He was proud of his family and its name, and Hugold, notwithstanding the great sacrifices he had had to make, had been a constant source of disquiet and concern. He forgave Holst for being the direct cause of the disaster; he wanted to forget everything but he was still deeply moved.

Jeannette, who was still living in Signora Montuori's apartment and went around as quiet as a mouse in sorrow over her little broken dream of happiness, sat silently in a corner of the living room. She didn't want to talk badly about Hugold, but she shivered whenever she thought about Annie's fate.

Holst had had an idea and turned to the equerry.

'Lieutenant Sjöström – you could do a good deed. This young girl is in a lonely situation in a foreign country and without a protector. Her father served Count Falkenberg loyally for many years; take her home to Sweden where her mother is still alive, and thereby correct the damage that Hugold has inflicted on her.'

The equerry gave it a moment's consideration while Jeannette wept quietly in a corner.

Bror Sjöström's good heart couldn't be denied and it didn't take long before he accepted the suggestion. Jeannette allowed Holst to decide; she was really sad, but Holst patted her cheek and stroked her hair away from her forehead.

'You must follow my advice, Jeannette. That's the best way I can pay my debt of gratitude to you.'

And so it was decided, although Jeannette still cried.

That same evening, she left Venice with Bror Sjöström and headed north. There was a position available in 'Arcadia', and during their journey, the equerry decided to offer it to Jeannette. Jeannette accepted – and it may be assumed that she would know how to hang on to Arcadia's resident for the rest of his days.

XVII

THERE WAS SUPPOSED TO BE A FESTIVAL in St Mark's Square and the music should have been playing between the pikes bearing the standards in front of the church, but it was noticed that the glorious Campanile had developed a threatening crack and the festival was cancelled.

The military blocked off the area around the square and people stood at a respectful distance, looking with concern at the bell tower. On the morning of the following day, 14th July, Holst ate lunch with the Ankerkrones at their hotel, and when they went to the Piazzetta to see how things were, they found the square full of people, so it was only with great difficulty that they could fight their way to the gondolas' landing stage at the quayside.

They were standing pinned up against the wharf, when suddenly a buzz from the large crowd of people, like a wave breaking, surged across the square. Holst directed his gaze towards the tower and saw to his surprise how the top, with the spire and the statue of St Mark in bronze slowly sank and, as the incessant buzz rose and grew like an ocean, the whole tower slowly began to sink, as if pushed into the ground by an invisible but mighty hand. The stones of the tower poured down like foam over the Logetta del Sansovino and its glorious sculptural work, while the dust swirled up into the clear sky. The doves from the peepholes fluttered around in fear and sought shelter on the domes of the cathedral. The mumbling from the crowd became a scream, and mixed into the din came the roaring sound of the tumbling stones. But the tower didn't fall; it slowly sank towards the ground, while its spikes pointed towards the sun, and suddenly, as the screams cut through the air, the noise grew to an almighty crash and dust whirled up in the air, while the stones cascaded like a waterfall across the square and into the broken gable of the royal palace. The air was filled with a fog of dust, and the crashing drowned out everything. Then suddenly, everything went silent and quite slowly, a menacing, sorrowful sound rose like a hollow sigh from the heaving sea of humanity and was carried by the wind across the lagoon.

Venice's slender clock tower, along with Sansovino's wonderful works of art, lay in ruins under broken plinths and stones, piled high, close to the procurator buildings like a rampart of rocks and dust, while Venice mourned and the sorrow spread like a wave over the whole world.

Captain Ankerkrone grabbed Holst's arm as the sea of people cascaded across the square and dragged him along with them, while Ulla pressed herself against him.

They didn't speak.

But when they had found seats in a gondola, which carried them away from the quayside out onto the water, where boats were darting off between each other in feverish haste, the

Captain sat with his head bowed in earnest thought. Ulla had taken Holst's hand, and turned towards her father.

'*Venedig – nenn ich mit doppeltem Recht heute Sankt Marcus im Koth*,'[10] she said to him in a subdued voice.

Ankerkrone looked up.

'You're right, Ulla, the mire has swallowed up the glorious Campanile, as it will swallow the City of the Doge and its beautiful buildings; the mire will absorb the city as it absorbs everything. We build in the mire that lies around us where our feet tread. The mire will erase every trace, every trace of our footsteps, and erase every trace of us all from the world as we sink deeper and deeper into it.'

The sorrow lay heavy and silent over Venice in the following days, and everyone's thoughts, everyone's talk, revolved around the great disaster that had happened to San Marco; San Marco's glorious bell tower, which the mire had swallowed up. No one had time to think of or talk about the Swedish lieutenant who had died in prison, or to investigate how he had died. His body was buried on Kurk's instructions on the island out there in the Adriatic, with his name on a simple marble slab along with the short inscription in Swedish:

'May God be merciful to his soul.'

The district magistrate was deeply moved by Sjöström's death, but not really dissatisfied. After all, it was probably far better this way. No one could know how much work, how difficult a battle, would have followed his extradition. His death was in all probability due to his brother's intervention; rich relatives in Sweden had wanted to prevent a scandal and it was best for all parties.

Ankerkrone avoided discussing the case with the magistrate, who ascribed this to it being a fellow countryman.

Holst didn't speak to Ankerkrone about Sjöström's death,

but the evening when the collapse of the Campanile was the only thing men and women in Venice spoke about, Holst and Captain Ankerkrone stood on the balcony and looked out across the lagoon, where the moon twinkled over the rippling water.

'Eigil,' said the Captain, 'the mire deletes the traces, it covers our footsteps, sticky and clayey, and nothing can be seen when we look back. Let the mire cover the tracks you have followed, so that not even the memory remains, and put our hopes in the harvest to come!'

Holst looked up.

'Sometimes I think you're like one of those Renaissance men as you sweep your way through life. And I think this last thing was unnecessary.'

'For me – yes,' replied the Captain. 'For you and her – no.'

Holst remained silent.

Ulla had come out to them on the balcony and Holst put an arm around her waist, while she turned her face to him and he kissed her lips.

Ankerkrone leant against the balustrade as his thoughts went back to Giulia and the days that were fading away and he whispered to himself, '*Alles was ich erfuhr, ich würzt'es mit süsser Erinnrung, Wurzt'es mit Hoffnung; sie sind lieblichste Würzen der Welt.*'[11]

A few days later, Holst and Ulla's wedding took place and they all set off north.

PART FOUR

Conclusion – Forest Lake

I

A SINGULAR FUNERAL WAS BEING PREPARED in the little church near Esrum Lake. It was late summer and the corn had turned yellow and was ready to harvest, while the treetops in the forest were darkening as autumn approached. The sun was clear in the sky, glittering above thin, greyish-white clouds, and the tiles of the little church reflected the light. A grave had been dug close to the white church wall and the gravedigger's men were lowering a yellow oak coffin into it, while the clayey soil was hidden under luxuriant wreaths and fragrant spruce. The priest stood tall in his black gown with the shining white collar; his voice was subdued as he prayed and his words were solemn as the earth fell with a hollow sound against the coffin lid.

'Ashes to ashes, dust to dust, in sure and certain hope of the Resurrection to eternal life.'

There were only a few people standing at the graveside: the district magistrate, Captain Ankerkrone and Captain Kurk and, between them, Eigil Holst and his young wife, with heads bowed. Ulla was weeping, while Ankerkrone was pale and relying on his friend's arm for support. A few of the people of the parish were present and stood back without taking part, but as solemn as the common people at a church service. Out of all these people, only three knew the deep secret hidden in the simple coffin and had followed the trail that was now being erased for ever while the earth fell on the coffin lid. A few scattered voices sang the hymn and the mourners spread out over the little welcoming cemetery where the gravedigger was hurriedly casting the earth that would cover Annie Bengtson's last resting place, far from home. The lonely grave would soon be forgotten and no one would suspect what the name meant. Arvid Ankerkrone bowed his head as he cast a last look at the grave, and recalled the magnificent marble cross at Gammalstorp where his wife was at rest.

All tracks disappear – all tracks are erased.

It was getting towards evening and the sun was sinking over the yellow fields. Eigil Holst walked with his young wife to the forest where they had first met. It was quiet and over the field rose a light veil of fog, while the bell rang in the tower of the old church. They crossed the stile, where the hazel and the blackberry bushes wove together over the granite boulders and the yellowish-green moss with the yellow stonecrop. A single sharp cheep-cheep came from a frightened bird that shot swiftly between the bushes and, as they finally emerged from the thickets beside the lake, which lay deep beneath the shoreline, they saw a strong roebuck standing with a bowed head by the water, which mirrored its slender body. They were downwind, so the buck didn't notice them. They walked noiselessly to the bench and sat down.

Not a word passed between them.

Suddenly, as if in thought, Ulla picked up a stone and threw it at the lake's mirror, which lay quite low, with little depth, despite the frequent rain. The buck's magnificent limbs tensed immediately; it lifted its head and flew startled away from the shore through the thicket in long, supple leaps.

There came a sharp cry from a forest bird, then everything went quiet.

And while the sun was setting, while the mist and the fragrance from a forest preparing itself to rest rose around the beech tree at the edge, Ulla leant her head on her husband's shoulder, and he told her in a subdued voice the strange, sad story of the trail from the lake between the beeches north of Esrum, which led across Småland's moors and its shimmering lakes between the heather and the stones, to the lagoon city where the mire was beginning to swallow and conceal it like the earth of Zealand concealed the coffin in the old cemetery behind the white walls.

The trail was hidden forever but, in the beginning, had played its part, which for these two ensured it against being forgotten as long as the sun shone over one of them; if it couldn't always shine over both of them, which is what people who are in love hope and pray for.

And that is what became of Forest Lake and the mystery hidden in it; it was their richest memory, the first one in their common ownership.

END

Endnotes

1. (p152) To waste money and time take a good look, At the comical guide in this little book. – Goethe, *Epigrams*, 1790.

2. (p152) I walked by the sea looking for mussels. In one I found a pearl; it has now secured a place in my heart.

3. (p154) I have often erred and come to my senses again, But never more happily; now this girl is my happiness! If this is yet another error, then spare me, you wiser Gods, And don't deprive me of it until yonder on the cold shore.

4. (p156) This girl was poor and without a stitch when I met her; Back then I liked her naked, as I still do today.

5. (p157) I once had a love, she was dearer to me than anything! But I have her no more! Be silent and endure the loss!

6. (p158) And so I philandered, separated from all my friends,
In the city of Neptune, days and hours pass,
Everything I experienced, I seasoned with sweet memories,
Seasoned with hope; it is the sweetest seasoning in the world.

7. (p160) Whatever happens to you, you growing youngster,
Love created you, so may love be a part of you.

8. (p161) It was jest enough, my sweetheart!

9. (p161) It doesn't surprise me that people love dogs so
much, For they are miserable rogues – people as well as dogs.

10. (p241, p278) There is a church called St John's-in-the-
Muck; today I have twice as much right to call Venice St
Mark's-in-the-Muck.

11. (p279) Everything I experienced, I seasoned with sweet
memories, Seasoned with hope; it is the sweetest seasoning in
the world.

Acknowledgements

To my wonderful wife, Lotte, for elucidation, brain-storming, proofreading and material replenishment.

To Lucy Moffatt, translator of Stein Riverton's *The Iron Chariot*, for the inspiration for this one.

To Scott and Kat at Abandoned Bookshop, for the clarity and speed of their communication.